The Radiance Trilogy

UNBOUND

Thanks for reading, I hope you enjoy!

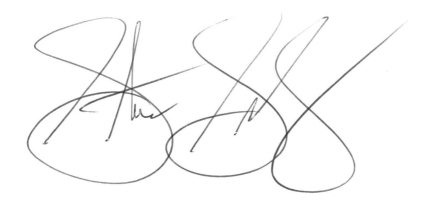

Steven Sandy

D0884735

UNBOUND

Copyright © 2019 Steven Sandy

Cover art by Aaron Little

Edited by Alana Joli Abbott

ISBN-13: 978-1-7340826-0-9

For Merrilee, my wife and encourager.

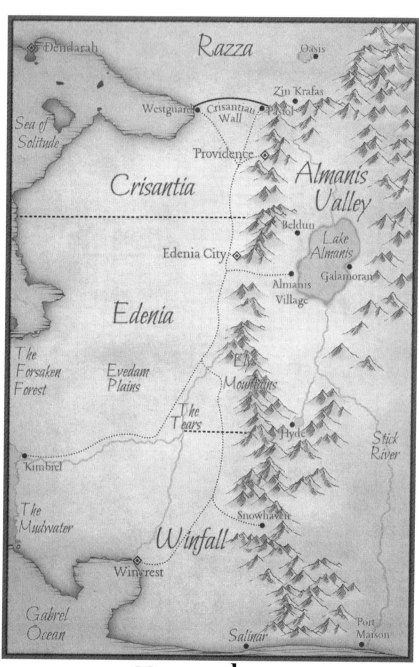

Map of Luoma

Prologue

The time has come. Paholainen opened his eyes. He had not been sleeping, for he never truly slept, but he did find solace in stillness. In his chambers, carved into rock deep underground, there was no light, as Paholainen had no need for it. He had spent many years in this place, and his eyes were well accustomed to the shadow.

Outside his chamber was a narrow passageway leading to the cell where the prisoners were kept. The circular room had six men chained to the wall, evenly spaced. They had been men of great renown once, but not anymore. These men should have been long dead, but Paholainen needed them alive, so he kept them that way. Some of them had hair long and gray, others had no hair at all. Shaggy beards grew on their faces and stretched to the ground. Their bodies were frail, wrinkled, and splotchy, and their heads drooped toward the floor. But they were alive.

Paholainen paced slowly toward one of the men and grabbed his chin, holding his head up to look into his sunken eyes. Though the man was barely conscious, his eyes still burned with the fire of defiance. Paholainen sneered. These men had possessed incredible strength, had reached the pinnacle of human potential, yet they were nothing more than insects to him. Some had broken slowly, some had remained obstinate, but this man was the most dangerous, despite his emaciated form. Even insects could bite.

The man could not see Paholainen in the pitch black, yet he stared directly into his eyes. "You... will fail." The man garbled the words, struggling for each syllable.

Paholainen smiled. "I have already succeeded." He drew a dagger from his belt and plunged it into the man's heart.

Chapter 1

"I can't believe you talked me into this!" Caelum shouted, clinging to the cliff wall. He blindly searched for any place to put his foot so he could take some weight off his violently shaking arms. It was another fifty meters to the bottom and, after this fool's errand was finished, would be a hundred-meter climb back to the top. He pushed that thought out of his head and focused on finding the next handhold.

"I thought you'd appreciate the fresh air!" laughed Daric. The brawny, dark-haired man was already on the ledge below him. "You spend too much time cooped up in that dreary study of yours."

Daric was Caelum's brother in every way but blood. After Caelum's parents died, Daric's family took him in and raised him as one of their own. The two of them had been nearly inseparable since. Daric was the kind of man every boy in the village over eight years of age wanted to be—and the kind every woman in town wanted to be *with*. Unfortunately for them, Daric was married and madly in love with his wife Sonya. And unfortunately for Caelum, Sonya's favorite flower happened to grow only in a beautiful garden at the very bottom of an ancient crater, nearly impossible to reach except by those who were extremely brave or incredibly foolish. Daric was the former; Caelum, regrettably, the latter.

"You know," Daric shouted up at him, "this climb would probably be a lot easier for you if you didn't insist on always wearing that thing."

Caelum rolled his eyes. As soon as his foot found a lip in the rock, he yanked his long overcoat—the "thing" Daric was referring to—around to the front of his legs so his other foot wouldn't slip on it. Scholars throughout Edenia wore their coats with pride, each color denoting a field of study. Caelum wore crimson, representing the study of Edenian history. It was uncomfortable and gaudy, and Daric took every opportunity to poke fun at it, but it was a symbol of his accomplishment. It was no small feat to achieve the rank of scholar in Edenia.

He found another handhold and shouted back, "What would make this climb easier is if you would keep your mouth shut!" He spared a glance down toward his friend, who looked as if he were enjoying himself too much, watching Caelum in his misery. But as he glanced past Daric at the long drop below, Caelum regretted looking down and barely caught himself as what seemed like sure foothold crumbled under his weight.

After what felt like an eternity, Caelum leapt down to the ledge that marked the end of the journey's first stage. Daric clapped him on the back and handed him his water skin and a couple of dried apples they'd had the foresight to bring along.

"If I'd known it was going to take you that long to climb down here, I would have brought more food," Daric teased. "At this rate we may not make it back in time to leave with the rest of our unit, and we'll miss supper for sure!"

Caelum was too tired, and too relieved that he had made it down the cliff alive, to be provoked. They still had the rest of today and all morning tomorrow before they would be leaving Almanis Valley to serve their three-year term in the Edenian Guard. Caelum was surprised by the pang of sadness he felt at the thought. He had known this day was coming, since all young men between the ages of nineteen and twenty-two were required to serve when the draft came around, and he thought he had prepared himself for it. Yet now, on the eve of their departure, he wasn't sure he was ready to leave behind the life he had built for himself in the valley. He knew his place here, but once they arrived in Edenia City, all new recruits would be assessed and given specific assignments within the guard, where they would serve until their term ended. Caelum was certain Daric would be among those chosen to serve amongst the most elite warriors. Daric worked as a master sculptor and seemed to be chiseled out of the same stone as his statues. He had a natural talent for almost everything he set out to learn, hindered only by an occasional lack of interest, and his skill was unrivaled at the mandatory weapons training in Almanis Valley. Caelum had been working hard to keep up, but he feared it wouldn't be enough to keep them together.

Another hour passed before they finally reached the bottom of the crater. Caelum stared in wonder at his surroundings. During their descent, he was so focused on his imminent death that he hadn't even realized what an incredible place he was stumbling into. This garden, if that was even the right word, was filled with a variety of flora unlike anything Caelum had ever seen before. He saw more shades of green in the plants around him than he thought possible. They began to wade through the dense foliage.

"This place is fascinating—more so than I had ever imagined!" Caelum said as he reached into his leather scroll case and pulled out a piece of parchment. He stopped and began sketching the likeness of a plant that grew no higher than his waist, yet had leaves large enough to engulf a grown man.

"I told you that you would like it here!" said Daric.

"I know, I know," said Caelum, wiping the sweat from his forehead before continuing with his sketches. Daric had been trying to convince Caelum to accompany him here ever since he had discovered the place, but it wasn't until Caelum uncovered a link between this crater and the legends of the Unbound that he agreed to make that insane climb.

Most people, including Daric, assumed the Unbound were nothing more than legend, but Caelum had dedicated his life to the study of the history of Edenia, and he believed otherwise. According to legend, the Unbound were magical beasts of great power, bent on the destruction of the human race. Historically, whenever one of these beasts appeared, the Edenian Guard would dispatch its six greatest warriors, the Knights of Radiance, to fight the creatures and banish them from the earth. While the Knights of Radiance remained an active part of the Edenian Guard today, they served primarily as officers and public figures in the military. There had been no reliable record of an Unbound sighting in over five-hundred years, and the ancient records that remained were largely dismissed as myths.

"That's a pretty picture you are drawing." Caelum jumped at the voice in his ear. Daric leaned over his shoulder, absolutely intending to spook him as he was caught up in his own thoughts. The big man wore a childish grin, obviously pleased with himself. "We should probably get going—"

Caelum shoved him away. "Hey, you made me smudge my sketch!"

Daric laughed and set off toward the center of the crater, whistling a jolly tune. Caelum reluctantly stuffed his pen and parchment back into the scroll case and hurried after him. A light breeze blew straight at their backs, as if it were encouraging them toward their destination.

"Next time we stop, you ought to hand me the pen and parchment so I can draw a picture of you. You are quite the sight," said Daric, eying him up and down. "I'm not sure if you have more twigs caught in your hair or in your coat."

Caelum glared at him, then ran his hand through his wild blonde curls to shake out the leaves. He opened his mouth to fire some choice words back about Daric's appearance, but Caelum could find nothing to say. Daric had a natural ruggedness that fit in this wilderness. He wore a leather vest over a simple white tunic with the sleeves rolled up to his elbows, which, to nobody's surprise, proved to be a much more functional outfit than Caelum's coat. And Daric had no leaves in his hair. "Well you smell awful," Caelum said finally. It was the best he could do.

Daric shrugged. "I can't argue with that. I am curious though," he said, scratching his head, "why do you *have* to wear that coat everywhere you go? Is it a requirement of the Scholar's Guild or something?"

"No, it is not required," Caelum answered. There were only three requirements for guild scholars, and none of them were difficult to keep. First, scholars were required to continue in their pursuit of knowledge throughout their lives. Second, every scholar had a responsibility to pass on their knowledge to the next generation of Edenians. Most scholars fulfilled this requirement either through direct instruction or by preserving their knowledge in written works, and many did both. Finally, scholars were prohibited from using their knowledge to aid the enemies of the empire. "I choose to wear this because it is a part of who I am." Caelum cleared his throat. "I am managing just fine, so can we please move on from my coat and get back to the whole reason we are here?"

Daric shook his head and muttered something under his breath. The two continued on in silence. The wind picked up slightly and whistled through the trees, the sun fell below the crater wall to the west, and dusk began to settle in.

"Say Daric," Caelum said as they walked, "do you think Mistress Jaena would bake a couple of pies to send with us when we leave for Edenia?" He heard a loud grumble from Daric's stomach.

"Aw, come on Cael, why'd you have to go and mention pies? I'm starving!"

Caelum laughed. "I sure am going to miss those."

Daric stroked his beard thoughtfully. "Do you suppose they'll grant us leave to come back for the Freshet Festival? I have never missed festival."

Caelum shook his head sadly. "I don't think so. If we're lucky we may be able to lift a glass with some of the other men from the valley, but that's about it." Caelum sighed heavily. "I guess there's a lot we're going to miss these next three years."

"What do you think you're going to miss the most?" Daric asked.

"Hmm…" Caelum thought a moment. "The people, I think. My students especially. I'll miss teaching and seeing that look in their eyes when they master a difficult concept." He laughed, remembering one recent incident. "Just the other day little Myrella Crawley's eyes nearly popped out of her head when she finally managed to count to a hundred."

"Are you sure there isn't something else?" Daric raised one eyebrow and nudged him with an elbow. "A certain young lady, perhaps?"

Caelum scoffed. "Olivette has never shown any interest in me. The only reason she ever talks to me is because I hang around with you."

"I don't know…" said Daric.

"Enough about me," said Caelum. "What about you? I mean, besides your wife, is there anything you are going to miss about the valley?"

"I haven't really thought about it," Daric said with a shrug. "I suppose I'll miss the mountain air, the smell of the pines, and swimming in the lake." His lips twisted in a wry smile. "Strangely, I don't feel as if I will really miss any of the people, aside from you and Sonya."

Caelum looked at him sideways. "You can't mean that. The people of Almanis love you, and you're friends with everybody."

"Maybe," he conceded, "but that's just it. Everyone thinks like you just said, and so people assume I have no need nor any desire for a deeper companionship. If it weren't for you and Sonya, I would have gone crazy here."

That was the last thing he expected Daric to say. "I think you are underestimating yourself," he said.

"Maybe," he said, and he shrugged. "Either way, I'm looking forward to our time in the guard."

Caelum climbed through a thicket after Daric, his coat snagging on a branch. *Perhaps he has a point about the coat after all,* Caelum admitted to himself, grateful that Daric wasn't looking, so Caelum didn't have to suffer an "I told you so." He yanked the coat free, cursing as he stumbled out of the thicket, and when he stepped into the clearing beyond, his jaw dropped. Just ahead of them grew a large tree, and around the tree grew hundreds of blue flowers Caelum did not recognize, each flower shimmering with an ethereal sapphire glow.

"Wow!" breathed Caelum. He had the uncomfortable feeling that he was someplace he was not supposed to be, yet at the same time, he felt strangely comfortable.

"I've never seen them glow like that before!" Daric said excitedly. "Sonya won't believe this!" Caelum hurried forward toward the center of the garden, but Daric grabbed him suddenly and pulled him back. "Be careful!"

"Why?" demanded Caelum.

Daric pointed at the ground just in front of them, and Caelum paled. There was no ground. There was a chasm, masked by the growing darkness, and he had almost walked right into it. He peered down into the pit but could not tell how deep it went, and he had no desire to find out. "Let's get that flower and go."

Daric went carefully around the chasm and picked a flower. "Whoa, it's still glowing!"

Curiosity tugged at Caelum. He felt there was much to learn here, but he couldn't shake the uneasy feeling that they should not linger. He made his way around the chasm and his dread grew. The wind was no longer at his back. As he moved around the chasm, the current always seemed to be trying to pull him down into the cavern, and the wind was picking up.

This wasn't natural. He went to Daric, took the flower, and placed it carefully in his scroll case.

"Let's go," he said, and Daric nodded in agreement.

As he turned back toward the way they had come, the ground shook violently, and he lost his footing. A startled cry escaped from his chest as he fell to the ground. *What is this, an earthquake?* he thought. Caelum looked around and found Daric on his backside as well, grimacing. The tremor passed, and the two of them looked questioningly at one another. Earthquakes were rare in Almanis Valley, and Caelum had experienced a few in his lifetime, but he had never felt one so powerful.

"Well that was fun." Daric smiled and got up, brushing himself off and extending his hand to Caelum. "But I think it's time we left this place." Caelum took it, and they made their way back toward the base of the cliff.

Caelum's growing sense of unease compelled him to walk more quickly, but they were now battling against the wind, which was still growing stronger. Caelum's crimson coat flapped vigorously behind him, and dust and small debris fluttered back toward the chasm, blowing in their eyes and obscuring their vision. They reached the base of the cliff and began to climb. Caelum's fear of heights was overshadowed by his fear of remaining any longer in the crater, and he climbed at a pace that even Daric could admire. They reached the first ledge and began climbing the second stretch of the wall, which would then take them to the top. Before they made it more than a few meters another violent tremor shook the ground, tumbling them down to the ledge. Daric struck his head on a rock as he landed and lay still. Caelum crawled frantically toward his friend, pulling him away from the ledge toward the cliff face. When Caelum determined Daric was still breathing, he slapped him gently on his cheek.

"Daric, Daric wake up!"

No response. Loose rocks fell from above as the tremor continued, and Caelum shielded his friend as best he could. An explosion roared in the distance. Caelum whipped his head toward the center of the crater, where an eruption of light and sound burst from the ground and into the sky, nearly blinding him. He closed his eyes and covered his ears, screaming. The image was burned into his eyelids. *What is happening?* he wondered, fearing that he already knew the answer.

Chapter 2

The earth trembled, and night turned to day as the beast was born. Not of flesh, but of wrath. Not of creation, but of destruction.

-Journal of Oleth Zandarion
Translation by Caelum Karasin
E.A. 967

Unbound. Caelum sat with his back to the cliff wall, furiously putting pen to parchment to record what he had seen. His eyes were wide, and he was trembling from the shock of it all. After the explosion, the wind had suddenly died, the ground stilled. Caelum checked on Daric, who was out cold but seemed to have suffered no serious injury, and laid him out comfortably with his head resting on Caelum's rumpled up coat. He would wake up shortly, and they could make their way back to Almanis Village. If it was still there. *Don't think like that! You don't know anything for sure.*

A low groan pulled Caelum out of his daze, and he went over to his friend's side as Daric began to stir. "What happened?" Daric mumbled, still groggy.

Caelum did not want to answer. Instead he grabbed their nearly empty water skin. "Drink this. You hit your head."

Daric took a drink and sat up, wincing. "An earthquake. I remember that. I fell, and I must have been knocked unconscious. The wind was powerful and strange. I remember all of that, but…" Daric paused, looking at Caelum. "I don't remember anything that would put that kind of fear into your eyes. What happened?"

Caelum looked back toward the center of the crater where he had seen the eruption of light, furrowing his brow. "I'm not sure exactly," he lied, "but I think we should get back to the village as quickly as we can." He felt guilty for not telling Daric what he suspected. His friend had always been supportive of Caelum in his research, yet Caelum knew Daric believed the Unbound to be nothing more than a myth, just like everybody else.

It was clear from his expression that Daric wasn't completely satisfied with Caelum's answer, but he just nodded. "Sounds good to me."

Daric had been out cold for most of the night, and dawn was fast approaching, giving them enough light to maneuver. They climbed the rest of the way out of the crater and made their way to the village. After the nightmarish events of the previous evening, the calm morning seemed out of place. By the time they reached the village Caelum almost convinced himself that it had all been only a dream. Everything seemed so… normal.

It was still early when they reached the outskirts of the village, so most of the other villagers were just starting their day's work. Daric and Caelum passed by a team of fishermen on the lake, hauling in their catch, and Daric went to greet them. Caelum was still too absorbed in his own thoughts to pay them any mind. But he focused when he spotted a guardsman on patrol, a fellow by the name of Jol Rustburn. Caelum had rarely interacted with the man personally, but he knew him as an occasional instructor for their weapons training. He reluctantly approached the man. "Good morning, Jol."

"Hello Caelum," Jol said politely, eyeing Caelum's ragged appearance. "Everything all right?"

Caelum wasn't sure how to answer, so instead he dodged the question. "I'm looking for Corporal Bek. Any idea where I can find him?"

Jol nodded. "He went out to meet the detachment on the road from Edenia. He should arrive back with them later this morning." When Caelum sighed heavily, Jol folded his arms. "Is there something I can help you with?"

Caelum hesitated. Jol was unlikely to take a report of the Unbound seriously, and even if he did, it wouldn't be enough. Caelum needed to tell someone who would not only believe him, but would have enough authority to do something about it. He would just have to wait. "No, thank you, Jol." The guardsman nodded and continued on his way.

"Seems like the folks in the village felt the earthquake, too" said Daric, returning from his conversation with the fishermen. "They told me nobody reported any damage other than some crashed plates and the like, but I'll have to check the structural integrity of the cabin when we get there. You'll probably want to check out the schoolhouse as well." Caelum nodded in silent agreement.

They continued toward Daric's cabin on the eastern side of the village, close to the lake's shore. Like most of the structures in the village, the cabin was constructed of local timber and had a comfortable, rustic feeling. It was a humble place, built by Daric himself after he married Sonya. Next to it was a small shed that served as Daric's workshop, where he kept his tools and some of his smaller sculpting projects. Most of his pieces were too elaborate for the small village of Almanis, but his work was in high demand among the nobles in Edenia. Caelum could see what looked like a flat, square piece of stone with many small figurines, which he suspected were pieces for the strategy game *Cross*, popular among many of his students at the schoolhouse. Caelum had never played the game himself. Daric went into the cabin, and Caelum followed.

"Where have you been?" a worried Sonya demanded, rising from the chair she had been nervously rocking. Her dull brown hair was tied back in a long braid, her pale blue eyes fixed on Daric with a disapproving glare. "You were gone all night! I thought maybe something terrible had happened to you, what with the earthquake and… and what happened to your clothes? It looks like someone dragged you two through the dirt. Are you hurt?"

As Sonya continued bombarding him with questions, Daric grabbed Caelum's scroll case and pulled out the flower he had stored safely there. "I brought you something."

The flower had a sweet scent, and Sonya fell silent when she took it. Her gaze softened, and a smile crept over her face. "Oh, it's even more beautiful than the last, and it's glowing! Oh, thank you Daric." Daric laughed and lifted her in a warm embrace. Caelum looked away; the two were obsessed with one another, and sometimes the only way to cope was to avert his gaze. "But you're not going to be off the hook that easily," she said, and Daric frowned. Sonya shooed at them. "You two both go rinse off and find clean clothes. You're filthy, and I don't want you looking like that when you are presented to the officers from Edenia." She smacked Daric's backside as he passed her.

Daric smiled and glanced at Caelum. "So much for getting some shuteye before we leave." Caelum laughed and they went to wash at the lake.

Once they were clean, Sonya prepared a hearty meal for the two men, and then Caelum headed to the schoolhouse where he taught the local children. The Guard would provide most of what they would need for their term serving, but Caelum didn't want to leave without some of his research. He felt especially compelled to bring it with him after what he had witnesses at the crater. If what he had seen had truly been the appearance of an Unbound, that beast would soon wreak havoc on anything that had the misfortune to cross its path. Once Caelum arrived at the training ground, he would tell the officers about his theory. *Studying about something so terrible is one thing,* he thought. *I never wanted to experience that terror for myself.* His skin prickled as he recalled what had happened at the crater, yet he couldn't help but feel a little excited at the prospect of witnessing an Unbound. Caelum said a quick prayer, thanking the Creator that Almanis Village had been spared its wrath—at least for the time being.

He arrived at the schoolhouse and went inside. He walked down the hallway past the large empty classroom where he had taught the children of the valley to read and write, among other subjects. Caelum had been the first inhabitant of the valley in a long while to be accepted into the Scholar's Guild, and after he returned home, the village council had decided that he would become headmaster of the schoolhouse before he had even unpacked. It had been four years since he had begun as headmaster, hoping to send more students from the valley to study amongst the scholars. He felt a small ache as he realized that, after today, he would no longer be there to oversee their instruction. He shook the feeling away and reassured himself that he would be back at the end of his three years of service.

Caelum climbed the stairs to the second floor, which held his personal quarters and private study. Light streamed in through the small window above his desk. Open books and scrolls were scattered across the wooden floor in a manner that would seem chaotic and unorganized to anyone else, but Caelum knew right where to look for the pages he desired. He was gathering the most important pieces of his research when a knock on the door caused him to nearly jump out of his skin.

"Excuse me, teacher," said a voice.

Caelum gathered himself and turned. "Oh, Fredric. I didn't know you were here." Fredric was a few years younger than Caelum and had served as his assistant at the schoolhouse. Fredric would be taking Caelum's place teaching the children of the valley once he had gone.

Fredric walked into the room. "I saw you come into the schoolhouse and thought I would come to say goodbye, seeing as how you'll be leaving today."

"Oh, well thank you. It certainly makes leaving easier, knowing you will be here to keep things going." Caelum could tell by the way Fredric was glancing about nervously that there was something else he wanted to say. "What is it Fredric?"

Fredric took a deep breath. "It's just that... I was thinking about that book you were showing me. Oleth's journal where he recounts witnessing the appearance of an Unbound. I know most people believe it is a work of fiction, and of course I know *you* believe it is a factual account." Fredric was rambling as he sometimes did, but Caelum waited patiently for him to get to the point. "I remember him mentioning an earthquake, and a flash of light. Obviously, we just had an earthquake, and I didn't see a flash of light, but some of the other boys say they did, and I was wondering—"

"You were wondering if there is anything to be worried about, if an Unbound may have appeared," Caelum said grimly.

"Erm... yes," he said, looking a little embarrassed. "I know it's silly."

Caelum paused before answering, a distant look in his eyes. "I was there, Fredric. I saw the explosion of light, felt the violent lashing of the wind and the churning of the earth. It... it was unnatural." He took a deep breath before continuing. "And something was there, in the light. It was barely discernable, but amidst the chaos I saw a creature. It couldn't be anything else."

The blood had drained from the younger boy's face as he listened to Caelum's recollection. "Then wha-what do we do?" he stuttered.

Caelum reached out a comforting hand and placed it on Frederic's shoulder. He was every bit as terrified as the boy, but he did his best to conceal it for Frederic's sake.

"You don't need to do anything. Just focus on your new role as the head instructor here until I come back. As for the Unbound," he said, "leave that to me. I am going to inform the Guard of the threat, and they will send the Knights of Radiance to deal with it."

That seemed to satisfy Frederic well enough, and the two of them said their goodbyes before the young man headed off to the rest of his day's errands. Caelum dug in his cluttered study until he found the journal of Oleth Zandarion, one of the few items he possessed that had once belonged to his father. It was written in a language that pre-dated the nation of Edenia, a language long extinct. Caelum had been working on translating the journal for many years, having had a breakthrough only in the last few months. Oleth's journal was a treasure trove of information regarding the Unbound, and it was through the journal that he had learned of the connection between Almanis Crater and the Unbound. He sat down in his reading chair and fingered through the pages.

Caelum couldn't believe he had finally talked his father into letting him and his mother travel with one of his trading convoys. He stuck his head out the back of the covered wagon he shared with his parents and gazed at the enormous cloud of dust produced by the four wagons trailing behind them. Each of those wagons was filled with a variety of goods to be sold off in Edenia City. He had never been to the city before, and he was already seven years old. Lonny had already been with his dad, and he was only five.

"Caelum, sit down!" his mother snapped from across the wagon. "One small rock catching the wagon wheel could send you flying right out onto the road!"

Caelum rolled his eyes before reluctantly pulling his head inside and sitting down with his arms crossed, pouting enough to be sure she could see it. It wasn't even ten seconds before the wagon suddenly lurched and bounced him hard enough to hurt his butt. "Ow," he said rubbing his behind. His mother arched an eyebrow at him and smiled knowingly, but said nothing.

His father laughed. "Come here son, I'll help you look. You won't want to miss this view." His father maneuvered to the back of the wagon. He beckoned for Caelum to come, and he crawled onto his father's lap. His father smiled and wrapped one arm around him, then pointed with his other hand. Caelum looked out and saw that they had emerged from the inland portion of the mountain trail to a section with a breathtaking overlook of the entire valley below.

"Wow," he breathed. He could see Lake Almanis gleaming amidst a sea of emerald trees. There near the lake was Almanis Village. "It looks so small from up here."

"Wait until you see what's on the other side of the mountains," his father said. "Edenia City is at least twenty times the size of our little village!" Caelum couldn't believe it. He tried to do the math in his head and visualize a city twenty times the size of his home, but decided instead to just imagine it as really big.

A faint rumbling sounded outside, followed by a commotion from the wagons behind them. Caelum noted the worry in his father's eyes as he glanced at his mother, then stuck his head out the back of the wagon to peer up the mountainside. A fist sized rock clattered to the ground, then another. His father hurriedly ducked back into the wagon. "Landslide!" he shouted. The rumbling grew louder, and Caelum's father grabbed him and held him in a protective embrace. The wagon lurched forward as the driver goaded the horses for more speed. A moment later something crashed into the wagon, knocking it onto its side, sending them all tumbling as they spun uncontrollably toward the cliff's edge.

Caelum clenched his eyes shut. He tried screaming, but his mouth and nose filled with dirt. They came to a stop, but he remained huddled as dirt and debris continued pouring over him. He only opened his eyes when he heard his father call his name.

"Caelum!"

He blinked the dirt out of his eyes and looked up at his father, who was reaching down through the wagon's torn canvas to hold Caelum's arm. The scene didn't register with Caelum. He looked down and screamed. He was suspended a thousand feet in midair. The landslide had tipped the wagon on its side and half buried it, knocking it far enough off the road so that it was now resting on the edge of the precipice. The tattered canvas covering hanging over the cliffside was the only support for Caelum and his family.

"Just look at me, son," said his father. "I'm going to pull you up."

The wind whipped all around him. Caelum whimpered as he focused on not looking down. As his father began slowly pulling him into the wagon, the canvas ripped, and Caelum fell a few feet before he jerked to a stop and let out a high-pitched yelp. His father had caught onto one of the arched metal frames that held the canvas and was now dangling with Caelum over the cliffside, grunting in pain.

"Jakob!" his mother called from above.

"We're ok!" his father responded. "Caelum," he said softly, "I am going to pull you up, but then you are going to have to hang onto the frame and climb out on your own. Can you do that?" Caelum bit his lips, trying to fight back his tears as he nodded. "Ok, here we go." His father's arm shook and his lips peeled back as he pulled Caelum up to the frame. Caelum grabbed it and pulled himself up to rest, wrapping his arms and legs around the thin metal band as he lay there. At the rear of the wagon, opposite Caelum and his father, he saw his mother lying on the canvas, trying to keep her weight centered on the frame. Her leg stuck out at an odd angle. She sobbed in relief when she saw he was unharmed.

His father pulled himself up enough to rest his arms over the iron frame. "Don't you worry. Help is on the way, son" he said. "We just need to wait."

The wagon shifted. Everyone's eyes snapped to the front of the wagon, where the horses lay on their sides, broken and half covered in dirt. One of them was hanging partially off the side of the cliff, but it was still connected to their wagon. It was sliding slowly over the edge, shifting the whole wagon closer to a long fall and a swift end. "Oh no," his father breathed. "If it falls, it could pull the whole thing down with it." He thought for a moment. "Caelum, I need you to do something for me," he said.

"Ok," Caelum agreed, terrified.

"I need you to climb next to the driver's seat and grab the toolbox. Take out the hatchet and hand it down to me. After you do that, I want you to climb the rest of the way out of the wagon, then wait for the men who are coming this way. Do you understand?"

"Yes, father," he said. The front iron frame had bent at the top from the weight of the landslide, blocking the way out, but Caelum thought he could squeeze through it.

"Good," said his father. "Now, climb across me." His father swung himself to reach the next iron frame support with his other arm, making a bridge with his body. Caelum crawled across cautiously until he could reach the wagon driver's seat. He had climbed on his father a million times at home, yet he trembled this time knowing that a fall would kill him. He reached the other side, found the toolbox, and took out the hatchet. Slowly, carefully, he handed it back down to his father.

"Good job, son. Now get moving," his father said. Caelum carefully climbed the rest of the way out. The wagon was covered by the dirt to the point that very little was visible from the top. All that dirt was likely the only reason the wagon hadn't already tumbled to the valley floor below. Caelum peered back into the wagon to see what his father was doing.

Jakob hung suspended from the first iron frame by one hand, holding the small hatchet in his other hand. He swung the hatchet with all his might and struck the wooden beam that extended from the front of the wagon to the harnessed horses, hoping to separate the horses sliding slowly of the ledge from the main body of the wagon. He pulled back and struck again, and again.

"Wait!" cried a weak voice. Caelum saw that lying there with the horses, half covered by the dirt, was the driver. He must have been thrown from his seat and landed among the horses. It was a miracle he was still alive, though he was in bad shape. He was tangled up in the harnesses. "Please...."

Caelum's father hesitated, knowing full well that if he cut the beam, the driver would fall with it to his doom. The other men of the convoy were close; Caelum could hear their voices. They were coming to help. His father looked up at him. "Go meet the men who are coming. We will wait for them to get here." He sighed and nodded to himself. "We can make it."

Caelum nodded and did as his father said, making his way carefully over the loose dirt toward the men coming his way. "Over here!" he shouted, waving his arms. He reached the edge of the landslide and stepped off. A loud snap sounded behind him, and as he turned, he saw the lead horse slide the rest of the way off the cliffside. The second horse followed, and Caelum watched in horror as the entire wagon plummeted to the valley floor below.

He awoke with a start, Oleth's journal falling to the floor with a loud *thump*. He must have dozed off for a few moments. Caelum hadn't dreamt of that fateful day on the mountain for years, but the vivid recollection of his parents' deaths stirred up many painful feelings he thought he had banished. The men in his father's convoy had called Jakob a hero for his "incredibly brave" sacrifice, giving his life in an attempt to save the wagon driver, but Caelum would have preferred his father had been a coward and still alive. And his mother…

Caelum clenched his eyes shut to stem the flow of tears, wiping them away. His apprehension about the Unbound must have triggered his old nightmare. He would feel better once he informed the captain of the guard.

"Aw, damn!" Caelum jumped out of his chair and looked out the window at the sun. He would have to hurry to make it to the training ground on time. He quickly grabbed the rest of his things, fastened his leather scroll case filled with his most important research over his crimson scholar's coat, and set out to meet Daric and the other recruits.

The training ground was at the southern end of the village. It consisted of an open field, an armory, and a small guardhouse where the members of the guard stationed here lived. Almanis was a small village, requiring only three sentries whose duties consisted mostly of training the local militia. Today, however, an entire company of Edenian Guards filled the practice field, and recruits from all over the valley were in line to register for their service term. Corporal Bek was standing with a man who could only be the leader of the company of Guards, taking registrations. Bek was a grizzled old man who commanded the small unit in Almanis Village. He had been stationed in the valley longer than Caelum had been alive and had looked a hundred years old for as long as Caelum could remember. Caelum found Daric and they took their place in line.

"What's the matter with you?" Daric whispered. "You look sick. Was it the stew Sonya made for us? Don't tell her I said this, but my stomach was churning something fierce until I finally managed to take a—"

"No, it's not that" Caelum cut him off, not wanting to hear details. "Last night, when you were out cold, I… I saw something." Daric got quiet. "There was an explosion, and something came out of the crater." Caelum met his friend's eyes. "I know you don't believe that they actually exist, but I think it may have been an Unbound, and I need to tell the captain here. I have to make him believe me."

Daric nodded. "Well, what are we waiting for?"

The answer caught Caelum off guard. He thought Daric would need more convincing, but Daric had already started off toward the front of the line, pushing his way through the other recruits. Daric had never been one to worry about how he might be perceived, preferring straightforward honesty and unfiltered bluntness.

"No, Daric wai—"

"Sir, excuse me, sir," said Daric as he walked right up to the captain's desk. "My friend has something important that he needs to speak with you about."

Caelum covered his face with his hand and sighed. This was not how it was supposed to go. Most people laughed in his face whenever he referred to the Unbound as anything more than fanciful stories. Daric never did, for which Caelum was grateful, but this man whom neither of them had ever met should probably have been approached with a *little* more tact. The captain looked up from his desk, first at Daric, then at Caelum. His thin lips were pursed, and he had a frustrated, impatient cast to his eyes. "Speak."

Nothing for it now…

"Sir..." Caelum gulped. "Last night, Daric and I—" Caelum glanced at Daric who gave him an encouraging nod. "—we were out at the crater north of the village. There was an earthquake, a flash of light, and an explosion, and well... I think there is an Unbound loose in Almanis Valley."

This was clearly not what the captain had been expecting him to say. His eyebrows rose and he addressed Daric. "You saw this Unbound as well?"

"Well, uh, no sir," Daric fumbled. "You see, I had fallen and was out cold sir, but I..."

The captain barked a laugh, "Hah! I've heard many stories from recruits trying to dodge the service, but never this dramatic. An Unbound? And I suppose I should delay the draft here and chase after this fantasy of yours?" He spat. "Get back in line."

"Of course not, sir," Caelum persisted. "But—"

"Now!" The captain left no room for argument.

Well, he had tried. Caelum didn't know what else to do, but he had to do something. As he and Daric walked defeatedly back to the end of the line, Corporal Bek pulled Caelum aside.

"I overheard you talking to the captain," he muttered under his breath. "How sure are you about what you saw, boy?"

A spark of hope reignited in Caelum, and he answered, "I am certain, corporal."

"An Unbound. Well I'll be..." Bek frowned. "Can't say I've ever heard a real sighting before, but I know you to be a good lad, just like your father. If you say you saw something, I believe you. But there aren't many in the Guard who will believe a storybook monster has appeared out of nowhere." Bek paused and thought for a moment. "If this thing really is an Unbound, as you say, then what can we do to stop it?"

Caelum hesitated. "There isn't anything *we* can do to stop it. From all of the accounts I've read, only the Knights of Radiance can take down one of the Unbound." Bek swore. "We could, however, send riders to warn the other villages, help them evacuate. If the Unbound didn't come here, my best guess is that it headed northward, toward Beldun and the other northern settlements."

Daric grimaced. "The people in those villages are as likely to believe the danger of the Unbound as the captain."

"Still…" Bek was thoughtful. "I'll take care of this boys. Well done." The corporal rejoined the captain at the registration desk and whispered into his ear. The captain's eyes narrowed at Corporal Bek, then at the two young men, before he reluctantly nodded. The captain stood and called for attention.

"Men! Corporal Bek has informed me that late last night this valley experienced an unusual earthquake, and after hearing the testimony of these boys, he is concerned that some of the nearby villages have been affected. He has asked that we stop in Beldun to assist the villagers as needed. As this will be slightly out of our way, we leave as soon as we are able. Dismissed." The captain walked straight toward Caelum and Daric. "You two, come with me."

Caelum followed apprehensively. The captain did not seem very pleased at the inconvenience of this detour.

"I respect Bek and will do as he has asked, but I will not give you two a chance to disappear. You will stay by my side on the way to Beldun and every day until we arrive in Edenia City. Understood?"

"Yes, sir!" Daric and Caelum said in unison. They looked at one another and grinned.

Chapter 3

What was is no more. What remains is Unbound.

-Journal of Oleth Zandarion
Translation by Caelum Karasin
E.A. 967

In less than a quarter of an hour, the captain led them out of Almanis Village on the road to Beldun. Caelum and Daric rode just behind him and to his right. True to his word, the captain hadn't let them out of his sight since his decision to take this detour.

The company had close to five hundred recruits from all over the valley, and about a quarter of those came from the three main settlements within the region. Almanis Village was the largest, followed by Galamoran on the east side of the lake, and their current destination, Beldun, which was farther north. Caelum and Daric had grown up with some of the other recruits from the village, but they were riding at the back of the column.

Daric attempted to make conversation with both Caelum and the captain, but neither responded with more than short, half-hearted replies. Daric eventually accepted their silence and hummed softly to himself in a rich baritone. Caelum couldn't stop thinking about what they would find in Beldun. Had the Unbound come this way? Would the villagers listen to his warning? Would the captain even give him an opportunity to tell them? Was he imagining things? Caelum opened his scroll case and fingered through his research until he found the page he needed. It was a half-finished translation of a poem from Oleth's journal regarding the Unbound. Repeated at the end of each stanza were the words:

What was is no more,
What remains is Unbound.

"What does that mean?"

Caelum jumped in alarm and nearly fell out of his saddle. Daric had maneuvered his horse so that he could peer over Caelum's shoulder at the text, and Caelum had been so engrossed in his study that he hadn't noticed. Daric had always enjoyed taking advantage of how Caelum would get lost in thought and startle easily. Caelum punched him in the arm, but he might as well punch a rock. "I hate when you do that."

Daric just laughed. "I can't help it. But I really am interested. What is what was? I'm confused even trying to ask the question!"

"What was is no more... it could be a lot of things. It may refer to a time or a civilization before the Unbound. Maybe it means something died, or changed, or was lost. I'm not entirely sure which theory describes our Unbound. Or maybe it is something else that I haven't even thought of."

"So you've got us chasing a giant, ferocious beast that may also be dead, and you gave me a hard time for making you climb down a cliff? I think *I* deserve an apology!"

Caelum rolled his eyes and went back to his study.

"Captain, look!" cried one of the soldiers from behind. Caelum followed the man's gaze through the trees to a cloud in the distance. *Wait, that is no ordinary cloud… it's smoke. Beldun is burning!*

The captain came to the same conclusion. "We must hurry!" he shouted, urging his horse to a gallop. Caelum and the rest of the company followed quickly behind. The air became thick with smoke and ash.

The captain was the first to see the desolation. He stared in horror. "No…"

Beldun was gone. Not a single structure remained intact. Splintered and smoldering timbers lay scattered among the ruins. The recruits from Beldun cried out upon seeing the ruins of their home. Some dismounted and ran toward homes that were burned to the ground, weeping for loved ones who had perished. The rest of the company rode into town in disbelieving silence.

"We were too late," said Caelum to Daric. "I… I should have gone straight to the captain first thing, or come straight here to warn them, or—"

"Caelum, stop," said Daric. "You did everything you could."

He shook his head slightly. "I… need to record what happened here," he said, yet he couldn't pull his eyes away. So much had been lost. As he watched the agonized wailing of the men around him who had lost everything, he couldn't help but think that this was only the beginning, and that the same thing would happen throughout all Edenia if the Unbound wasn't stopped. "How is it that something so evil can exist and nobody even believes it is real?" He slammed his fist into his hand. "They had no idea what was coming.... how could this happen?"

The captain dismounted and walked over to a pile of rubble. Caelum paled as he realized that the captain was staring down at the charred remains of one of the villagers. It looked as if the man had been torn in half. Without waiting for orders, Daric took a shovel from one of the packhorses and began to dig. Other men slowly recovered themselves to help him. Caelum pulled out a pen and some parchment from his belongings and documented all that he saw. He examined the trail of destruction encompassing Beldun. The creature came from the east, from the direction of the crater, and the trail of scorched earth led northwest toward the Elys Mountains. *Away from Almanis Village.*

Caelum did not hear the captain approach. "Son," he hesitated, "I may have misjudged you, and I nearly made a grave mistake because of it. If this slaughter was really the work of an Unbound, as you say, then I need to know everything you can tell me about the creature." The captain had regained his composure. Caelum had not, and shuddered as he replied.

"Sir, it is said the Unbound care only for destruction. What we see here...." He gagged at the smell of burned meat clouding the air. "What we see here is what we can expect to find everywhere in its wake. The trail it left suggests that it is heading toward the mountains, and fortunately for us there are few settlements in that direction."

The captain nodded. "What would you suggest we do?"

There is nothing we can do, Caelum thought. Instead he said, "The Unbound can only be stopped by the Knights of Radiance. All we can do is try to warn people. If we send out a few riders to try to reach the villages before the Unbound, we could tell them to evacuate to somewhere safe, maybe to Almanis Village. Beyond that, I think we should make haste in our return to Edenia to request the aid of the Knights of Radiance."

"You are telling me not to pursue this creature, to simply allow it to roam freely in these woods and potentially happen upon another village?" the captain demanded. "We should hunt this thing down now before—"

"We would all die, Captain, and accomplish nothing."

The captain stood, calculating. He turned and shouted.

"Bern! Quentin! Ride toward the mountains, stopping in the surrounding villages to tell people to get the hell out of here and make for Almanis Village. The rest of you, get ready for the ride of your life. We are returning to Edenia. You, scholar—" He pointed at Caelum. "—you will ride with me and tell me everything you know about the Unbound."

Before they left, Daric and some of the others finished digging the mass grave in which they buried what remains they could find amidst the rubble. The captain had offered the men from Beldun the chance to stay behind, to pay their respects in whatever way they chose, but they all refused, stating that there was nothing left for them there. They were determined to reach Edenia, as word had spread that the Unbound scholar who rode among them claimed they needed the Knights of Radiance.

Caelum had spent nearly a day in the saddle riding beside Captain Bradford before he learned the man's name. The captain had been grilling him for everything he knew about the Unbound, Knights of Radiance, and anything else that might prove useful against the creature.

So Caelum explained. The oldest manuscripts suggested that the Unbound used to appear regularly, and there were seemingly many different types. But there were commonalities. Sometimes Caelum would discover descriptions of the beasts that were remarkably similar, yet those descriptions would be found in documents written decades apart and in different parts of the world. Their appearances became less regular, and the last account of an appearance had occurred over five-hundred years ago.

"And the Knights of Radiance are supposedly the only ones with a weapon or a power to stop them?" Captain Bradford asked, as though hoping to get a different answer.

"Yes sir," Caelum said apologetically. "All of my research suggests that apart from the Knights of Radiance, these beasts are unstoppable."

"Hmph." Captain Bradford wore a thoughtful frown and was quiet for a moment before he shrugged his shoulders. "Well, that is enough for one day. We will continue this discussion in the morning. It seems I have a lot to think about." He turned to his second in command. "We will make camp here for tonight." The officer saluted and called the company to a halt.

They stopped in a clearing close to a stream that flowed down from the nearby mountains. As the recruits set up their tents, the sun dipped just below the peaks, their shadows creeping eastward. The sound of the water rushing by masked Daric's footsteps as he approached. "Caelum?"

Caelum turned and faced his friend, who looked concerned. "What is it?"

"I've been wondering… is Almanis Village safe? I can't help but remember Beldun, and then I imagine the same thing happening at home, and Sonya is there…"

"The beast headed in the opposite direction." Caelum put a hand on his friend's shoulder, doing his best to comfort him. "Almanis Village is as safe as anywhere for now." He spared telling Daric that nowhere was truly *safe* while the Unbound was free. Daric seemed to calm slightly, but worry was still plain on his face.

"I feel like I should be there with her, in case anything was to happen. I…" Daric looked around to make sure nobody could hear before continuing. "I have to go back."

"Don't be a fool, Daric!" Caelum said. "If you leave, you will forever be branded as a deserter."

"I don't care," Daric growled in frustration. "Maybe there was a part of me that didn't believe you before, or maybe I simply didn't understand the full ramifications of what you were talking about. But, now that I have seen what the Unbound is capable of—"

"I understand how you feel," Caelum said, trying to calm his friend and talk some sense into him, "but there isn't anything we could do there to help. The best thing we can do is to bring word to the people who can make a difference." Caelum looked westward, toward Edenia City. "As soon as we get to the capital, the Knights of Radiance will take care of things. You'll see."

Daric looked at him a long time, then sighed. "You have to promise me, Cael, that you know what you're doing."

"I promise," he said.

"Right," Daric replied with a forced smile. He returned to his bedroll.

Caelum had trouble getting to sleep. He had studied these creatures his whole life, was fascinated by the stories of what they were capable of. Reading about the sort of terror the Unbound wrought upon the world was exciting. Burying the greasy black bones of the dead left in its wake was horrifying. When sleep finally found him, Caelum dreamt of Daric digging a grave and filling it with the bones of all the people of Edenia.

Chapter 4

Nestled in the western foothills of the Elys Mountains, the capital city of Edenia has stood as a symbol of its people's strength for a thousand years. Home of the Edenian Guard, a military force unequaled by the nomadic nations of the north and the loosely affiliated peoples of the Western Wildlands, the city provides a stable centralized government that has ensured peace for citizens throughout the entire Edenian territory. However, Edenia's power does not solely lie in its military might. The city is also home to the Scholar's Guild, a premier institution of learning unlike any before or since its conception. Its focused pursuit of knowledge has led to the development of many breakthrough achievements in fields such as medicine and engineering.

-A History of Edenia and Its People
Headmaster Barius
E.A. 627

The rest of the journey to Edenia was uneventful. The city lay on the other side of the Elys Mountains, which meant the company would take the route through the Nauru Pass. The last time Caelum had traveled the pass had been on his way back to Almanis after completing his studies to become a scholar. The paths became a little too high and narrow, in his opinion, but presented a stunning view of the landscape where he would pause to marvel at the beauty of the valley and the artistry of its Creator. Yet he could not make this journey without also recalling his first journey through these mountains. If there were in fact a Creator, he couldn't possibly be as benevolent as the priests claim. Not after what happened to Caelum's parents.

The pass followed a stream before beginning its steep climb. Captain Bradford continued to interrogate Caelum, determined to learn in a few days the knowledge it had taken Caelum years to acquire. Caelum was happy for the distraction, as it kept him from focusing on the tantalizing sensation that comes from walking a meter away from a sheer cliff drop.

Daric rode close behind them, already friends with the soldiers nearby. He was telling one of his favorite stories, learned in his time as an apprentice sculptor, about an Edenian lord who had contracted his master for a statue depicting a knight carved in the heroic tradition. Daric explained that the "heroic tradition" meant completely nude. The other recruits found that to be quite amusing; most of them grew up in smaller villages around the valley and had never experienced the extravagance of Edenian culture.

Daric continued, "When the statue was finished, the Lord presented it as a gift to Lady Amera, who was so shocked by the nudity she demanded that Lord Kensington commission my master to form a proportionally accurate leaf--" Daric squinted and held his thumb and forefinger in front of his face, practically touching. "—to hang on the sculpture, to restore to it a sense of decency." Daric chuckled, "My master was furious at the insult and refused to make the change. He sent me instead, and they were so pleased with my work I was given the title of Master Sculptor." The other recruits laughed and showered Daric with questions about his travels and creations. It was good to hear the men laughing again.

As the pass led higher into the mountains, the company rounded a ledge overlooking the valley. There was Lake Almanis, shining like sapphire, and the great pines rolled out over the landscape as far as he could see. A sinking feeling came over Caelum when he looked north and saw the scorched path the Unbound had created on its rampage through the forest. It had continued north as he had expected, which loosened the knot in his chest. He had feared that the beast might turn back toward home, but it looked like Almanis Village was safe, for the time being. He heard Daric sigh in relief beside him.

Evening found them through the pass and out of the mountains. They made camp for the night, and it seemed as if Caelum had only just drifted off to sleep when he was awakened by the captain's call to saddle up.

As the city came into view, the recruits erupted into an astonished clamor, clapping each other on the back, pointing fingers, and standing in their saddles to get a better look at a real city. Edenia City was built in the foothills north of the pass. The castle, keep, and Temple of the Creator sat behind an immense wall atop a hill steep on three sides; a gentle slope on the western side led down into the main city. Caelum and Daric shared a knowing grin at the commentary of their fellow recruits, remembering their own excitement when they had first come to the capital as a couple of country boys. Daric had been apprenticed to a master sculptor in the city, and had since been called in many times by some lord or lady for a commissioned work. He had met Sonya in the city, wooed her, and brought her home. Caelum had spent a few years of his studies at the Scholar's Guild in Edenia City. Yet despite their familiarity, it was still spectacular to behold.

The company took the main road through town up to the castle. The capital was a bustling city, filled with people from all across the empire. Merchants' stalls lined the cobbled street on either side, offering an eclectic mix of goods and services. There were clothiers from southern Winfall, clad in bright garments that complemented their ebony skin and striking blue eyes, and beside them an olive-skinned fletcher from the northern province of Crisantia, showing off a set of finely made arrows to potential buyers. There were shops for exotic perfumes, herbal remedies, leatherwork, and all manner of things rarely seen in the valley, each of them with youngsters out front shouting their wares, doing whatever they could to entice the hustling crowds. Caelum recognized the road that would take him to the Scholars' Guild and hoped he would have time to visit, though he didn't think it very likely.

The crowds parted easily for the mounted soldiers, and they soon found themselves riding through the castle gates. Captain Bradford issued commands to another officer and hastened toward the keep, probably anxious to report about the Unbound and what they had encountered in Beldun. The new officer in charge led the recruits to the southern end of the courtyard toward the barracks. Each recruit was given a bunk, small storage compartment, and standard issue military uniform. Caelum folded his scholar's coat and placed it into his locker, donning instead the green and gold tunic worn by all the basic infantrymen. The message they were trying to convey was clear. Whatever the recruits had been before they arrived was to be put aside. They were soldiers now.

Captain Bradford paced impatiently as he waited in the small anteroom for an audience with the king. *There is a rampaging monster loose in the northern territories, and I am forced to wait for him to finish his supper!* Bradford knew that most people dismissed anything related to the Unbound as mythology. He himself would have done the same, before Beldun.

The door to the king's council room opened and a servant appeared, ushering him in. His Majesty Cedric Torrendus III, King of Edenia, sat at the end of the long rectangular table centered in the room, resplendent in a green and black robe and thick golden crown upon his brow. He was in his middle years, his dark hair and neatly trimmed beard showing only the slightest hints of gray.

Bradford recognized few of the other men around the table who were part of the king's council. Most were nobles from powerful houses in Edenia, with a few exceptions, including a scholar of crimson as well as the recently added Archpriest of Edenia, Einhold La'Rathia. About five hundred years ago the former king, Cedric I, had expelled the church from any role in government after a dispute between the king and the Archpriest. However, the recent appointment of the Archpriest's son as Knight Commander of the prestigious Knights of Radiance seemed to have smoothed over the hostilities. Bradford wondered what the original argument had entailed, but he pushed the thought aside, as there were presently greater matters to discuss.

The king cleared his throat. "I am told you bring news claiming that the beasts of legend may actually be quite real. Make your report."

Captain Bradford knelt before the king. "Your majesty, I have seen what this beast is capable of with my own eyes. An entire village burnt to the ground, no survivors. We believe the beast headed north of the valley into the mountains. There is a young man among the latest recruits, a scholar wearing crimson, who seems to be a specialist on Edenian mythology and history of the Unbound. He is convinced that the monster is in fact an Unbound and claims they can only be stopped by some weapon or power the Knights of Radiance possess. I don't know if that is true, but I have come to trust the boy. I suggest we send the Knights of Radiance to respond to this threat immediately." Bradford had never heard of any special power the Knights of Radiance might wield, but they were damn good warriors, the best in the Guard.

"Interesting," said the crimson scholar, stroking a thin beard. "I wonder… would the scholar you mentioned be a young man named Caelum?" Bradford nodded, and the scholar smirked. "Of course." He leaned back in his chain and addressed the king. "Sire, this Caelum is known to me. He showed great potential during his time at the guild, yet upon completing his studies he chose to focus his research on fables rather than anything useful. It wouldn't surprise me if the boy fabricated this tale to legitimize his research."

Bradford shook his head. "Respectfully, I must disagree. I've spoken to the lad at great lengths and he didn't strike me as the type who would lie about something of this magnitude. And his fear was genuine. If there is even a chance that Caelum is right, we need to act."

King Cedric's expression darkened. "Remember your place, captain."

"Forgive me, sire."

The king stared at him a moment before folding his hands, wearing a thoughtful frown. "I have heard the stories of these creatures, but I don't recall anything that relates them to the Knights of Radiance." The king paused. "Still... word of this *supposed* Unbound is spreading, and if it is left unchecked, we will have mass panic among the citizens in the city.

The king stood, taking a moment to look at the men around the table before he continued. "Let us send in the Knights of Radiance to deal with this threat, and let us do so with all of the pomp and circumstance we can muster. This will help to reassure the people." Nods and murmurs of agreement came from each of the advisors. For a second it looked as if the Archpriest might object, but he expressed his support of the king's decision along with the rest of them. Bradford suppressed his annoyance as he waited for the king to continue. "We must also send in a supporting force to assist them."

Bradford stood. "Your majesty I would like to command the force accompanying the Knights of Radiance." He hoped he didn't sound too eager, but he had chosen to listen to the scholar's advice and halt his pursuit of the beast in Almanis Valley, and he felt responsible for any destruction the beast might have caused since. He had to get back.

"Very well Captain Bradford. But know this." The king's expression hardened. "Should this expedition turn out to be nothing more than a wild goose chase, you will be held responsible. Understood?"

"Understood, sire."

"Good. Prepare your men, you leave tomorrow." The king sat back down at the table and waved his hand. "Dismissed."

Bradford bowed and walked out of the council room.

Chapter 5

While Edenia's military and intellectual might both serve as a potent deterrent to their enemies, the third power in Edenia is the key to its domestic success. The Church of the Creator provides a moral foundation upon which the government rests. Many lords and ladies, including the former king himself, have included amongst their advisors a representative from the Church. However, this practice has dwindled in recent years for unknown reasons.

-A History of Edenia and Its People
Headmaster Barius
E.A. 627

The ring of the morning bells echoed through the hallowed halls of the Temple of the Creator as Callus La'Rathia, leader of the Knights of Radiance, sat alone in the great cathedral, thumbing through the scriptures as he waited for his father to arrive. A bouquet of light streamed down through the stained glass all around him, bathing the white marble columns in a variety of striking hues. The temple was an artistic and engineering masterpiece, a creative offering to the Divine Creator to whom Callus had dedicated his life.

Yet aside from the Knight Commander, the building was empty, as was typical in this church at the capital. Not like the way it had been in Snowhaven, where he had grown up with his sister Halia. People were simpler there, more focused on enjoying the little things in life, not burdened with the politics of city living. The temple at Snowhaven was a humble place compared to here, but rarely was it empty. Children gathered there for daily lessons, as Callus and his sister had. Townsfolk stopped in to offer prayers. And there were weekly gatherings in which the entire town would come together in thanksgiving to their Creator for His many blessings. It would never have been a convenient place to set up a private meeting.

"Hello Son."

Callus closed his book and stood to face his father, Archpriest of Edenia.

"Father," he said, embracing the man awkwardly. Callus had been told all his life that he was a spitting image of his father, Einhold. The two were of the same height and shared the same golden La'Rathia hair, though his father wore a thick beard that Callus refused to imitate. Yet they had their differences. His father was a slender man who had never held a sword in his life. Callus, on the other hand, had held a sword since he was old enough to carry one, and had trained his body and mind in order to become the perfect soldier.

His father held the embrace a little too long, so Callus broke it and stepped away, noting the new creases in his father's brow and the slight buildup of moisture in his eyes. He had rarely seen his father so shaken. Something was wrong.

"What is it, Father? Why have you summoned me here?"

Einhold struggled to find words, but reluctantly they came. "Callus, I assume you've received the king's orders...."

Callus nodded. "Yes, I am to lead the Knights of Radiance to battle against a creature believed to be one of the legendary Unbound. We are scheduled to depart in less than an hour."

"You mustn't go!" his father said forcefully, reaching out to grab hold of Callus's tunic.

Callus pulled away. "Father what has gotten into you? Of course I must go!"

"No, I cannot allow it!" Einhold said relentlessly, looking as if he wished to say more, but hesitating.

Callus couldn't believe what he was hearing. "What's gotten into you Father?" he asked angrily. It was his father who had wanted him to become a soldier in the first place, who had chastised him for the slightest demonstration of disobedience to his superiors. "My whole life you have impressed upon me the importance of duty—"

"And I am now asking, no, I am *begging* you not to do this."

His father's posture, usually so certain, now stooped, as though he were a common beggar, not the Archpriest. Callus almost hesitated, but his sense of duty prevailed. "You would have me do what then, defy the king? Bring dishonor upon myself and our whole family?" He scoffed. "No, Father. I have spent my entire life trying to please you. It was *your* ambition that I become a Knight of Radiance, not my own. Now you would see me throw everything away—"

"I would see you *live!*" he cried.

Callus was taken aback at the anguish in his Father's voice. "You know something," he said, putting the pieces together.

Einhold flinched at his words and looked around nervously. "It is dangerous to say more," he said. "You will simply have to trust me."

"That's not good enough, Father," he said. "Every mission comes with its own risks. That is the nature of being a soldier. This is no different, and I will go."

Einhold's eyes shifted to something behind Callus. The Knight Commander turned and saw that an acolyte had entered and was lighting candles to prepare for the morning prayers. Callus hadn't realized it was getting so late. He turned to face his father once more and noticed how pale and fragile the archpriest looked. His father rarely showed any sign of weakness, but perhaps the years were catching up to him.

Einhold spoke with a weak smile. "I am proud of you, son. I still remember the day I caught you and your sister in the library at Snowhaven. You both had stolen four pies from one of the bakers. I don't know how you managed to get inside, though I suppose your sister might have been given the key by your uncle, for her studies." He closed his eyes sadly. "What I wouldn't give for the three of us to go back there now."

Callus frowned, unsure how to handle his father's strange rush of nostalgia. He couldn't recall ever seeing the archpriest like this, so vulnerable, and it made Callus uncomfortable. But now was not the time for reconciliation, nor reminiscence. His duty was clear, and Callus steeled his resolve.

The acolyte had finished lighting the candles and approached Einhold. "Your Holiness," the woman said, "might I have a moment of your time before the afternoon's service?"

Einhold's gaze never left Callus, but he nodded. "Then that is all."

"I must be going," Callus announced. He bowed low. "If you'll excuse me, Father?"

Einhold nodded. "Farewell, son."

Einhold watched as his son left the temple, full of regret for the things left unsaid and for his selfish and cowardly actions that now brought his family to the edge of ruin.

"Our master suspected you might betray him," the woman dressed as an acolyte said. "You know the price of betrayal."

Einhold stared ahead defiantly. "I know it well," the archpriest answered, doing his best to keep his voice from quivering. "But Callus knows nothing."

"Which is why I allowed him to leave this place alive," said the sinister acolyte. "Though if our master didn't still have need of him…" The woman smiled viciously, then shook her head slightly and shrugged. "His time will come soon enough."

A dagger appeared in the false acolyte's hand.

Forgive me Callus… Halia….

Chapter 6

Those among us who have proven themselves worthy, heroes of great renown, now ride forth with the blessing of all our people, bringing with them the hope that one day we shall be free from despair.

-*Journal of Oleth Zandarion*
Translation by Caelum Karasin
E.A. 967

Caelum stood at attention along with the rest of the recruits from Almanis Valley. They lined the King's Road near the main gate, watching as the parade honoring the Knights of Radiance approached the city exit. The whole city was celebrating the beginning of the quest to slay the Unbound. Most citizens knew very little about what had occurred in Almanis Valley, but the Knights of Radiance were heroes of the people, and the mixture of adoration, curiosity, and over the top ceremony created an excitement that rivaled by anything the citizens could remember.

Musicians marched in front, their shining trumpets blaring a triumphant fanfare. Next came the Knights of Radiance all six of them, riding proud atop white destriers, horses and knights both resplendent in the green and gold of Edenia. Callus La'Rathia, Knight Commander of the Knights of Radiance, rode at their head. Captain Bradford and his company followed at the rear, along with the pack animals and supply carts. The captain's dark expression was in sharp contrast to the surrounding festivities.

Caelum had hoped for a long time that he would have the opportunity to speak with one of the Knights of Radiance. He longed to ask some of his unanswered questions about their relation to the Unbound, but perhaps he would find the opportunity when they returned from their mission. The recruits all raised their swords in a salute as the parade passed, and watched as they disappeared through the gates, the music slowly fading in the distance.

Master Hamen, the master-at-arms responsible for training the new recruits, motioned for them to fall into marching formation. Caelum had expected they would return to the training yard, but instead Master Hamen led them out the gates after the parade. He was filled with a glimmer of hope, thinking that perhaps they would follow Bradford and the Knights of Radiance to pursue the Unbound, until Hamen halted to address them.

"It is time to turn you men into soldiers." Caelum didn't like the sound of that. "For the rest of today, you will march in formation around the city. Every morning, until I am satisfied, we will march in formation until midday." Some of the other recruits visibly slumped at the command. Caelum wasn't enthused himself, but he recognized the necessity. Infantry needed to be mobile, moving as a compact fighting force. Mastering this simple exercise was crucial, but knowing that didn't help his aching feet feel any better. One recruit let out a particularly despairing sigh.

"Is there a problem soldier?" Master Hamen demanded.

The recruit paled as he stammered, "No... no sir."

"Good. Now march!"

Caelum spared one last glance toward the soldiers in the distance, wondering what it would be like to face an Unbound, to see the Knights of Radiance in action, before Master Hamen reprimanded him. It would be almost a month before the Knights of Radiance would return, he estimated, and until then he would just have to focus on his training. At least now he could be sure that Almanis Village would be safe.

Jeremiah Bradford had led men into battle many times, but never had he experienced the sort of uneasiness that plagued him this mission. It had been clear from the start that most of the men accompanying him on this journey did not understand or believe the gravity of the task before them. The first few days out of the city consisted of lighthearted jesting and boasting from the soldiers about the heroic deeds they would perform while assisting the Knights of Radiance in vanquishing the Unbound.

They sobered quickly upon their arrival at Beldun.

Bradford still couldn't believe the destruction the beast was capable of. He watched the Knights of Radiance as they rode through the village. Each of them wore a grim expression, but there was something else there... determination. *Good.*

Bradford respected the Knights of Radiance. Each had been chosen for demonstrating exceptional character and talent. He had even recommended two of them for the position. They were the best soldiers Edenia had, capable of extraordinary feats of bravery and leadership. If anyone in Edenia had a chance at stopping this beast, it would be these six.

Bradford led the men northwest, following the trail of scorched earth and blackened trees. It looked more like they were tracking a wildfire than a beast. The air was thick with ash stirred up by the horses. Bradford tied a kerchief to his mouth to keep from choking.

Two days after they began tracking the beast from Beldun, his first scout returned. The scout led them to the remains of one of the soldiers he had sent out during his first visit to Beldun, but the body was burned to the point that he could not tell whether the soldier had been Quentin or Bern. They buried his remains, said a prayer, and continued the hunt. The morale of his men sank steadily as they began to realize what they were facing.

A week later, the scouts rode back and reported that they had found the beast—or, at least, what they assumed must be the beast. They led Bradford and the Knights of Radiance to the top of a nearby hill outside the scorched trail. Bradford could see in the forest below him the trail they had been following, and in the distance, he could see what looked like a fire blazing against the wind, moving to the northwest. "That is where we will find our monster."

Callus La'Rathia, Knight Commander of the Knights of Radiance, approached Bradford on the hilltop. He was a hand taller than Bradford, with golden blond hair and icy blue eyes. He wore an emerald green cloak over gleaming silver armor, an elaborate sword belted to his waist. Many young lords liked to wear such impressive blades, but few could wield them effectively. Callus was one of the few. Bradford had never known a man more dangerous with a sword, but there was more to the young man than his skill in battle. He was also a *good* man, and that was why Bradford had recommended that he be chosen to serve among the Knights of Radiance.

Callus looked out at the source of the fire. "So, there waits our quarry."

"So it would appear," Bradford replied. "Are you and your men ready for this?"

Callus nodded. "We are, though it would help to have some more information about this creature. We should sneak in close. I want to see exactly what we are dealing with."

Bradford nodded in agreement. "I'll have my scouts lead you as close as they dare."

"A moment, sir," said the younger man, withdrawing an envelope from where it had been tucked in his gauntlet. "I can't shake an uneasy feeling I have about this mission. I have… written a letter, for my sister, Halia." He held the letter out to Bradford. "I would like for you to deliver it to her, should anything happen to me."

Bradford drew back from Callus' outstretched hand as if it were holding a diseased rat. "Callus, I've made it a habit to never accept such a thing from any man I've commanded. You can deliver that letter to her yourself when this is over."

"Ah, but I am not under your command anymore, sir," Callus said with a small grin. "In fact, on this mission I believe *you* are under *mine*." He pushed the letter into Bradford's chest, and the captain reluctantly took it.

"Fine, dammit. I'll hold on to it for you until this Unbound is dealt with. Then you can have it back."

Callus smiled. "Thank you."

Bradford shook his head and grumbled. He tried to shake off his own growing apprehension about this mission, but

Callus' admission of his own concern was making it difficult. "All right, enough of that. Let's get moving." He started off down the hill.

"Wait Bradford, look!" Callus pointed at the fire. Captain Bradford turned back toward the source of the fire. It had been moving northwest, but was now traveling southeast. Traveling back toward his men.

Bradford didn't believe in coincidence; the beast must know it was being followed. He didn't know how it had become aware of them, but he was sure of it. He commanded one of his scouts to return to the men and call them to arms. He then turned to Callus. "Son, do you have any special secret you would like to tell me that relates to how you intend to take this thing down?"

Callus met Bradford's eyes and calmly replied, "No."

Bradford grimaced. "I was afraid of that."

Callus gripped his sword. "We'll do what we can."

In short order Bradford stood in a clearing atop the hill alongside his men, staring out at the smoke rising above the treetops—smoke from an unnatural fire that headed straight toward them. His men were divided into two units, one holding long pikes and the other carrying hunting bows, everyone wearing a cloak that had been soaked in a nearby stream. They still had not seen the Unbound, which worried the captain more than he was willing to admit, but it was obvious the beast could start a fire, so they took what precautions they could. He remembered the scholar mentioning that there were records of a fire-breathing Unbound and assumed that the foe they faced today was something similar. The plan was simple. They would lure the

Unbound to this spot, the pikemen would take the initial charge and then surround the beast to cut off any escape route, and the Knights of Radiance, equipped with modified boar spears, would slay the beast. Simple, but not easy.

He hoped that the scholar had been right about the Knights of Radiance, that they would be able to handle the beast without incident. They certainly looked like heroes of legend, proudly standing at the head of the formation, armor gleaming in the sunlight. If they failed, a hundred pikes should skewer the monster into oblivion. One way or another, they would take this creature down. If things were to somehow go sour, he had his fastest riders prepared to send word to Edenia of what happened here. But that seemed unlikely.

Then why can't I shake the feeling that something is wrong?

A noise like thunder shook the ground. Frightened glances and mutters spread throughout the soldiers' formation.

"Hold your ground men!"

This thing must be immense.

"Remember your training!"

We are not prepared for this.

"Close ranks, set pikes!"

With a loud crack, the Unbound burst into the clearing, charging through tree trunks as if they were twigs. Bradford's eyes widened at the sight of it. The beast had the body of a serpent covered in scales the color of blood, but it ran on four powerful legs, tipped with menacing claws as long as daggers. It was easily ten horses long from head to tail, and its whole body emanated an ethereal red glow. Of all the soldiers, only the Knights of Radiance maintained their composure in the face of the nightmarish creature, and Bradford gained a newfound respect for the knights who could stare this charging demon in the eye without flinching. Their bravery inspired him enough to bring him back to his own senses. "Archers, ready! Loose!"

Arrows rained down upon the stampeding beast and bounced off harmlessly, succeeding only in enraging the beast further. The Unbound closed on them fast. After another volley of arrows, the archers retreated behind the pikes. Bradford was proud to see his pikemen now holding their ground alongside the Knights of Radiance, knowing that taking the oncoming charge from the Unbound would likely claim their own lives as well as the beast's. With a roar the Unbound collided with the pikemen, sending bodies and shattered spears flying. The men quickly closed ranks to fill the gap the Unbound had created. Bradford watched as the beast slowed and came to a stop, and he searched for signs that it had been dealt a lethal blow.

The Knights of Radiance wasted no time, immediately rushing to the Unbound, spears ready, to finish the beast swiftly. Callus stopped suddenly, stretching his free hand toward the others and crying out, "Wait!"

He was too late.

The Unbound spun at remarkable speed. With one swing of his claw, it sliced the first of the charging knights in two. There was not a scratch on the beast. The other Knights of Radiance turned to flee and were engulfed in flames as fire spewed from the creature's maw. Bradford winced at the heat from fifty meters away and watched in horror as Callus unsheathed his sword and engaged the beast with a vengeful fury.

Callus ducked under the first swipe of the Unbound's claw and slashed at the beast's arm. The Unbound drew breath as if to unleash another spray of deadly flame, but Callus swung his sword at the beast's jaw, knocking it away so that the deadly flames were fired into the air above him. In the split second the beast was recovering, Callus drove his sword up and into the beast's mouth, but once again the blade glanced off the monster, leaving no injury. The Unbound clamped its jaws, sinking its teeth deep into Callus's sword arm, and he screamed in pain. Callus grabbed the dagger at his side and jabbed at the beast's eye in one last desperate attempt to damage the creature, but to no avail. Callus lowered his head, defeated, as the Unbound opened its fangs, wider than its mouth should have been able to stretch. Bradford gasped as the maw closed over Callus, completely devouring the Knight Commander.

Just like that, hope was dead.

"No!" shouted Bradford.

This can't be happening, he thought to himself. It was chaos all around him. All six Knights of Radiance were gone, and most of his men were dead or fleeing. It was a scene from a nightmare. *What can I do?* He could not find the messengers he had prepared, which he hoped meant they had gotten away and were already riding hard for Edenia. *This thing will destroy us if we try to fight it head on, but I can't risk letting it wander loose to destroy everything it comes across.* Bradford watched as the beast massacred those closest to it, then stared helplessly as it pursued some of the fleeing men back into the forest. Then he steeled himself for what he knew he must do.

Chapter 7

Edenia's citizens enjoy numerous benefits. Guardsmen are stationed across the empire to ensure peace and protection. The Scholar's Guild provides trained educators to the nation's larger cities. A system of justice provides a platform to settle disputes. These and other benefits do not come freely, however. In addition to standard taxes, every young man born in Edenia, with few exceptions, must serve in the Edenian Guard for a term of three years.

-A History of Edenia and Its People
Headmaster Barius
E.A. 627

Caelum grinned as he selected a wooden practice sword from the rack outside the training yard. Over the past few weeks their training had consisted mainly of hours spent marching, practicing formations, running, and swimming, and then doing it all over again while carrying their gear. He couldn't deny the noticeable difference in his physique since his training started, but the training had been strenuous, painful, and dull. In between conditioning exercises, they had been put through various written tests to evaluate their strengths and weaknesses, as well as their interests in different areas of service within the guard. But today was different. Today, the recruits would finally get a chance at combat, and would be evaluated on their proficiency with various weapons.

All men in the Edenian Empire were required to train in various forms of combat when they reached a certain age, but Caelum and Daric had been watching the men practice swordplay since they were young boys. They would often find sticks and reenact what they had seen the older men doing, stopping only when one of them would get smacked a little too hard and start crying. As they grew into young men, they continued to hone their skills with one another until they outclassed every other boy in Almanis Village. Caelum waited in eager anticipation to see how they would each fare in a contest against men from all over the Empire. He was sure Daric would rise to the top of the rankings, and he hoped he would win a few bouts himself.

First, they had been tested on their ability to use a bow. Daric naturally took top marks, whereas Caelum was unremarkably average. From there, they were evaluated on their pike formations, which were relatively basic. Caelum assumed everyone received an adequate ranking. Finally, they were to be tested with a blade.

The recruits were divided into many small sparring groups, each with an officer to oversee them. Each group member would be evaluated and separated into new sparring groups based on his skill level, and the process would begin again until Master Hamer was satisfied with the rankings. Recruits would then be given their assignments once all of their units, where they would serve out the remainder of their time in the Guard.

Caelum took his place on the dusty training yard across from his first opponent. The rules for sparring were simple: deal your opponent five clean blows before he did the same to you. If opponents landed blows at the same time, no points were awarded. Disarming or knocking down an opponent would count as an automatic win.

The man Caelum faced was slightly bigger than he was, but Caelum could tell his stance was awkward. The man advanced and raised his practice sword for an overhead slash, which Caelum easily ducked under and countered with a thrust to the man's stomach for his first point. This angered his opponent, who quickly turned with another fierce swipe that Caelum narrowly dodged. Caelum took advantage of his opponent's off-balance stance, crouching low and kicking his feet out from under him, knocking the bigger man down and winning himself the fight.

Master Hamen shouted from behind them, "Hubert, you imbecile! Quit waving that blade around like you're a dog trying to snap its neck, and instead pay attention to your feet!"

"Yes, sir!" Hubert used his practice sword to help him regain his feet and glared at Caelum as he moved back into formation. Master Hamen nodded at Caelum and continued pacing along the lines of recruits.

As the day continued, Caelum never lost a match. He came close against an incredibly fast, dark-haired opponent from north of the capital, but finished just ahead with a five-to-four victory. At the end of the day, Master Hamen had placed all the recruits in groups of various sizes, some containing more than one hundred recruits. Caelum was in a group of seven.

Daric was also in his group, as well as the dark-haired recruit he had struggled against earlier. Daric smiled wide when he saw Caelum.

"Nice going, Cael," he said.

Caelum laughed in return. "I never thought I would make it this far." He ran his hand through his hair, shaking his head. "I'm just glad I didn't have to spar with you."

"Oh?" said a deep voice behind him. He turned around and there was Master Haman. "I didn't realize I had given you an unfair advantage."

"Sir, that's not what I—" Master Haman cut him off before he could finish.

"It seems we have one final matchup for today. You two recruits—" He pointed at Daric and Caelum. "—take up your positions opposite one another. Now"

Caelum winced. He wished he had kept his stupid mouth shut. Now he would have to embarrass himself in front of his fellow recruits and the master at arms. As he got into position, he saw Daric looking at him apologetically.

"Don't hold back on me Daric," he said.

Daric almost looked offended. "Have I ever?"

Daric launched himself forward. Caelum had only a moment to react. Was it a feint? Daric would know that's what he would think, so instead he raised his sword to intercept the blow. Their swords connected with a loud crack that sent Caelum stumbling, dangerously close to losing his feet. While he recovered Daric tapped him for his first point.

"Sorry Cael," he said.

Caelum gritted his teeth and took up his position again. His hands were ringing from that single blow he blocked. Daric certainly wasn't holding back, and how recruits from other groups were crowding around to watch their fight. As Caelum watched his friend ready himself for another bout, he paid careful attention to Daric's posture. He couldn't match Daric's strength, but he could outthink him. Daric charged a second time, and this time Caelum was more prepared. He anticipated the feint, countering with an attack of his own, but Daric recovered swiftly and parried Caelum's thrust, slicing him at the wrist.

"That's two for Daric."

Caelum growled. He wasn't about to go down *three* to zero. This time, Caelum made the first move, launching himself at Daric with his sword held high. Daric was caught off guard and raised his sword to deflect an overhead slash, but instead of slashing down, Caelum twisted his wrists and whipped his sword sideways, striking Daric hard on his helmet. The recruits around them cheered. Many of them had faced Daric earlier in the day, and Caelum wasn't sure if anyone had landed a single hit on the big man.

"Not bad, Cael," said Daric, wearing a savage grin. "Not bad at all."

Caelum looked at Master Haman to see if he had garnered the old soldier's approval, but the man showed about as much expression as a rock. Caelum would have to show him something truly impressive to get a reaction out of him. He would have to beat Daric.

He felt more confident as they faced one another again, knowing that Daric wasn't invincible. They charged one another once more, and Caelum felt adrenaline pulsing through his body as he closed the distance. Daric raised his blade to strike, but Caelum ducked underneath and slashed back at Daric's legs. Only Daric had never intended to strike at

Caelum. It was a feint, and Caelum fell for it. Daric blocked Caelum's slash and grabbed his wrist, squeezing until Caelum dropped his weapon. It was over; he had lost.

The recruits around them cheered, clapping Daric on the back and asking him all sorts of questions about his technique. A few came to offer Caelum their condolences or encouragement regarding his loss, but he didn't want to hear it. The dark-haired fighter he had faced earlier stood next to him and stared sourly at Daric, seemingly oblivious to Caelum's mood.

"I loathe this feeling," he said, scowling, "and I know you must feel it too. I've worked hard my entire life to become the best swordsman among the recruits in Crisantia, and I was. Yet now I have been bested by you, and you have been bested by another." He shook his head. "We were apex predators, but now we disappear in the shadow of a new alpha. It seems as though we will have to work even harder to be the leader of this pack."

Caelum clenched his fists, annoyed. "You are mistaken. I don't know the feeling, because I have lived in Daric's shadow my whole life. And, can I give you a word of advice?" he said, echoing the words he often told himself. "Give it up, because you will never be better than Daric." Caelum walked away from the other recruit to stand alone. The rest of the recruits dispersed back into their own groups, and Master Hamen gathered their small group of seven to address them.

"Excellent work to all of you men. I am glad to know that at least some of the officers responsible for training men of the Empire take their job seriously. You have demonstrated today exceptional combat skill with the sword. This and the results from your other evaluations have led me to believe that training you with the rest of the recruits would be a waste of your time and talents." Master Hamen stood a little straighter, and the recruits mimicked his posture. "From this point forward, you will be training as initiates in the Edenian Elite Guard."

Caelum's jaw dropped. He couldn't believe it. He turned to look at his friend and saw that Daric wore the same wide-eyed look of disbelief. The Elite Guard was a unit comprised of the finest warriors in all Edenia. Their talents were reserved for only the most important missions for the Empire. Many of the soldiers who had accompanied Captain Bradford and the Knights of Radiance had been from the Elite Guard.

Master Hamen continued to speak to them about the high honor it was to be recommended to the Elite Guard, but reminded them not to let it get to their heads. They would have to pass the initiation training before becoming full members of the Elite Guard. After that, he dismissed them to gather their belongings and move to their new quarters with the other Elite Guard, which was to say another barracks that looked exactly the same as the first, but on the other side of the training yard.

The room was mostly empty when they arrived, as most of the Elite Guard from the keep had been sent out with Captain Bradford, but there was a small group gathered between bunks gambling with dice, and another guardsman in the back of the room reading by the light of a candle.

One of the gamblers looked up from his game and saw the initiates enter. "Hey, new guys!" He eyed them all up and down. "Why don't you come over here and wager some of that nice stuff you brought with you?" The other men around the dice laughed and jeered, waiting for the recruits to join. Daric and the other initiates headed over to the game. Caelum had never been much of a gambler, but he wanted to make a good first impression, so he went over to join them.

The first man who had spoken started poking through each of the initiates' belongings. The initiates objected but he ignored them and pulled out anything he liked, tossing it into the wager pile. He found a flask of brandy, a knife, and one of Daric's small sculptures. He came to Caelum and took his bag, pausing when he found Caelum's crimson coat.

"What's this?" He unrumpled the coat and held it up to show it off to the rest of the men. Caelum grabbed for it, but the gambler jerked it away from him. "We have a scholar among us boys!" The men laughed, and one of them shouted, "Try it on, Merv!" The man, Merv, put on Caelum's scholar's coat and strutted around the room, mockingly impersonating his idea of a scholar's grandiose mannerisms. Caelum flushed.

"Give that back," he said, but Merv ignored him. Then Daric stepped up to Merv, who ran into the big man, then took a step back when he realized just how thick Daric was.

"Well, well, well," said Merv. "It looks like we have another tough guy around here, eh?

"We don't have to have a problem," said Daric, sounding very diplomatic. "Take that off and give it back. That coat is important to him."

"Or what?" Merv jeered.

Daric's eyes narrowed, and it looked like he was deciding whether to reshape Merv's face with his fists. Caelum started forward to try to settle this peacefully when he heard a voice from the back of the room.

"Enough."

Caelum turned as the man who had spoken rose from his bulk and walked over to the rest of them. He had a stern look, and though he was shorter than any other man in the room, and younger than the other Elites, he had an air of command that made even Daric seem small. Everything about him looked meticulously well groomed, from his clean-cut black hair to his spotless black boots. The man looked at each of the new recruits as if he could deduce everything about them from a single glance. His gaze lingered on Caelum longer than any of them. Finally, after the silence that had everyone holding their breath, he spoke again.

"Merv, give the initiate his coat back. You are all members of the Elite Guard. This kind of horseplay does not belong in our ranks. And you, recruits, are not Elite yet. I don't know what Hamen saw in you, but until you have proven yourselves, you will treat the members of this company with the respect they deserve." He turned to Daric and Merv, his narrowed eyes conveying his disapproval. "There will be no more trouble from you two." Daric and Merv both nodded. "Good. Now, everyone get some sleep. We start early tomorrow." And with that, he turned and went back to his bunk.

Caelum, feeling thoroughly cowed, picked up his things and chose a bunk on the other end of the room with the rest of the initiates, away from the trained guardsmen. The other initiates began to chat quietly amongst themselves, but Caelum kept to himself, still feeling humiliated from before. One of the gamblers, a man the size of an ox, came over to him as he unpacked.

"Hey, don't worry about the guys. They just enjoy giving any new initiates a hard time. I'm Kurt, by the way." Kurt extended his hand out to Caelum.

Caelum took it. "I'm Caelum."

Kurt nodded. "You're the scholar that came in with Bradford. The one who saw the Unbound?"

"Yeah that's me…"

"A lot of the boys are restless and angry about being left behind while the rest of the Elite went with the Knights of Radiance to fight that monster, nobody more so than Flex."

"Is Flex the commander?" Caelum asked.

Kurt chuckled. "No, but he does come across that way sometimes. Our commander went with the rest of the Elite Guard to fight the Unbound. Jon Tomkins over there is the highest-ranking Elite left in Edenia City." Kurt nodded toward a soldier who was already asleep in his bunk. "Flex, however, is the best warrior among the entire Elite Guard, and we all respect him. He would have surely been chosen as a Knight of Radiance had he been old enough during the last choosing. He was out on patrol when Bradford chose his men for *this* mission and came back into town just a few hours after they had left. The poor guy has the worst luck."

"Is that why he gave us such a scolding?"

"Nah, he's always that way." Kurt laughed. "But he is a good friend and a good soldier. Do well in your training and he will come to respect you too." Kurt crossed back to the other side of the barracks and lay down to sleep in his bunk. To Caelum's shock, the man immediately began snoring so loudly Caelum wondered how any of the other soldiers ever got any sleep, but he looked around at the other men and saw that they weren't having any trouble.

Caelum could understand how Flex was feeling. He was a great warrior who missed his chance at becoming a Knight of Radiance and missed his chance to accompany Bradford. But there was no reason for Flex to be there now, as only the

Knights of Radiance stood a chance fighting the Unbound. Caelum, on the other hand, had spent years of his life studying everything known about these creatures, and he was sure that his knowledge could help them, but he had been left behind also.

It had been almost two months since Bradford had left, and over a month since any word had come about their mission. Caelum was beginning to worry. *I hope they are all right.*

Chapter 8

For years we lived in terror, hiding from that which cannot be deceived. Fleeing that which is inescapable. Fighting that which cannot be killed. The people have given it a name: Unbound.

-*Journal of Oleth Zandarion*
Translation by Caelum Karasin
E.A. 967

Bradford was tired. Two weeks had passed since the nightmare of the first encounter with the Unbound. After the Knights of Radiance fell in the battle, Captain Bradford had done his best to gather the remaining troops and organize a retreat while the beast fed on their fallen comrades. It sickened him. He had lost one hundred sixty-two men that day. They had left the bloody scene and traveled ten leagues south, making camp atop a foothill, only to have the lookout alert the company that the Unbound was once again heading straight for their. They set out, changin out time and time again, only to realize that the beast had tripled their pace to move, and it was gaining on them. It was still then Bradford began forming an idea. He called the remaining officers and some of the veteran soldiers to ride with him.

"We cannot keep on like this. That beast doesn't seem to need food or rest, and we do. We still don't know how it is tracking us, and at the monster's present rate, it is only a matter of time until we're caught."

One of the younger officers, a man named Hal Dennix, spoke up. "Captain, if that is the case, then let us stop running away! We can wait for the beast and make our last stand here. At least we can die honorably."

Bradford shook his head. "Dennix, I admire your courage, but dying here in a pointless battle will not serve anyone. We need to formulate a plan to contain this beast. Every second it spends following us is a second that it is not wandering free to terrorize any unfortunate soul it comes across. If we can lead it deeper into the forest and mountains, away from civilization, then we give the king more time to develop a permanent solution."

"But sir, we are all exhausted," said Randal, next in command after Bradford. "We have hardly had a moment's rest since our retreat. We won't last another day."

Bradford knew Randal was right, but he wasn't ready to give up. "We will do what we must."

"Captain!" Bradford turned to find the lookout racing down the hill toward the officers.

"What is it now, man?"

"The Unbound has changed course, sir, and is now heading southeast!"

"Southeast? But why?" *There isn't anything to the southeast for leagues. Unless… oh no.* "We have to stop it!"

Bradford halted and shouted the order to turn around, back toward the Unbound. He could see the looks of bewilderment on his men's faces, but there was no time to explain, and the soldiers under his command knew better than to question an order. The captain spurred his horse to a gallop, and the rest of the company followed his lead. Bradford spared a glance to his right to find Dennix riding next to him with a wild grin on his face. *The fool can't wait to die for some ill-conceived notion of glory. Though it does feel good to once again become the hunter rather than the hunted. I just hope we aren't too late.*

To the west Bradford could begin to make out the smoke from the fiery trail that the Unbound left in its wake, and he shivered at the thought of facing the monster again. *The Knights of Radiance, the best soldiers the empire has, supported with pikes and archers, were completely annihilated by the monster. What do you think you can do? It's suicide.* He pushed the thought aside.

Soon after, He spotted the first sign of what he was looking for and slowed briefly to adjust his course. *Tracks. Not much further now.* Back at Beldun, Bradford had sent two of his men to alert the villages in the valley to the threat of the Unbound, and to assist them in their migration to Almanis Village. The company had stumbled across the blackened remains of one of those men a few weeks ago. The tracks they now followed suggested the other messenger had been successful, and one unlucky migrating party had attracted the attention of the Unbound. Bradford was not going to allow another slaughter like the one witnessed both at Beldun and on the hilltop where they first encountered the beast. He urged his horse for more speed.

The smoke thickened, making it difficult to breathe. Faint cries rose above the sound of their eighty thundering horses. *Damn, it has found them!* The trees around them burned, the heat of the fire almost too intense to bear. Just when he thought they could travel no further, they came upon the beast and the chaos surrounding it. People ran screaming, trying to escape in every direction, but they were all on foot and the Unbound easily picked them off. It looked like some of the men from the group of travelers had tried to gather and fight off the beast, but now they were either dead or fleeing. Bradford watched as the Unbound snapped up one of the fleeing villagers in its jaws, shaking its head and sending a spray of blood raining down before devouring the man whole. It then turned to pounce upon the next closest victim.

Bradford looked at his officers. They were in no condition to engage the beast. It was a death sentence to have them ride into this slaughter, but what else could they do? He couldn't just leave these helpless villagers to such a gruesome fate. *We will do what we must*, he thought to himself. He saw the same determination in his men. "We can't kill this creature, but we may be able to draw it away from the villagers. Randal, I want you to—"

Bradford's gut sank as he noticed a small girl crouched near a burning, abandoned wagon. She clutched a doll to her chest and kept her eyes tightly shut, unaware that she was now the closest person to the Unbound who was still breathing. The enormous beast turned its head and fixed its gaze directly on the girl, snaking its way toward her with a snarl.

Before he had time to think Bradford was charging at full speed at the beast with a primal roar of his own, aiming his lance at its glowing red eyes. The Unbound crouched low, ready to pounce. It sprang, but Bradford was there, smashing his lance into the creature's head and knocking it away from the girl. The lance shattered, and Bradford rounded back to the creature, jerking the reigns to lead his disciplined warhorse into a practiced jump, unleashing a powerful hind kick mid-air and striking the beast once more. "Run!" he shouted at the little girl. To Bradford's relief she got up and ran toward the rest of the fleeing villagers, crying hysterically. The Unbound paid no attention to the girl's flight. Bradford had gotten its full attention now.

"Come on, hellspawn!" he shouted.

The beast growled low, then whipped its tail faster than Bradford believed possible, striking his horse square in the chest and sending both horse and rider flying back. Bradford landed with a hard thud, and he heard a snap before his leg flared with excruciating pain. He cried out once, then gasped for breath, pinned to the ground underneath the mangled corpse of his longtime companion.

"Captain, hang on!"

Bradford heard his men riding to his aid, but he knew they would be too late. The hellish creature was upon him. It slammed its razor-sharp claw down, piercing through both the dead horse and Bradford's trapped leg. He screamed in pain. The Unbound spun and rose on its hind legs, lifting both horse and rider high into the air as if to devour them. Despite his agony Bradford drew his sword, and with a grunt and all the strength he had left, he swung, striking his leg just above the knee and severing it from his body, just before it disappeared into the beast's awful maw. The world slowed down as he fell to the ground, and then everything faded into darkness.

Chapter 9

The Edenian Empire consists of three provinces: Crisantia in the north, Winfall on the southern coast, and the central province of Edenia. While the king rules the empire from Edenia proper, each other province is locally governed by its own duke. The king and dukes each have the allegiance of five vassals within their territory. This comprises the entirety of Edenian nobility. While original court rank was bestowed upon individuals at the nation's founding, the king retains the authority to revoke lordship for serious offenses, and to promote someone of an entirely different family to the rank of duke or baron. This shift in nobility happens quite infrequently, with the most notable occurrence being the recent appointment of Malthier Mantell as Duke of Crisantia.

-A History of Edenia and Its People
Headmaster Barius
E.A. 627

Any pride Caelum had acquired from his initial placement training was unmercifully beaten out of him in the first day training with the Elite Guard. Flex took each of the initiates out early that morning for a short one on one "lesson" in swordsmanship, which essentially meant he knocked them around the yard until they could barely hold their practice swords. After that humbling experience, the initiates spent many grueling hours conditioning, practicing formations, and learning technique for a variety of weapons. Caelum struggled at anything outside of the sword, though he had been working hard to gain some competency with a bow. Of course, Daric took naturally to everything, much to Caelum's chagrin, though he was somewhat used to it by now. Since they were boys, Caelum had lived in the shadow of Daric's numerous successes. His scholarly pursuits were the one area in which he shone, probably only because Daric chose to pursue something entirely different. Caelum might never be able to match Daric, but if he worked hard enough, maybe he could make a name for himself as a soldier as well.

There were about fifty of the Elite Guard still in the city, and each day one or more of them was given the duty to train the initiates. Some days were worse than others, though nobody was as hard on them as Flex had been that first day, which made every day after much more tolerable. There were twenty-one initiates total: the seven from the new recruits, including Caelum, eleven soldiers who had been promoted from different units, and three men who looked like they must be sons of lords. These last three had come into training with a swagger and a cocky smile, but now looked more ragged than anyone.

Caelum was paired with one of them — Daxton Preavic, son of Valdemir Preavic — now, working what was called a press drill. The drill was all about leverage. The two combatants kept their swords pressed together and tried to gain a position in which they could make a cut on their opponent.

"This is stupid!" the lordling hissed. He thrusted toward Caelum's chest, and Caelum countered into a smooth cut that would have sliced the nobleman's hands clean off in a real fight. Daxton's face reddened, contorting with rage. He screamed, whipping his practice blade at Caelum's head. Caelum barely got his own blade up in time to block it.

"Whoah, Dax!" Caelum shouted, shuffling back. "Calm down. It's only training." The nobleman didn't relent; instead he pulled back and struck again. Caelum began to panic as Dax continued his assault, struggling to focus on repelling each chaotic attack. One wild swing slipped through Caelum's guard and slammed into his torso, knocking the wind out of him and sending a throbbing pain through his already bruised body. He wouldn't recover in time to stop the next attack. As Daxton swung, Kurt grabbed his sword hand and punched the lordling square in the face, knocking Dax to the ground clutching his nose, blood seeping between his fingers.

"Get the hell out of here Daxton!" Kurt roared. "And I don't care who your father is, if I see you do something like that again, that punch will seem like a goodnight kiss from your mother compared to what I will do to you, understand?"

Daxton pushed himself back up and swung his practice sword at Kurt, who stood unarmed, with enough force to crack his skull. Kurt tilted his head slightly and the wooden blade missed by a hair's width. As Daxton stumbled forward, Kurt raised one thick arm into an arm bar, catching the lordling hard in his throat. Kurt grabbed the smaller nobleman, picking him up and tossing him toward the gate. Daxton squealed before landing sprawled in the dirt a few paces behind them. The initiates around the training yard all stared in stunned silence.

Kurt shook his head in disgust. "Leave, Daxton. Don't ever come back. You have no place amongst the Elite Guardsmen of Edenia."

Daxton wiped blood from his face and sneered, looking up at Kurt. "You'll pay for this!" Kurt started toward him, and Daxton scrambled to his feet and retreated, looking over his shoulder only once to make sure Kurt wasn't following. Kurt spat as he stared after Daxton, waiting until the lordling left the grounds before turning back toward Caelum with a laugh. Caelum could only gape at him.

"Can you do that?"

"What, kick him out of the Elite Guard like that? Under normal circumstances yeah, but Daxton's father is an important man and knows our commander, so I'm sure he will be back. The commander will probably have my hide, but that boy has been pissing me off. And did you see the look on his face when he was leaving?" Kurt let out a deep chuckle. "It was worth it, just for that." Caelum grinned. "Now, you've been practicing with pretty boy this whole time, why don't you see how you fare against me?"

This was more of the kind of challenge Caelum hoped for. He had been training hard after being humiliated by Flex on that first day and was determined that nothing like that would happen again. He took his stance opposite Kurt and they locked swords.

"Go."

Caelum wasted no time and pushed high with his sword, angling his blade back down toward Kurt. But Kurt shifted his feet and kicked, sweeping Caelum's feet out from under him and knocking him to the ground. Caelum pushed himself back up and readied himself again, determined.

"You focus too hard on our swords and forget everything else. You need to be aware of everything around you and be prepared for anything." Caelum nodded and they began again. This time Kurt pushed first, and Caelum pivoted, using the big man's power against him. Kurt lashed out again with his foot, but Caelum was ready and stepped gracefully around him. They continued their give and take struggle in a wavelike dance, and Caelum noticed the other initiates watching. Kurt tried kicking again, which Caelum nimbly avoided, and the big man gave an approving nod. He then forced Caelum's blade to the ground, stepped on it, and mock-sliced his feet.

"Not bad Caelum. Not bad." The big man lowered his training sword and wiped his brow with his tunic. The other initiates went back to their own training and Kurt pulled Caelum aside. "You've got a real talent for that blade."

"It doesn't feel like it," he said. "I still feel helpless against you, and Flex, and all the rest of the Elite Guardsmen. Not to mention Daric."

"You can't expect to be the best after only a few weeks of serious training." Kurt clapped him on the back and Caelum tried not to wince. The man had inhuman strength. "With some hard work and discipline, you could become a fine swordsman, and a valuable member of the Elite Guard."

"Thank you." Caelum felt a swell of pride. He liked Kurt. All the men in the Elite Guard, including Flex, respected the big man. To receive his praise meant a lot.

Kurt nodded. "Meet me here tomorrow morning an hour before regular training begins. Bring your pal, Daric, and be ready to work." He tossed his practice blade to Caelum and called an end to the day's training.

After dismissal, Caelum found Daric and went to the mess hall. The cook served some sort of potato mush with vegetables and a piece of bread. Caelum, hungrier than he realized, practically inhaled his meal. He turned toward his friend, but found that Daric had already gone back to the cook to ask for seconds. Caelum followed suit.

After they both had had their fill, Caelum told Daric about the invitation to a special training session with Kurt.

"He asked for both of us?" Caelum nodded. "That's great! You and me are going to go all the way." Daric grinned. "When I'm commander, I will promote you to be my personal assistant. You can shine my boots, saddle my horse, wash my undergarments…"

"Keep dreaming." Caelum shook his head. "And besides, I'm here to serve my term and then I am heading back to Almanis Village." Daric and Caelum both got quiet and stared at the ground, avoiding the unvoiced concern that gripped them both. Was the village safe? Why had there been no word from Bradford? The mess hall was filled with raucous laughter and loud conversation, but every now and then, during the quieter moments, Caelum could hear the murmurs of the men around him, hushed speculation about the fate of Bradford's company and the Knights of Radiance. Caelum couldn't shake the feeling that something was wrong.

"Do not fear for your home," said Flex, jolting Caelum out of his melancholy. Caelum was surprised by the compassion in his voice. Flex, normally so cold and strict, slid onto the bench next to them. "I trained with Callus, Knight Commander of the Knights of Radiance, and he is an incredible man. And Captain Bradford is an experienced soldier. He will make sure that what must be done, will be done."

Caelum sighed. "Yeah but it's been too long since we've heard any word from them. What if…."

Flex shook his head and rose from the table. "Stop worrying about what you can't change. I suggest you get some rest. I hear you have an early start tomorrow."

As Flex left them, Daric whispered, "That didn't sound like a suggestion."

Caelum laughed. "No, it didn't. Let's call it a night."

They made their way back to their bunks, but Caelum couldn't sleep. Instead, he lit a candle and looked over his research on the Unbound. He began again the slow process of translating Oleth's journal, searching for anything that might prove useful, until sleep overtook him.

Chapter 10

We were not soldiers. We were farmers, singers, builders. We were fathers, brothers, sons. We knew not the ways of war. But we would learn.

-Journal of Oleth Zandarion
Translation by Caelum Karasin
E.A.967

Kurt's fist struck home and sent Caelum back to where he spent much of his mornings now: the dusty surface of the training ground. Caelum gritted his teeth in frustration and spat red as he regained his feet.

"Never lose your feet," Kurt reminded him.

Gee, that is so helpful, Caelum thought bitterly. *He is so strong... I can't keep this up.*

Kurt studied him and replied almost as if he could read Caelum's mind. "You're trying to fight me the same way Daric fights me, absorbing my attacks, but you're not strong enough." Caelum could hear Daric chuckling behind him. Kurt arched an eyebrow and turned. "Oh? And what is so funny back there, tough guy? Haven't you two been sparring partners for quite some time? If you didn't strike about as hard as my aged grandmother, he would have already adapted to handle this."

"I do *not* hit like your grandmother…" Daric grumbled, but Kurt ignored him and resumed his instruction.

"There are four elements to swordsmanship every soldier must develop and learn to recognize in their opponents. First is strength. By now you should recognize that I am stronger than you." Caelum half-chuckled, half-groaned. "If you cannot match your opponent's strength, you must compensate with swiftness and smarts. It won't matter how strong he is if he can't hit you, and the smart swordsman can turn any situation to his favor using momentum and redirection. Use your opponent's strength against them." Kurt motioned for Daric to approach him. "Daric, attack me with an overhead slash and use all of your strength."

"Why do I get the feeling this is going to end poorly for me?" Daric joked. This "special training" hadn't been easy on him, either.

"No complaining," ordered Kurt. "Just do it." The two men took their positions, Daric with his practice sword high above his head in both hands, Kurt holding his steady in one hand.

Daric roared and unleashed a bone-shattering downward swing, but Kurt angled his blade and lightly deflected the blow, just enough to spin to the side and elbow Daric in the back of the neck, sending him to the ground. This time Caelum laughed as Daric dizzily came back to his feet.

Kurt smiled. "I'm glad you enjoyed that, Caelum, because now it's your turn." Kurt raised his sword and stared at Caelum expectantly. "Do exactly as I did."

"Oh great."

* * *

Paholainen stood in a dark corner of the balcony, overlooking the courtyard where three young men pitifully practiced at the sword. One of the men was inconsequential, one a possible inconvenience to his plans, and the third the key to his success. He had to resist the urge to reveal himself and slaughter the nuisance with his own hands, but now was not the time. The situation required delicacy, and he was still vulnerable, so instead he left the balcony, resumed his guise, and prepared to make his next move.

"Better," Kurt said after Caelum managed to turn another ferocious swing from the big man.

They had been at this for almost an hour, and though he was exhausted, Caelum was pleased with his progress. Kurt swiped at him again from another angle and Caelum barely managed to parry the blow, feeling the *whoosh* of the blade as it narrowly missed his skull and instead struck him hard on the shoulder.

"Ow!" Caelum grunted and grabbed his shoulder. "You know you could kill me like that, right?"

"That's the point," Kurt said, and Caelum stared at him dumbfounded. "To live is man's greatest motivation. Threaten a man's life, and it is amazing what he becomes capable of. Your technique has improved tremendously in the last hour simply because you had no choice *but* to improve."

"You are crazy," said Caelum.

"Haw!" Kurt guffawed, and clapped Caelum on the shoulder- thankfully not the injured one. He put an arm around Daric's neck as well. "Welcome to the Elite Guard. If you aren't half insane already, you soon will be!"

The morning bells tolled, echoing over the city from the high spire of the Temple of the Creator. Caelum had been so engrossed in the morning's lesson that he hadn't noticed the rest of the city was now awake. Soldiers filed in for their morning training, townsfolk hustled to accomplish their morning tasks in the city below, and the sun rose in the sky, driving away the morning chill. Summer was fast approaching. A young, dark-skinned woman entered the training yard with two small children in tow.

"Daddy!" shouted the older of the two children. She let go of her mother's hand and ran to Kurt, who swooped her up in his arms and swung her around.

"You're getting so heavy! What did you eat this morning?"

"Apple tarts."

"Did you bring me any?" Kurt asked.

The girl giggled. "No, Mommy said they would make you fat." Kurt's eyes widened.

"That is not what I said!" protested the woman, ruffling the little girl's hair. "I said that your father needs to eat healthy food so he can stay strong and protect us."

"Mm-hmm," Kurt chuckled and hugged the woman, then turned and introduced them. "Boys, this is my wife Noretta. And the two squirrely ones are my kids, Kayla and Nico."

"Hi!" said the little girl, while the young boy hid behind his mother's dress, peering at Caelum with a furrowed brow, as if the boy might pounce any moment.

"It is very nice to meet you all," said Caelum.

"And you as well," said Noretta. "I've brought Kurt breakfast, but there ought to be enough to share, seeing as how he kept you so long that you've missed breakfast at the mess hall."

"Wow, thanks!" said Daric, who had probably been well aware of the fact that breakfast had come and gone.

"You're welcome," she said with a smile. She lifted up on her tiptoes to kiss her husband on the cheek. "I'll let you all get back to your duties. Will we see you for supper tonight, Kurt?"

"I'll do my best," he answered, squeezing her hand. Noretta guided the children back out of the training yard and down into the city.

"I don't know about you guys," Daric grunted, "but I'm dying to find out what is in that basket." He reached over to pull off the cloth covering it.

"Breakfast is going to have to wait." Flex strode into the courtyard to join the three men. "A scouting party from Razza has been seen making their way into the Elys Mountains, which, if true, is a blatant breach of the Peace."

Caelum frowned. Razza was Edenia's neighbor to the north, a nation with a long history of war with Edenia. The Peace was a pact made hundreds of years ago between the two nations, brokered by the Duke of Crisantia, to essentially restrict any and all trade, travel, or interactions of any kind between them.

Flex continued, "The rest of the guard is nearly ready to march. Our task is to capture these scouts, by whatever means necessary, and learn their purpose."

"Understood." Kurt hurried back to the barracks to grab the rest of his gear.

Flex turned to look at the two initiates. "And what are you two standing around for?"

"Well," Daric began, "if you all are going on a mission, I figure we have the day off—ugh!"

Caelum cut off Daric's rambling with a discreet elbow to his ribs. "Sir, do you mean... are we to join you for this mission?"

"If you think you can handle it." Flex raised a questioning eyebrow, and he almost smiled as the two men began to understand his meaning. "Be outside the front gate in a quarter of an hour."

A dismissive gesture sent Daric and Caelum racing back to don their initiate uniforms: a black oak tree on a field of green, trimmed in gold. Caelum buckled his sword belt and dashed past a bewildered Kurt back to the front gate to join the rest of the guardsmen, ready to join them for the first time as an equal.

Chapter 11

Fear was our first enemy. In the comfort of our homes, we knew fear, but now we faced it. Many fell prey to its whispers in those first days, vanishing in the night. Like the beast before us, this foe could not be killed. Yet the Creator, in His wisdom, instilled a weapon within us against such an enemy. Courage. We had but to wield it.

-Journal of Oleth Zandarion
Translation by Caelum Karasin
E.A. 967

Caelum, Kurt, and Daric arrived at the front gate to find mounts already prepared for them. Kurt was amused to learn that Flex talked Tomkins into promoting Caelum and Daric to full-fledged members of the guard, but he congratulated them both with a hearty slap on the back, knocking the wind out of Caelum. The other guardsmen welcomed them with a brief nod or a handshake, but before long the company was on the move.

Caelum and Daric weren't the only new faces amongst the guardsmen. Six of the other initiates were riding with the Elite Guard today, including the three young nobles. Including

Daxton. Daxton sneered when he saw Caelum staring, and Caelum quickly looked away. Daric leaned over and said in a hushed voice, "I can't believe Tomkins is letting that slimy nobleman join the Elites. He's nothing but trouble."

"I doubt he had a choice," Caelum said. "Daxton's father is a powerful man. He probably threatened to have Kurt kicked out of the guard and tossed in a cell unless they promoted his son." Daric just shook his head angrily.

The capital passed out of sight behind them, and the company turned northward. The Elys Mountains towered high above them to the east, their tops still glistening with spring snowfall. Caelum rode next to Merv, who began filling him in on their mission. "Apparently some old farmer claims he saw a small party of about twenty Razzan men moving through his land, headed for the northern pass." Merv shook his head. "People report seeing things all the time, but this farmer used to serve on the Crisantian Wall. He's one of the few people alive to have actually *seen* a Razzan before, so Lord Mantell took the claim seriously."

"Who is Lord Mantell?" Daric asked, looking first to Caelum and then to Merv.

Caelum didn't know much about Lord Mantell, other than he was the Duke of Crisantia, though he did know he was one of the nobles who served on the King's Council. He didn't want to look uninformed, however, and so he kept quiet.

Merv looked at Daric incredulously. "You've been in the city how long? And you don't know who Lord Mantell is?"

Daric shrugged. "I tend not to pay much attention to the nobility, unless they are paying me for my services."

Merv shook his head. "Lord Mantell is a hero. He saved the former king's life when a band of assassins tried to murder him in his own quarters. He fought and killed four of the would-be killers while the king was unconscious on the floor with a knife in his ribs."

Daric looked impressed. "I'd like to meet that guy."

Merv chuckled. "Keep dreamin' country boy. He's one of the most powerful men in all of Edenia. Though his reputation is incredible, few of us have ever actually seen the man, let alone talked to him. He has a seat on the King's Council, but he's rarely in the capital. I guess he's here now though..." Merv paused to think before continuing. "Anyway, we are going to try to intercept the Razzans on the mountain path we believe they will be taking, but in order to catch them, we can't take the King's Road—it would take too long. Instead, we're taking a more direct route, up Blind Man's Ridge."

"Up...." Caelum stammered as he noticed the path ahead ended in a sheer wall of stone. "Do you mean...."

Merv smiled. "Time to climb boys."

The company halted and the soldiers began to dismount. Daric approached Caelum with a worried look on his face. "You going to be all right Caelum? I know how you feel about heights."

"That didn't prevent you from talking me into climbing down the Almanis Crater." Caelum feigned a chuckle, but he was trembling, and his friend's concern made him feel like even more of a coward. He hated that he was afraid. He was a member of the Elite Guardsman of Edenia, a part of the finest fighting force in the known world. "I..." he started, but his response was cut off with a choke. He cleared his throat and tried again. "I will be fine." He would be. He had to be. He tried another chuckle. "At least I'm not wearing my coat."

Daric looked unconvinced, but mercifully didn't press him on it. "Thank goodness for that," he said instead.

Kurt dismounted and walked his horse over to Daric and Caelum, noticing something was wrong. "You boys all right? Caelum, you look sick." Caelum couldn't meet the big man's eyes. Kurt glanced back at the cliff, then looked at Caelum. "You worried about the climb?" Caelum was too ashamed to answer. Kurt took Caelum's silence as confirmation. "Don't be!" He waved his hand. "We've made this climb dozens of times. We still have stakes in the rock to make the climb easier." That did make Caelum feel a little better, though he still dreaded entrusting his life to a couple of spikes and a rope.

As they approached the cliff face, the guardsmen broke up into groups of three. Each group would tie themselves to the same rope as they climbed, so that if one fell, the others could support him while he regained his hold. Kurt approached Caelum and clapped him on the shoulder. "Each of the newbies will be with two of the veteran guardsmen." He smiled warmly. "You'll be with me."

Caelum gave the big man an appreciative smile. "Thanks."

"Who am I climbing with?" Daric asked.

Kurt grinned wide. "You get to be in Merv's group, first up the clifftop."

"Ah, not Merv!" Daric didn't even attempt to hide his disappointment.

Kurt laughed. "Caelum and I will be climbing last, so make sure to have a stew ready for us when we reach the top."

"The way Daric eats, I wouldn't be surprised to reach the top and find nothing but an empty pot," Caelum said, which earned a horrified expression from Kurt.

"Don't worry, I'll save you some," said Daric, laughing.

Though Caelum dreaded the climb, and he wished Daric were the third man on his team, he was glad that he would be with Kurt. Daric nodded encouragingly before leaving to join his assigned trio. Caelum watched him go before turning back to Kurt. "Who is our third man?"

"Flex."

Caelum groaned inwardly. Just when he thought Flex was beginning to warm up to him, as much as Flex *could* warm up to anyone anyway, he was going to embarrass himself by climbing right next to the man like a frightened child.

"Take a few minutes to pull yourself together. We will be climbing last." Kurt squeezed Caelum's shoulder. "You can do this." The big man left him to go help some of the others with their ropes. Caelum was grateful for the time to himself. He hated being seen as a coward, and the thought of exposing himself, coupled with his fear of heights, was enough to make him dizzy.

The first two groups began to climb on two different paths set with stakes running parallel up the mountain. Caelum closed his eyes and breathed slowly. Time stretched on as each group waited for their turn to climb. Some of the other newer guardsmen looked nervous about the climb as well, which eased his mind somewhat. Caelum saw one man lose his footing near the top of the cliff and fall, dangling perilously from the rope tied around his waist, but his two climbing partners were able to support his weight and help him regain his hold. Caelum nearly vomited at the sight, remembering the terror and helplessness he felt on the day of the landslide, so many years ago. *Just look at me, son,* he heard his father say. *I'll pull you up.*

Surely it wasn't vital for him to do this. There were already plenty of guardsman on the cliff top who could—

"It's time to go."

Kurt's voice broke Caelum out of his nervous inner ramblings. Caelum worked himself up for what he was about to do. He had made worse climbs before, right? Flex gave Caelum an odd look as the three of them were tied in. *Of course, he would; he has seen me panicking this whole time. He knows I am afraid.* Caelum was grateful Flex did not voice his thoughts aloud.

Daxton, however, one of the three others still left on the ground, was not so kind. "What's wrong Caelum?" he snickered. "You look scared!"

Caelum ignored him, and the two groups began their ascent. Flex was the leader of their group, followed by Caelum and then Kurt. *One step at a time,* Caelum told himself. They started out at a steady pace, but about half-way up the cliff face, the group beside them stopped. Their leader, a man called Yowin, called out to Flex and gestured to his rope.

"We have to go to ground." Yowin was shouting, but Caelum could barely hear him over the wind. "One of my men has a broken clasp. I don't want to take any chances, so I'm going to get a replacement." Equipment malfunction was the last thing Caelum needed to hear about, but Flex just nodded and signaled he understood. Caelum checked his own clasp.

"You don't need to worry," Kurt said from below him. "I checked all of our equipment; everything is in good shape."

"Right," Caelum said. He was beginning to ache, first in his arms, then everywhere. They had only stopped for a moment, but every moment they delayed prolonged his misery. He took a deep breath, letting the air out slowly. "Let's keep moving."

Kurt chuckled. "That's the spirit!"

They set out again, more quickly than they had started. The clifftop still seemed so far away, he was beginning to think they would never reach the top. *We have to be at least halfway there...* He glanced downward, and his heart raced as he felt a sudden rush of fear shoot through his entire body. *Why did I look down? Come on, Cae—*

His foot slipped as his foothold crumbled underneath him. He screamed as he fell, but it was cut off when the rope connecting him to the other men reached its length. Flex let out an annoyed grunt as he bore all of Caelum's weight, while Kurt grabbed Caelum's arm and helped him swing back to the wall. Caelum's hands found a grip, and he clung to the wall, breathing heavily with his eyes closed tight, too terrified to move.

"Soldier," said a stern voice from above. Caelum, still trembling, looked up at Flex. The Elite stared back down at him, scowling. "We must keep moving." Caelum wanted nothing more than to do just as Flex said, but he just clung there, frozen.

"Caelum," Kurt's voice came from below. "It's ok to be afraid. Hell, this mountain makes me uncomfortable! Just don't let that fear keep you from doing what needs to be done. Right now, we need to be at the top of this wall, so howbout we get moving, eh?"

Caelum took a few slow, even breaths. "I... yeah." In and out. "Sorry."

Kurt smiled up at him. Caelum nodded weakly and reached to steel himself on the next spike. Before he could secure his grip, he was ripped away from the wall by a heavy weight at his waist. Flex cried out in pain above as he was once again bore Caelum's weight. For a moment, they both fell, until Flex was caught by the rope he had anchored into the spike above them. Caelum's head whipped back as the rope again became taut.

Flex shouted through gritted teeth. "Agh… what the hell is going on down there, Kurt?"

Caelum stared down at the big man, hanging limply from the bottom of the rope. A glimmer of sunlight glinted off of the tip of an arrow that was protruding from just below Kurt's chest.

"Flex!" Caelum cried. "Kurt's been shot!"

"What did you say?" Flex shouted, annoyed.

"Kurt's been…" *Whoosh.* An arrow whizzed by Caelum's ear. Caelum grabbed for the wall, scanning below and to his left, the direction from which the arrow seemed to fly. There, on a small ledge jutting out from the cliff wall not forty feet below them, stood Daxton Preavic with a bow in hand. He smiled maliciously as he pulled back his bowstring and loosed another arrow. This arrow flew higher over his head, closer to Flex.

"That bastard!" Flex shouted, and as Caelum watched the arrow pass overhead and clatter against the rock wall, he noticed something even more terrifying.

"Flex, the stake is coming loose!"

Flex looked at the stake to which their rope was anchored. It was the only thing keeping all three men from plummeting to their doom. The stake twisted ever so slightly as they swayed gently back and forth on their rope, and it was wriggling free of the rock. "We have to swing back to the wall and find a hold!" Flex shouted. Caelum nodded, hoping fervently that their efforts wouldn't aggravate the stake further and hasten their demise. The two men swung to build momentum, reaching out to find any place to grab on to the wall. Caelum was trying desperately not to think about the small sliver of metal that was their only lifeline, nor the lunatic trying to kill them from the ledge below. More arrows whizzed by, and one nicked his calf, but that sharp pain was nothing against the terror in his chest. After seconds that felt like hours, Caelum managed a solid grip on the wall and pulled himself close, grasping now with both hands. He found a strong foothold as well. Flex was still scrambling to find his own when the stake slipped free. He fell with a shout, jerking to a stop when he reached the full length of the rope that linked him and Caelum, and slammed hard into the wall below.

Caelum screamed with agony as the rope around him tightened even more. He was now bearing the weight of both Kurt and Flex, holding on for all their lives. He could hear faint shouts from the cliff top, as the other soldiers realized what was happening on the wall.

Another arrow narrowly missed Caelum's hand, instead shattering against the rock in a spray of splintered wood. Caelum felt a flash of pain beneath his left eye, and warm blood dripped down his face. *I'm going to die! We are all going to die!*

Caelum could hear Flex below him crying out in pain. He dared to look down, and he saw the man bleeding from a nasty cut on his face, one of his arms hanging limp as he swung. Flex was trying in futility to regain a hold on the wall with his good arm.

Caelum gritted his teeth, his arms feeling like they were on fire. "Flex, I can't hang on any longer!" A crash sounded to his left, followed by a shrill scream and another crash. Caelum could hear shouts from above. He looked up and saw Daric preparing to repel down the cliffside to help them. *He won't make it in time.* Caelum was terrified. He looked down at the two men depending on him. Flex, who was still desperately trying to find a hold, fighting against the pain of his broken arm, and Kurt, who almost looked asleep, his chest slowly rising and falling. He was dying.

Or is that just your way of justifying what you are about to do? Caelum was scared, he couldn't think straight.

Flex's eyes met Caelum's, then flickered to Kurt and back. "No, Caelum don't do it!"

If I don't all three of us will die!

Caelum let go of the cliff with one hand, trembling with both fear and exhaustion as he reached down to pull the knife from his belt.

"He's still *alive!*" shouted Flex. "Help is on the way. We can make it!"

Caelum's father had said nearly the same thing all those years ago. "I can't!"

Flex continued his vehement pleading as Caelum grabbed hold of the line connecting him to Kurt, the man who had taken him under his wing, shown him kindness, and believed in him.

Flex was desperate. "Cut me down! Cut me, not him!"

"I'm... sorry." Caelum cut the rope.

"No!" Flex screamed, and Caelum closed his eyes, shaking and sobbing as his friend fell to his death.

"What have you done? What have you done!" Flex shouted angrily below him, but Caelum couldn't hear anything. He was lost in the darkness of his own mind.

He wasn't sure how long it took Daric to reach them. Daric tied a rope to them, and they were pulled the rest of the way to the top. Once they were safe on solid ground, Caelum collapsed to his knees and stared out into nothing. Flex marched straight over to him and punched him square in the jaw with his good arm, grunting in pain.

"You coward!" He punched him again, knocking him to the ground, before the other guardsmen restrained him. Caelum just felt numb.

I killed him.

Daric helped Caelum back to his feet and gripped him by the arms. He shook him and forced Caelum to meet his eyes. "Cael, you did what you had to do."

"Did I?" Caelum snapped at him, as his icy numbness transformed into fiery anger.

Daric flinched at Caelum's sudden aggression and paused, choosing his next words more carefully. "Of course, you always do! If you hadn't—" Daric stumbled to find the words, twisting the dagger of self-loathing Caelum already felt between his ribs. "—acted decisively," he continued, "all three of you could have died. Kurt would be grateful for what you did."

"Maybe," Caelum replied. "Flex doesn't see it that way."

"He's just in shock, like all of us. He will come around and see that what you did was reasonable."

"Reasonable." Caelum laughed bitterly. "Would you have cut the rope and let Kurt fall to his death, had you been in my place?"

"I..." Daric's voice trailed off under the weight of Caelum's gaze and he looked away, confirming what Caelum had always suspected about himself. What everyone in the guard had now seen about himself. He was a coward.

Chapter 12

All glory to our Creator,
He who was in the beginning,
shall be in the end,
and will remain forevermore.

Who creates life amidst death?
Breeds strength from weakness?
Forges majesty from oblivion?
None but our Lord.

Though we do not see Him, He sees all.
His understanding exceeds what we can fathom.
Yet He is with us, and His voice will guide us in the darkness.

-Book of Creation
Author Unknown
Before the Alliance

Kurt's death was a tragedy that weighed heavily on all the soldiers. He had been universally well-liked and respected among the Elite Guard. Shortly after the rescue, men were chosen to escort the wounded Caelum and Flex back to the capital, and to retrieve the bodies at the base of the cliff. Daric was one of the volunteers.

Caelum, Daric, Flex, and two other guardsmen split off from the rest of the company and began the trek back to Edenia City. The party walked in silence. The company had left their horses at the base of the cliff with hostlers who would have already taken them back to the city. Flex and Caelum were in no condition to make the climb back down, so they had to take the long way back by way of the King's Road.

Nobody spoke a word the rest of the day. They set up camp at sundown, and at their pace, it would take another three full day's walk to reach the city. Daric started a fire and began preparing supper. Flex went off into the darkness to be alone. Caelum stared into the fire, lost in his own dark thoughts. A loud clang sounded, and Caelum spun around in response, thinking they had been ambushed by bandits, but it was only Roger, one of the other guardsmen, who had dropped his canteen.

"Sorry," said Roger, taking a seat next to Caelum by the fire.

"It's all right. It's just been so quiet," Caelum said, grateful that the uncomfortable silence had finally been broken. He hadn't spoken with anybody since he snapped at Daric earlier, and he had some burning questions. "Roger, when we were there on the cliffside, Daxton was shooting his bow at us. I remember hearing a scream, and I assume he fell…"

"He didn't fall. He was crushed," Roger answered.

Caelum stared at him, puzzled. "I don't understand."

Roger took a bite of his stew and continued. "I was responsible for keeping an eye on everyone as they finished their climb. I saw Daxton's group start to head back down, and I didn't think anything of it. They started their climb again, and when they had reached that ledge, Daxton stabbed both of his partners in the back, cut their ropes, and pushed them off the ledge.

Caelum was stunned. He knew Daxton was sleezy, but he never expected him to kill his own team for petty revenge. He said a short prayer for his fallen comrades.

"At that point I called over some of the men. We saw Daxton pull out his bow and begin shooting at you three. It was your friend Daric who kept his head and quickly took action." Roger gestured with his spoon over to Daric, who was rifling through his pack.

"What did he do?" asked Caelum.

Roger couldn't hide his admiration as he described the scene. "He tore a boulder out of the ground, walked over to the edge of the cliff above that bastard and dropped it. His first one missed but it sure did get Daxton's attention!" Roger laughed, and Caelum remembered the shrill scream he had heard. That must have been from Daxton. "He didn't miss with the second." Roger tilted his spoon and dropped a large chunk of potato back into his bowl with a splash.

Caelum sighed and dropped his head into his hands. It was his fault that Daxton had come to kill them. He had made a fool out of Daxton in the practice yard, enraging the nobleman and forcing Kurt to come intervene in their quarrel. Though he despised the man for what he had done, in the end it wasn't Daxton who killed Kurt. I did.

"I'm sorry." Caelum said, though it sounded pathetic.

Roger seemed to understand his meaning. He took a deep, slow breath and sighed. "Caelum, I'm not going to lie. I hate what you did." Caelum lowered his eyes. "But I also understand why you did it. I can forgive you for doing what you believed you had to do."

Caelum was thankful for that, but he wasn't sure he could ever forgive himself. *Did I have to do it?* He thought again of his father. Had his father thought through things logically, as Caelum had, when he chose to risk everything rather than sacrifice a man's life? Could his father have made the right decision? But he was dead, as was his mother and the man his father had tried to save. Caelum had hated his father for years for making the wrong decision, yet now, having made a different choice himself, he was not sure anymore which was right or wrong. There was no easy answer, and he wrestled with his thoughts until he fell asleep.

They rose early the next morning, resuming their slow trek back to the city. The day passed uneventfully. An air of melancholy still weighed heavily on the party. Midafternoon on the third day, Caelum noticed a dust trail rising behind them. He pointed it out to Daric, who then informed Flex. Caelum was not ready to speak to Flex, who had shown nothing but contempt toward him since he had cut Kurt's rope, and Caelum didn't blame him for it.

Flex called the party to a halt and they waited. "It's probably a farmer bringing in his crop," Flex said, addressing the entire group. "We can pay to borrow the cart and use it to help us bring back the bodies of our fallen brothers."

It wasn't long before Caelum could make out the shape of a wagon, led by two horses, but to his surprise this was no farmer's wagon. The wagon was pure white, as were the horses. The driver's garments were white as well, and they bore the emblem of the Church of the Creator, a golden hammer. Two more riders wearing white and the golden hammer, guards by the look of them, rode on either side of the wagon.

"Now there's something you don't see every day," Roger grumbled.

He was right. It was rare to encounter church officials outside the Temple grounds. The clergy lived and worked at the Temple, and any business they conducted was usually done there as well. Caelum believed in the Creator, but after so many unanswered prayers he was not sure the Creator was *good*, or that his religion was worth adhering to. Not after the suffering he endured as a child, nor the horror he had just experienced at Blind Man's Ridge. He had to admit, however, that he didn't actually know a whole lot about the religion. His interaction with the Church had been limited, as there were only a handful of temples outside of Edenia City, and none anywhere near Almanis Valley. The clergy were a peculiar lot, and, despite his lingering guilt over Kurt's death, Caelum felt a spark of curiosity toward these strangers.

Flex hailed the newcomers, and the wagon slowed to a stop in front of them. One of the riders stared down at Flex and spoke in irritation, "What do you want?"

Flex narrowed his eyes at the man. No one in Edenia City addressed Flex in such a rude manner, as far as Caelum could imagine, but Flex dismissed it and continued. "My fellow guardsmen and I have been struck by tragedy. We lost good men, and you can see that we have been injured. I request that you consider retrieving the bodies of our fallen comrades and transporting them back to the city. You will be properly compensated for your aid upon our arrival."

The man on horseback eyed them haughtily. "We have more important things to do than helping you riffraff clean up your mess." He started back down the road.

Flex, now fuming with a controlled fury, started after the man. "You heartless piece of scum! In the name of the king I *demand* that you—"

"Garret, stop!" said a female voice from behind them.

Both the rider and Flex came to an abrupt halt and slowly turned to look back at the wagon, where a woman stood. She was a slender girl with golden hair, and Caelum thought she looked somewhat familiar, yet he was sure he had never seen her before. She wore flowing white robes, the type that every priestess of the Creator would wear, and she was one of the most beautiful women Caelum had ever seen.

The priestess was staring at Garret, her escort, with a look of mixed incredulity and anger. "How can you ignore these people in their time of need? You should be ashamed of yourself." Garret just rolled his eyes as the woman shifted her gaze to Flex and the rest of the guardsmen.

The anger in her eyes changed to compassion as she spoke to them softly. "I am so sorry." She said those words as if she could see into the very heart of Flex's grief, as if she shared the same pain that he felt. Her sincere remark made Caelum sad, but rather than the despairing sadness that had plagued them since the tragedy on the cliffside, this new sadness hurt in a good way, like the cleansing of a deep wound.

Flex seemed shaken by the priestess' display of honest compassion. He lowered his head, and Caelum thought he spotted tears at the corners of his eyes. Seeing calm, cold, seemingly-unfeeling Flex this way was jarring. Caelum found himself wiping away tears of his own.

"Forgive me, my lady. I did not mean to intrude," said Flex after a moment, regaining his composure. "I would not ask this of you and your men were we not desperate."

"Please, do not apologize," she said. "Of course we will help you."

Flex bowed graciously to her. "Thank you, priestess. You and your men can wait here while we go to gather—"

The priestess shook her head and held up a hand. "We shall all go together."

Flex persisted, "But, my lady, these men died a violent death. It will be a gruesome scene, no need for—"

"I appreciate your concern for me, but I am familiar with death, and I wish to offer a blessing for your fallen. I am coming with you." Her tone left no room for argument.

Flex nodded in acquiescence. "As you wish, my lady."

"Very good," she said. "And you may call me Halia."

It wasn't long until the party reached the base of the cliff, and the sight would haunt Caelum the rest of his life. Four mangled corpses lay scattered in pools of dried blood, crows picking at their remains. Flex let out a cry as he ran to the largest mound, chasing the crows away, and he sank to his knees. The rest of the men spread out amongst the other bodies. Halia went first to the corpse where Flex knelt, and Caelum followed. Kurt was unrecognizable except for his size and the arrow still lodged in his chest. Halia knelt and laid one hand on Kurt's body and said a prayer, though the words were lost to Caelum. He continued to stand staring as Halia moved on to the next body.

Flex stood and began to carefully lay Kurt's corpse out upon his black cloak, solemnly wrapping him. When he had finished Caelum bent to help carry him.

"Don't touch him!" snapped Flex, his eyes a vicious warning.

The reaction caught Caelum off guard, bringing all the guilt he had been smothering flooding back to his conscience in full force. He stood up slowly and left while Roger took his place and helped Flex to carry the big man's remains to Halia's wagon, to be buried back in Edenia City. Caelum helped Daric to bring the body of one of the other men, Gus he believed, though he had hardly known the man. Gus had been climbing on Dax's rope, murdered by the deranged nobleman simply so that Daxton would have an opportunity to exact his revenge on Caelum and Kurt. After the three bodies had been loaded into the cart Flex signaled for them to make for the city.

"Wait!" said Halia from behind them. Flex turned back to her and raised a questioning eyebrow. "There is one more body!"

Flex sneered. "Leave him for the crows," he said, and he spat.

Halia gave him a disapproving glare and shook her head. "I will not."

She turned and walked over to the last corpse, Dax's corpse, said a short blessing over him, and began to wrap up the young man's body. Halia's white robe was stained with mud and blood, and she struggled to move Dax on her own, yet in her dishevelment the purity of the priestess seemed to shine all the brighter. It was Daric who moved to help her carry the man the rest of the way.

Flex scowled as they loaded Dax's body onto the wagon next to the other men, but all he said was, "Move out!" and they started back toward Edenia City.

Paholainen was annoyed. He should never have trusted the useless boy with such an important task. Yet even though the outcome had not been exactly as he had desired, Paholainen had already made arrangements to make up the difference. All would be well, and the boy would trouble him no more.

The party was exhausted when they finally reached the gate of the city. The sun was dipping below the mountain peaks to the west, and merchants were closing their shops for the night. Halia and her escort left the group and made for the Temple of the Creator, along with the bodies of the slain, which they would see buried. Caelum and the remaining guardsmen made for the barracks.

Upon reaching the door to the barracks, Flex placed his outstretched hand on Caelum's chest and spoke without emotion. "You will gather your things and go. The Guard has no place for cowards such as you."

Caelum was stunned. He couldn't mean it. "Flex, I..."

"There is nothing more to say. I am going to report to the king, and I don't want to see you when I return." Flex's tone left no room for argument. Caelum stood, feeling numb. It was Daric who came to him and spoke up in his defense as Flex walked away.

"Sir, you can't possibly mean that ..." Daric trailed off as Flex turned his head over his shoulder to glare icily at him, cutting him off. Daric hung his head in silence, defeated, and Flex set out once more toward the palace.

Daric turned to his friend. "Caelum, I… I don't know what to say. This doesn't seem right."

"It's ok Daric. I can't say that I disagree with him." Caelum lowered his eyes before continuing, "I don't belong here, and I'm not sure I ever did. I am a coward, and if I hadn't been so slow on our climb, Kurt might still be here." Daric started as if to say something, but Caelum shook his head. "I'm better suited for books than battles. Now I can return to focusing solely on my study of the Unbound, and I can return home to Almanis to check on everyone there."

"So you're going home then?" Daric asked.

Caelum sighed, then nodded. "First, I'll spend a little bit of time at the grand library at the Scholar's Guild. I want to see if there is anything more there that will aid in my research. It has been a long time since last I visited."

Daric smiled sadly. "I am sorry that things had to work out this way." He extended his arm. "I am going to miss you my friend. I wish you the best." Caelum grasped his friend's arm and smiled.

"Same."

And with that, Caelum gathered his things, donning his crimson coat once more, and he left.

Chapter 13

About half of the current nobility are descended from original noble households. Sometimes referred to as "true nobles," these houses are often afforded an extra measure of reverence by the more conservative members of society. Contrarily, newer lords and ladies have gained a measure of popularity among the younger generations.

-A History of Edenia and Its People
Headmaster Barius
E.A. 627

Flex had never experienced the range of emotions he was now feeling. He had always been the one who was calm and controlled, cool to a fault, yet since Kurt's death....

He leaned against the wall outside the training yard, covering his face with his good hand. His other arm had been broken when he slammed into the cliff wall at Blind Man's Ridge, though the pain he felt in his arm was nothing compared with the agony of losing his best friend. He and Kurt had been recruits together, had served in the same unit since the beginning. Death was not unfamiliar to members of the

Elite Guard. Flex and Kurt both knew what it might cost them to serve and protect their country. But they were prepared for death in battle. Kurt had been slain by his own brothers in arms: betrayed by a noble brat and condemned by a cowardly scholar. Flex slammed his fist into the wall before setting out once again for the palace.

It was getting dark. The guardsmen posted outside the palace lit the torches on either side of the gate as Flex approached. He passed through unchallenged. If they'd intended to give him space because he was distraught, it was the wrong choice. Flex made a mental note to chastise them later for letting anyone, even himself, enter the palace unchallenged. For now, he needed to report to the king's council about what had happened on the cliffside.

Upon reaching the door to the council chambers, Flex was relieved to be challenged by the guard posted there. *At least this man knows how to do his job,* he thought. "I am here to see the King and his council. I have important information that they must hear regarding our recent mission."

The guardsman nodded. "They are expecting you. Leave your sword." The guardsmen opened the door and announced Flex to the men inside. Flex entered to find the entire council present, although oddly, the Archpriest's place was taken by another clergyman Flex didn't recognize. Flex put it out of his mind as he fought back the lump growing in his throat, and he prepared to address them. He knelt and awaited the king's invitation to speak.

King Cedric sipped his wine glass before speaking. "Soldier, we have heard troubling rumors about your return to the city. By the look on your face I can see there must be some truth to these rumors. Please, tell us why you are here."

"My Lord, I'm afraid our unit met with betrayal and tragedy as we traversed Blind Man's Ridge. One of the other soldiers sharing my lifeline, Kurt…" He could feel himself choking up and did his best to put aside his emotions, focusing instead on simply relaying the facts. He felt a fool—this was so unlike him. He cleared his throat and tried again. "Kurt Vester took an arrow in the back from a recently promoted guardsmen who betrayed us, one Daxton Preavic."

One of the lord's sprung from his seat. "This is outrageous! My son would never betray this kingdom!".

"Lord Preavic, sit down," the king commanded.

The lord did nothing of the sort. "But Your Majesty, this accusation is baseless and false. Surely—"

"We have not heard the whole story," said the king. "Let the soldier finish his report."

Lord Preavic sat back down, his face flushed, and he stared at Flex with eyes of fury.

Flex ignored him and continued, "As I said, another guardsman, Kurt, was shot in the back, and was grievously injured. I was also injured in the exchange." He gestured to his broken arm, now in a sling. "The other soldier on my line, despite my insistence to the contrary, cut the rope supporting Kurt, seeking to lessen our burden so that we might save ourselves. As the arrows continued to fly, other guardsmen who had reached the top took action and struck down the traitor."

"Do you mean to say my son is dead?" Lord Preavic rose again and moved toward Flex.

The king reached out his hand to stop the nobleman. "Lord Preavi—"

"You killed my son!" Lord Preavic cried in rage. "My only son!" He lashed out and grabbed Flex by his throat. Flex was surprised at the strength of his grip, and he grabbed the nobleman's arms, trying to free himself without hurting the man too badly in the process. He struggled to speak but could only make garbled sounds.

"Lord Preavic! That's enough!" the king shouted, but Flex could feel that the councilman was lost in his anguish, intent on choking the life out of the man he held responsible for his son's death.

Flex couldn't breathe. If he didn't do something quickly, he was going to die. He didn't like the idea of hurting a superior, even the father of a traitor, but he had no choice. He prepared to escape and send the man to the floor with no more than two broken arms, hopefully.

Another councilman, this one dark and wearing a magnificent silver cloak glided into Flex's now blurred vision, grabbing Lord Preavic under his arms in such a way that his grip softened, and Flex was able to break free. Lord Preavic collapsed to his knees, sobbing. Flex rubbed his throat, which felt like it was on fire, and he gasped for air, fighting off his shock. He found it unimaginable that a councilman could lose his composure in such a fashion. He looked back up to the king, who was staring down at Lord Preavic menacingly. The other councilman, the one who had come to his aid, broke the silence.

"My king, I ask your forgiveness for our Lord Preavic. There is no grief like that of a parent losing his child. Show mercy for his outburst and let him go to bury his son. I assume you have brought back his body?" The man looked to Flex, who had been staring at Lord Preavic. Flex felt no pity for Daxton; the boy had been a traitor. He could, however, pity the loyal father who had been shamed by his son.

"Yes, my Lord," he croaked, his voice still hoarse.

"Very well," said the king. "See to your son."

The silver-clad councilman beckoned to the guard at the door. "You there, escort Lord Preavic back to his quarters, then see to it that he is brought to the place where his son is to be prepared for burial."

The guard raised a fist to his chest in a salute. "Right away, Lord Mantell."

Lord Mantell....

Flex stared at Lord Mantell as the other councilman was escorted out of the chamber, unable to completely hide his surprise. Lord Mantell, greatest of the Lords of Edenia, second only to the king. He was said to be a fierce warrior and a brilliant tactician. Despite his widespread reputation, he was rarely seen outside of his own estate in the northern province of Crisantia. Flex had always admired the man, but he had never had the good fortune to meet him in person. It bothered him that they were meeting under such troubling circumstances, and he was afraid Lord Mantell would bear a dishonorable impression of him.

Lord Mantell stood and walked gracefully back to take his seat as the king spoke, clearly agitated. "Continue your report, soldier."

"Yes, your majesty," Flex replied dutifully. "Upon reaching the summit...."

The doors to the council chamber slammed open behind Flex with a loud *crack*, jolting the king and council to their feet in surprised outrage. Flex, with teeth bared, reflexively spun, reaching to draw his sword before remembering it wasn't there.

A single soldier stumbled into the room, haggard and filthy. He took three steps before he slumped to the floor. The man looked weak, as if he had had nothing to eat or drink for days. Flex moved to grab the man as he pathetically tried to stand.

"What is the meaning of this?" the king demanded from across the room.

"Dead," the man mumbled. "They are all dead."

"Who is dead?" the king demanded. "What are you talking about? And who are you?"

Even as the king spoke, Flex felt an icy pit forming in his stomach. "Sire…" he began, each of his next words weighed heavy with dread. "I know this man." Flex couldn't believe it was the same man he had served with in the Elite Guard for years. He was too thin, unkempt, and had a hollow look in his eyes that chilled Flex to his bones.

"Well, who is he then, and what is this madness he keeps muttering?" The king's voice grew louder and more impatient with each question.

Flex now supported the full weight of the newcomer, the poor man's arm wrapped around Flex's shoulder. Flex tore his eyes away from the haunting gaze of the soldier to once again address the king.

"His name is Lawrence, and he was one of the men sent out along with the Knights of Radiance to slay the Unbound." The ramifications of the man's identity were not lost on the council members around the table, nor the king, and nervous muttering broke out amongst them. Flex noticed Lord Mantell staring pensively down at the wounded soldier.

"Quiet, quiet!" The king stood and slammed his hands down on the table in front of him, and the men around the table ceased their frantic chatter, turning to face the king. Lawrence was still muttering incoherently under his breath. The king looked at him and demanded once more, "Tell us what happened."

Lawrence continued his babble, showing no indication that he had even heard the king speak. King Cedric's expression darkened, and Flex turned to Lawrence hoping to get him to speak before the king's fury was unleashed.

"Lawrence, it's me, Flex," he said gently. "Can you tell us what you saw? What's happened to Callus and the others?"

The man responded, looking first at Flex, then up at the king, cowering. "They are all dead, sire," he whimpered. "We engaged the beast first with our archers and pikemen, but they fell to its hideous charge. The Knights of Radiance assaulted the devilish creature next and were obliterated...." Flex heard a councilman gasp; another dropped his head into his hands. All of them were speechless. "After that..." Lawrence's eyes had a faraway look. "The onslaught continued. That demon killed them all...." The man collapsed in Flex's arms, his eyes glazed over. Flex laid him down gently, staring down at his lifeless body in disbelief. He was dead.

The man must have come here straight from the encounter with the Unbound. The trauma of what he had seen, combined with a lack of food and sleep, had taken its toll. The overwhelming need to deliver his message must have been all that had sustained him this long. Flex reached out a hand to close the man's eyes. "You did well, my friend."

The council chamber was chaos. Frenzied councilors argued with one another over what course of action should be taken next, shouting their suggestions to the king. King Cedric stood motionless amidst the noise, never taking his eyes off the corpse lying before him, ignoring everyone else around him.

Flex was overcome with grief. He closed his eyes as he knelt, gripping Lawrence's arm. He could feel the warmth leaving the man's body. This was the second friend he had watched die in the last few days, and now he learned that even more of his comrades had perished in the battle with the Unbound, Callus, the man who had been his mentor, among the fallen. He wiped away the tears welling in his eyes before standing. The council seemed to have regained some semblance of order. One councilman, Lord Faris, was addressing them now.

"…which is why we need to focus our efforts on preparing for the inevitable arrival of this beast."

Nods of approval came from a few of the men around the table. Lord Mantell was also standing, shaking his head, and Flex felt as if his own presence had been forgotten amid their debate.

"I understand your concern, Andro, but you forget that there are many innocent people who would be left to fend for themselves should we be complacent. Shall we abandon them while we cower behind our walls?" Some of the men who had been supporting Lord Faris lowered their eyes in shame. Lord Mantell turned toward the king as he continued. "Sire, we cannot allow this beast to take any more lives. We must attack now, with everything we have. There is no time for half measures. New Knights of Radiance can be appointed, if that is in fact what is needed, and they can march with the full force of the Edenian Legion. This threat must be ended, now. Whatever the cost." Cheering erupted among the councilmen, and Lord Faris slumped back into his seat, clearly defeated.

King Cedric raised both of his arms, palms outward, and the room became silent. He faced Lord Mantell. "Once again, my friend, your wisdom is sound." Lord Mantell bowed his head in gratitude, and the king turned back to address the entire council. "Lord Mantell is correct. We clearly underestimated the threat that this beast represents. Tomorrow, Lord Mantell will depart with the entire Edenian Legion to crush this menace once and for all." The councilmen around the table cheered once more, and Lord Mantell approached Flex.

"Soldier, return to the barracks and have the men make preparations to march."

"Yes, sir," he replied and put his fist to his chest in a salute. "When do we leave?"

Lord Mantell glanced down at Flex's broken arm in its sling, then back up again. "*We* leave at dawn," he said, and his tone left no doubt as to his meaning. Lord Mantell flicked his silver cloak back over his shoulder and exited the council chambers.

Flex felt numb. Once again, his brothers in arms would be facing the greatest threat they had ever known, and once again, he would be left behind. He turned dejectedly and walked out of the room to follow his orders, as he always did.

Chapter 14

Our companion Gemmel has died, succumbing to the sickness he acquired as we traversed this barren wasteland. Death is a curious thing. Men will do anything to escape it. Even terrible things. Yet for a noble cause, many people will gladly give up their lives. Perhaps it is not so much that a man fears death, but rather that he fears a life spent for nothing.

-Journal of Oleth Zandarion
Translation by Caelum Karasin
E.A.967

Jeremiah Bradford opened his eyes, his vision blurry at first. He blinked a few times and then tried to sit up, but sharp pain from his right leg caused him to draw in a quick breath and flop back down on his mat. Bradford lifted himself more carefully this time and pulled up the blanket covering him to examine his right leg, only there was no leg. There was a stump, wrapped in linen just above where his knee used to be.

Memories of his encounter with the Unbound flooded back into him. He remembered his reckless charge at the creature, remembered the frightened little girl that left him no alternative. He remembered being struck aside by the beast, trapped under his dead horse, and being lifted toward the Unbound's hideous maw. He remembered the sick feeling of flesh ripping from hacking off his own leg.

Bradford shuddered, leaning over his bedside and vomiting. He sat up, wiped his mouth, then examined his surroundings. He was in a makeshift tent with sunlight streaming in through the cloth, warming the space nicely. There wasn't much inside, only a small table with a bowl of water and a cloth for washing, a small stool, and the cot Bradford was sitting on. Bradford noticed he was bandaged in other places on his body and grunted with pain as he spun to place his one good leg over the side of the cot. There he froze, realizing he had no way to stand.

The tent flap opened and a woman approaching her middle years ducked inside. She was short and her long brown hair was braided in the style common among country women. She frowned as she saw Bradford. "You should be resting."

"Where am I?" Bradford asked, half grunting.

Her expression softened, and she sat in the stool next to him, checking his bandages as she spoke. "You are in the refugee camp just south of the place where you battled the Unbound. We are on our way to Almanis Village." She helped him lie down, and after checking his forehead with the back of her hand, she put the wet cloth on his brow. "You have been unconscious for three days since the attack." She noticed the mess Bradford had made beside the bed and began cleaning it up without comment.

Bradford rolled his head to the side to look at the woman. "What happened to my men?"

"After you fell in battle, your men came swiftly to your aid. They rushed the monster and drew it away from you. They…" She paused, looking down at her hands, folded on her lap. Her voice softened as she spoke again. "Many died. Those who survived led the beast away from the refugees, deeper into the forest. A few of those who were wounded are here in the camp."

Bradford closed his eyes and said nothing. He knew the danger of this mission. He had seen what the Unbound was capable of in Beldun, then again at the ambush on the hilltop, and now more of his men were dead because he led them into a battle that they could not win. *All of our efforts have been for nothing.* Several minutes passed in silence before he spoke again. "Thank you for tending to my injuries."

She looked up, and Bradford could see tears forming in her eyes. "Do not thank me. I should be thanking you. You saved us. When we were attacked, most of the men in our group tried to fend off the creature with whatever they could find, but there was nothing they could do" She sniffed, trying to maintain her composure. "My daughter broke away from me and tried to reach her father. My husband was dead—he sacrificed himself to try to buy us some time—and I thought I was about to lose my little girl as well." She smiled at him through her tears. "You saved her," she said, her voice quivering.

The woman's words rekindled a fire in Bradford that he thought was gone for good, and he had to fight back tears of his own. There had been so much death, and there seemed to be no hope of stopping the catastrophe the Unbound had wrought, but this was something. He *had* accomplished something, and he could do more.

The tent flap swung open again and a little girl darted in and stood behind the woman, clutching at her dress, peeking out from behind her to stare at him. She couldn't have seen more than six or seven summers.

"Lily, say hello to the man who saved your life."

"Hullo, mister." The girl's voice was muffled as she spoke with her face still buried in her mother's dress.

Bradford smiled as warmly as he could—he had never been very good with children—and reached out his hand to the girl. "Hello Lily, I'm Jeremiah."

The girl snuck out from behind her mother and grabbed his hand, shaking it slightly. "I see'd a bird once with one leg, just like you. It had to hop everywhere. Are you a good hopper?"

"Lily! That is not a polite thing to say!" her mother snapped, aghast at her daughter's bluntness.

Bradford burst out laughing, which set the little girl to giggling and earned her a frown from her mother. "I guess I will have to be," he said, still chuckling. Bradford looked at the little girl smiling at him, and he knew he would gladly give his other leg if it meant she could live and smile for even one more day. *I don't know if we can stop the Unbound, but I know I can buy these people time.*

He looked back to the woman. "I need parchment and a pen, and any maps of the valley that you may have. If there are no maps, maybe one of you locals can draw us one. Also, send word to my men. Tell them that anyone who is able is to join me in the tent as soon as possible."

The woman stood and nodded, "I will. Lily, let's let Jeremiah get some rest." She took Lily's hand and turned to leave. "Wait," he said, and she turned back to him. "I never got your name."

"My name is Lissa." She turned to leave once more.

Bradford's stomach growled angrily, and he called to her once more. "Lissa," he said hesitantly, "do you have anything to eat?"

It was a little less than an hour before Captain Bradford, now satisfied after three bowls of stew, was joined in his ramshackle tent by eighteen other men, which was more than he had expected. They crammed in as best they could, but some were forced to stand outside. Eleven of the men were his soldiers, all with injuries, but Bradford had the worst injury of those who survived. The rest were men from the refugees who had served their term in the military and were volunteering to assist him in any way necessary. Bradford admired their courage and wished that he wasn't about to lead them all to probable death. Bradford cleared his throat and the men became silent, waiting for him to speak.

"You men have all witnessed the terror that we face. What I am about to ask of you will not be easy, and it is likely to cost you your very lives. If you are not prepared to die so that others may live, you may leave now, and I would not blame you for it." Nobody moved. Captain Bradford nodded his approval. "Good, then let's get started."

He resettled himself on the cot, wishing he could stand to deliver his plan. He'd have to make do. "Our attempts to neutralize that damned Unbound have been largely unsuccessful, but despite our failures, we have managed to learn a few things about our enemy. First—" Bradford held up one finger. "—the beast seems to have one single insatiable desire, and that is to kill every human being it encounters." He held up his second finger. "The beast also seems to have some uncanny ability to sense us and track us from a distance, and it doesn't seem to tire. That means it will pursue its prey relentlessly until we are no more." Bradford raised his third finger. "And lastly, nothing we have done to stop the creature seems to have dealt it any noticeable harm."

The room was quiet.

"So what's the problem Cap?" asked a sarcastic voice.

Bradford didn't have to look to know the voice belonged to Brick, a known prankster in the company who was a little too friendly around women, in Bradford's opinion, but nevertheless a good soldier. He chuckled along with the other men, and the nervous tension in the room was dissolved.

"That's the spirit Brick." Bradford smiled, grateful for Brick's levity, even amidst the hopeless situation. The man played the fool, but Brick was intentional in his efforts to boost morale. Bradford continued, "We face an invincible foe who seeks to hunt us down and destroy us all. Our mission is no longer to defeat this beast, as I believe we are ill equipped to do so." *If it even can be defeated,* he thought, but kept that to himself. "Instead, we will do everything in our power to keep this demon from taking any more innocent lives until somebody discovers a way to slay that hellspawn once and for all."

"How are we going to do that, Captain?" asked one of the men.

Bradford pulled out a piece of cloth and laid it out on the table. "How many of you have played the game *Cross*?" Several of the men nodded, raising their hands slightly. It was a popular game throughout Edonia. Each player had twelve stones that they used to maneuver around a game board in order to capture their opponent's leader. While an attacking player would focus their efforts on capturing their opponent's leader, the defender could perform a maneuver called a *cross* by passing one of his pieces over his own leader, thereby transferring the leader title to the new stone, completely changing the game.

The cloth Bradford unrolled was a map of Almanis Valley, hastily drawn. Bradford placed a stone on the map. "This is us." He then placed two more stones slightly to the north of the first. "This is where we believe the Unbound and the rest of the survivors from our company might be, according to the last time we saw them when they appeared to have been heading further east." He didn't tell them that it was very possible there were no survivors left. Bradford moved the stones representing the Unbound and their missing companions farther east, then moved the third stone northeast until they met. "We will intercept them here. The men will be exhausted and frightened. We will perform a *cross* and draw the beast away from them, forcing it to pursue us and giving our weary comrades a much-needed respite."

Some of the men looked concerned, not yet fully grasping Bradford's plan. He continued, "We will set up camps here, here, and here." He circled three areas on the map, forming a triangle with points approximately three leagues apart. "We will also split into three parties. Those of us here will compose two of the parties, and those we intercept will form the third. Since this beast seems to function without need for sleep or sustenance, we will lead it in an endless chase, performing cross maneuvers near each camp with fresh troops and horses. This will continue indefinitely until reinforcements arrive, or we are all dead." He looked up from the map and back to his men. "Any questions?"

They spent the next half-hour refining the plan, discussing contingencies, and dividing into groups with specific assignments. Then Bradford dismissed them to begin preparing for their departure. A few more of the refugees were going to accompany Bradford and his men to take care of the needs at camp while the soldiers rested and recovered between their shifts. Lissa was among them.

Bradford had been helped into the back of one of their supply wagons, and he was sitting up as he was attended by one of the other refugees. He called out to Lissa as she passed by. "You should stay with the rest of your people. It will be dangerous out there, even for those of you who plan to stay at camp."

Lissa changed her direction and walked over to the wagon. "I will take over from here Mayra, thank you."

The woman who had been attending Bradford nodded and gathered her things before climbing down out of the wagon. Lissa replaced her at Bradford's side.

"You're one to talk." She gave him a disapproving glare. "You shouldn't be out of bed for at least another week."

Bradford shrugged. "I can't ask these men to risk their lives while I am resting comfortably attended by beautiful women." Lissa blushed. "You, on the other hand, have a daughter who needs you. Stay here, with her."

Lissa began working on changing Bradford's bandages. He had to grit his teeth as she gently pulled away the old, bloody wrap that covered his stump. This was the first time he had seen his wound. He had seen other men lose limbs in battle and thought he had become accustomed to blood and gore, yet his stomach churned as he stared at the ruined, scabby flesh.

She gently cleaned the wound before she wrapped it again in a fresh bandage.

She spoke as she worked. "I wish I could stay behind. I hate to leave Lily for any reason, especially after losing her father. But if you soldiers fail, there will be nothing stopping that monster from following us wherever we go, and then there would be nothing at all I could do for her. If I go with you, perhaps my small talent in healing will be helpful."

Bradford nodded his understanding. If they were unsuccessful in containing the Unbound, he was almost certain the beast would head straight for Almanis Village, and from there straight into the heart of Edenia. Even if they were successful, there was no telling how long they would be able to last out here alone. He hoped one of his messengers had reached the capital by now, and he hoped that scholar had something else up his sleeve to counter the Unbound.

The wagon driver poked his head into the back of the wagon. "We're ready to go, sir."

Bradford nodded. "Then let's go."

The wagon lurched forward and then continued at a steady pace. Lissa finished wrapping his leg in fresh bandages and discarded the nasty old wrappings. Bradford laid his head back to rest, not intending to fall asleep.

He awoke sometime later to Lissa gently shaking him by the shoulders.

"Jeremiah," she whispered. "Your scouts returned. They say the Unbound has come farther south than we expected. It will be upon us any minute."

Bradford cursed as he sat up, then again from the jolting pain in his ghost leg caused by his careless movement. "Tell Brick to get squad one saddled and…."

Lissa held up a hand to cut him off. "Your men are mounted and ready. They told me not to wake you, but I thought I should tell you anyway." She bit her lip, waiting to see his reaction.

He smiled at her. "Thank you."

She relaxed a little and smiled back, nervously. "I guess this is it."

"This is going to work, Lissa," he reassured, as much to himself as to her. "It has to. Now help me up."

She put her arm under his shoulder and supported him as he managed to carefully scoot to the edge of the wagon. At Lissa's request, someone back at the camp had fashioned a crutch for him, and with the crutch and her help, he hobbled to the place where the first twelve men were preparing to *cross*. They stood at the edge of a large clearing, the foothills of the Elys Mountains rising to the west, thick forest covering the landscape all around them. Bradford had chosen this area intentionally for the *cross*, as there was plenty of room to maneuver. The men would later attempt to redirect the Unbound to the north, along the road leading to the next staging area. Should anything go wrong, the men could leave the road and try to lose the beast in the dense forest. He hoped it would not come to that.

Brick sat on his saddle at the head the group of riders, and Bradford was impressed with their composure. They had all chosen to be a part of this desperate endeavor and had made peace with the fact that they were unlikely to survive. Each rider was outfitted for speed, wearing no armor and equipped only with bows, lances, or anything else they could find that might be useful in provoking the Unbound from a distance to draw its attention, rather than for attempting to harm the beast. They knew better than that now.

Captain Bradford approached Brick with Lissa still supporting him as he went. Brick sat calmly in his saddle at the front of the group of horsemen. He brought his fist to his chest in a salute. "Fine evening for a ride, sir."

Bradford grinned. "It's a bit cold for my liking."

"I reckon things will be heating up for us pretty quickly."

Brick stared out over the horizon, where a faint glow emanated from over the hilltop, almost as if the sun were rising from the west. A nervous buzz spread through the camp. The men on horseback shifted uneasily and gripped their weapons tighter, but even though they were afraid, they looked determined. *At least that strange glow that surrounds this thing might provide some light for the riders,* he thought. Riding through the darkness could be treacherous for the men. A few of them carried torches, and they were fortunate to have the light from the full moon, but it was still dangerous. Even so, they had no choice.

A red glow shone through the trees to the west, and from this distance it looked just like a raging wildfire. Bradford could make out a few small shadows moving in front of the flames, which meant that there were at least some other survivors from his company. *Good, now let's just hope they continue east.* Hopefully the scouts he had sent earlier would see to that. He patted Brick on the leg and nodded reassuringly, then saluted him and the rest of the men preparing to ride. He raised his voice to address them.

"This is it boys!" he bellowed. "This is what we have prepared for. Every second that we distract this beast is one more second that our loved ones are safe. Have courage, and trust in the wisdom of our king! Help is on the way." Bradford hobbled away, leaving Brick to command the riders. The blaze to the west was getting nearer, and the small shadows were almost recognizable.

"Ready, men!" Brick shouted, riding along the line of horsemen. He turned forward and shouted, "Charge!"

Mud flew from the explosive power of the horses' hind legs as they burst into movement. They rode in formation toward the center of the clearing. The other riders and the Unbound came close enough for Bradford to clearly distinguish them. There were six riders, including the two scouts he had sent out as guides, though they were too distant still for Bradford to identify, and they didn't appear to be carrying anything besides the clothes on their back. The Unbound was terrifying, loping behind them menacingly, closing the distance between them with every one of its tremendous strides. Bradford realized his first mistake. In the forest, men on horseback were smaller and could outpace the larger creature. Out here in the clearing, the Unbound was faster. The beast's entire ruby-scaled, serpentine body was glowing an ethereal scarlet, and its four muscular, sharp-taloned legs tore the ground with each step. Fire blazed from the top of the hellish creature's head down the length of its body, and more flames burst from its mouth as it roared its fury, revealing razor sharp fangs. The flames overtook the rear most rider, and horse and man went down in a burning heap. The Unbound pounced, letting out another deep roar as it set to devour its prey.

The remaining three riders took the opportunity to change course, heading for Brick and his men. Brick waved an arm to the wagons and shouted something, and the three riders galloped away from their rescuers and back to Bradford and the rest of the onlookers. Brick set his archers and gave the command to loose. The Unbound was just finishing his quarry when the arrows bounded harmlessly off its scales. Its head snapped up, and it roared in frustration. The beast whipped its head toward Brick and his men, then it swung it back to lock its gaze on the three retreating riders. Its thunderous roar shook the air as it charged after fleeing riders. Toward the caravan.

Seven hells….

Panic spread through the camp as the onlookers rushed to escape the path of the raging beast. Bradford took his arm away from Lissa's shoulder and growled, "Run, woman!"

She took his arm back and said defiantly, "I'm not leaving you." Bradford scowled and looked back at the Unbound. Brick led his men back toward the caravan, his archers firing at will, but the beast paid them no heed. It had found its new target.

The Unbound lumbered toward the caravan. The refugee volunteers scrambled back into the cover of the trees. The three men on horseback were close to reaching the wagons when the Unbound let out a terrifying howl and leapt, landing just in front of them and crushing a supply wagon under its enormous bulk. The exhausted horses carrying the men reared in fright, and two of them collapsed, their riders frantically crawling away. The Unbound reached out with one vicious talon and slashed at the horse still standing. The man on its back jumped away as the beast closed in and crushed the poor animal with its powerful jaws.

Lissa clung fearfully to Bradford's arm. He pried her loose and shoved her back behind him, toward the trees.

"Go now!" he yelled at her.

The three unhorsed soldiers ran for their lives toward the cover of the trees. The Unbound inhaled heavily and Bradford recognized the precursor to its hellish, fiery breath that would engulf all three of the men before they made it. He hurled his rude crutch with all his might, and it struck the beast below the eye with a loud crack, then fell to land in the burning heap of the crushed wagon where the beast stood. The Unbound lowered its head and stared directly at Bradford, stalking toward him with a furious roar, forgetting about the other three men now reaching the cover of the forest.

The pain from Bradford's stump was agonizing as he stood there, balanced on his one good leg. Bradford beckoned tauntingly at oncoming behemoth and shouted, "Come get the other one, hellspawn!" He stared up into the gaping maw of the Unbound, now barely more than a few yards away from him.

I failed them. I'm sorry, Lissa.

Bright orange flame exploded. Bradford raised his arms to hide his face and felt the rush of hot air wash over him. Time seemed to slow down. Something heavy hit him, driving him to the ground and away from the flames. He screamed in pain as his stump struck the hard-packed dirt. Lissa was on her knees kneeling over him, using her bare hands to pat out the patches of flame on his tunic. Bradford could hardly see, his vision blurred by tears and the thick smoke all around them. He blinked and saw the beast preparing to unleash another stream of fire.

A single rider leapt through the blazing inferno surrounding the Unbound and slammed the tip of his lance into creature's chest. The lance shattered into a thousand flaming splinters, knocking the beast off balance. Brick circled wide around the beast, shouting every obscenity he could think of to try to keep its attention focused on him. The Unbound roared in outrage. Some of the archers joined Brick, firing a few shafts at the monster from horseback, infuriating it further.

Bradford was being dragged under one of the supply wagons that remained untouched in the mayhem. Lissa grunted with effort as she did her best to pull him to cover. The pain he felt all over was unbearable, and his head swam as he fought back against the blackness that threatened to overtake him. They reached the cover of the wagon, and they both laid flat against the cold earth, watching the nightmare continue to unfold before them.

Brick and his riders had successfully captured the Unbound's attention this time. They began backing away slowly, trying to lure the creature away from the wagons. Without warning, the beast unleashed a wave of flame that swept over the two archers who were closest to it. Brick and the others spun on their mounts and galloped northeast into the clearing, toward the path they had chosen as the route to the second camp.

Maybe they can still pull this off, but this is our last chance.

The next few seconds seemed an eternity as Bradford waited to see if the Unbound would chase Brick and his men. If not, then there was nothing more he could do. The Unbound would have free reign to terrorize the people in the more densely populated areas west of the valley. He watched as the beast rose to peer menacingly back at the caravan, surveying its surroundings. Bradford breathed a sigh of relief when the beast loped off into the night after the decoy, its furious roar fading into the distance.

"It's gone," Lissa whispered next to him.

He nodded. "For now."

The two of them lay with their backs resting against the wagon wheel, too exhausted to move. People trickled back out from the cover of the trees to save as much as they could from the burning wagons, putting out fires where they could. Bradford hurt everywhere. He looked down at himself and saw he had been burned along the right side of his torso, as well as along his arm. Some of his skin was peeling around his ribcage, and it hurt like hell. He rolled his head to the side to look over at Lissa, her face glistening with sweat where it wasn't covered by grimy black soot.

"You look terrible," he grunted, and she laughed, coughing from all of the smoke. He smiled back at her, half grimacing as he did so. "Thank you for saving my life. I guess I owe you one."

Her eyes were closed as she spoke. "I like honeycakes," she said with a smile.

Bradford chuckled. "Honeycakes it is, then." He reached out to grab her hand. Lissa flinched when he touched her and sucked in a sharp breath, pulling her hand away.

"What's wrong?" he asked.

Lissa was nursing her hand in her lap. "It's nothing," she said.

Bradford frowned and scooted for a closer look at her hands, which were black and blistered. She must have suffered the burns when she was trying to put out the fires that had threatened him earlier.

"Your hands are burnt! We need to get you to a healer."

"Have you looked at yourself?" she quipped, raising an eyebrow at him.

He grunted. "I've had worse."

That wasn't true, and the skeptical look on Lissa's face proved he wasn't fooling either of them. She chuckled, then Bradford grinned, and they both burst out into uncontrolled, delirious laughter. They heard footsteps approaching, and a young man, one of the three who had just returned to them, bent down to peer under the wagon. His boyish features were somewhat tempered with new lines of exhaustion around his eyes and brow.

"Are you all right, sir?"

"Hal Dennix!" Bradford exclaimed. "It's good to see you, son." The young man smiled, still in surprisingly good humor after what he must have been through.

"You too, Captain," he said, then he turned to shout over his shoulder. "Garit, bring a healer over here quick. We have two wounded."

"So Garit made it back too," Bradford said thoughtfully. "Who is the third man with you?"

"Felman, and that was Randal who fell out there to the beast."

Bradford sighed. Randal had been his second, and a good friend. He could have used him in this mess.

"Sir," Dennix continued, "there may be other survivors. We scattered early in our flight. The beast surely got to some of those that separated, which is probably the only reason we were able to elude it for so long, but I doubt it has taken them all. If you would allow it, sir, I would like to lead a search party to find them."

Bradford nodded. "Find them and bring them to the place we have chosen for our camp. One of the other men can show you where that will be. But first, I need you to tell me everything that happened since last we spoke."

Chapter 15

Everything made by the Creator is good and is cherished by Him. None moreso than mankind, to whom he hath given both love and the ability to love. And if we are so highly regarded by the Creator of all things, how then can we declare the life of a brother to be worthless? How can we say a man is so shattered that he is beyond saving? For the Creator delights in reforming that which is broken into something beautiful.

-Book of Creation
Author Unknown
Before the Alliance

Caelum sat alone at a small wooden table within the great library of the Edenian Scholar's Guild, where he'd spent every waking hour since he was expelled from the Elite Guard three days ago. The library was immense and contained the most extensive collection of knowledge in all Edenia, and Caelum doubted there was a place like it anywhere else in the world. Many of the ancient texts were extremely brittle and required the utmost delicacy when handled, thus it was forbidden to remove them from the premises. Caelum had transcribed some such texts, indirectly related to the Unbound, when last he had visited the guild, and he was determined this time to finish the rest in order to produce his own complete record of everything known on the subject before he left for Almanis Village. *And maybe I can find something to help Daric and the other soldiers defeat the Unbound.*

Word had spread quickly of the second mobilization to destroy the beast. When he left the dormitories this morning, Caelum had heard the news about a man galloping into the city at night to inform the king that the Knights of Radiance were annihilated. The entire garrison was now preparing to march, leaving just enough troops to manage the city. They would depart later that day.

Caelum slammed his fist down on the wooden table, earning disapproving glares from the other scholars nearby, mostly wearing the jade overcoats representing the field of biology. It was foolishness to send these troops to face the Unbound. One thing was very clear in his research; nothing could bring down an Unbound except the Knights of Radiance. *But why did Callus and the others fail?* The question had plagued him since hearing news of the massacre. If he was unable to discover what he was missing, he feared this second attempted attack on the creature would result in even more lives lost, including Daric's. He had tried to gain an audience with the king, or anyone in authority, to tell them these things, but nobody would lend him an ear. The Knights of Radiance's failure was partially attributed to him, and Caelum's own disgrace at Blind Man's Ridge made that two marks against him. He turned his attention back to Oleth's journal, and the passage he was studying.

> *Bearing the gift of the first, the renowned*
> *Shall face death incarnate, and tame the Unbound*

He believed this passage held the key. "The renowned" was a term used in some of the other older texts to refer to the Knights of Radiance. The part that puzzled him most was the "gift of the first." He had found mention of "the first" in other sources and had been able to link the phrase to another word, *Enkeli*, but he had no idea what that word meant. He suspected it was some sort of ancient city or people, maybe even a specific person, but nothing he could find contained any sort of description or explanation. Whatever "gift" the Enkeli might possess could be the missing link.

The door to the great library opened and closed with a loud boom, the only sound in the otherwise silent room. Caelum heard soft footsteps echoing through the chamber, and he was surprised when the priestess Halia rounded one of the enormous bookshelves and walked straight to him at his little hideaway table. She wore a new set of the same pure white robes Caelum had first seen her in, her golden hair braided and resting over her shoulder. Her eyes were red and puffy, as if she had been crying, and Caelum was both concerned and a little uncomfortable, not sure what he should say.

"Halia, what's wrong?" he asked, rising from his chair.

"My brother is dead," she said, voice quivering slightly as she tried to maintain her composure. She practically collapsed onto the chair across from Caelum, and Caelum sat back down slowly.

Caelum ached for her. Both of his parents had died when he was very young, and he knew the pain of losing a loved one. "What happened?"

She blinked as if that was the last thing she expected him to say, before realization set in. "I'm sorry, I assumed that you would know. My full name is Halia La'Rathia, daughter of Einhold La'Rathia, the Archpriest. My brother was Callus La'Rathia."

Callus La'Rathia, Knight Commander of the Knights of Radiance. Caelum was stunned. She did bear a shocking resemblance to the man, though Caelum had only seen him during the parade celebrating their departure to face the Unbound. "I'm so sorry, Halia."

She tilted her head slightly and looked at him with a mixture of confusion and sorrow. "I set out for Edenia when I heard my brother had been sent on such a strange quest. I wanted to be here when he returned…" Her voice trailed off, and she had to take a moment to regain her composure. "They say that you have spent your life studying these creatures, even when nobody else believed that they even existed. And I have been told you are the one who claimed that the Knights of Radiance were the only ones who could defeat the Unbound." She held him captive with her pleading gaze. "If that is so, then why is Callus dead?"

She gave voice to the question that had burned inside him. "I'm sorry, Halia, I don't know," he said, feeling partially responsible. "I have been in here trying to find some answers, anything to help end the threat this monster brings. My best friend is leaving with the rest of the garrison to fight another hopeless battle, and I haven't gotten any closer to a solution." It sounded pathetic, he knew, when he had so confidently claimed that the Knights of Radiance would be able to defeat the Unbound. It was because of him that Callus was sent on the failed mission in the first place. "I foolishly assumed the

Knights of Radiance would have the knowledge they needed. I failed them."

She reached across the table to gently take his hand. "I do not blame you for my brother's death. I know you are trying to help. I simply seek answers as well, and I believe that the Creator may yet use Callus's sacrifice for good." Caelum was thankful for her kind words, and while they didn't completely assuage his guilt, they did help.

"Thank you," he said. The idea that the Creator might have a plan for Callus's death troubled him, however, so he voiced a question he had had for many years. "Halia, if you don't mind me asking, how is it that you choose to follow this Creator of yours? For an all-powerful, benevolent being to create a world with creatures of terror such as this Unbound, where terrible things happen to good people like your brother, or my parents, or—" He closed his eyes and let out a breath, "—or Kurt."

Halia lowered her gaze and sat quietly a moment before answering. "It's not always easy," she said softly. "I've asked that question many times and have found comfort in two truths. First, that evil is not a part of creation, but rather a distortion of it. And second, that even the worst acts of evil can be used by the Creator to make something of greater beauty."

Caelum wasn't convinced. "I fail to see how anything good can come from such senseless deaths."

She sighed. "I do not understand it either, but I don't have to right now. It is enough to trust that good can come from this, and, in the jo hey to discover what that good might be, there are lessons to e learned. Perhaps our meeting here is one such blessing.' She nrled weakly and let her fingers trail across his research spread across the table. "Perhaps I can help you find some answers."

Caelum chuckled and immediately regretted it. Halia frowned at him.

"You find something funny?"

Caelum sobered as he answered. The woman was grieving, and here he was flaunting his own arrogance. "I'm sorry, it's just that I have been studying these texts for years, and I doubt you have set foot in this library before today." Her frown deepened. Clearly, he had chosen the wrong words. He had always been awkward around women, especially pretty ones. "But… um," he scrambled, "perhaps a fresh pair of eyes may see something I have missed." He slid the book he had been reading across the table to Halia. "It couldn't hurt," he said. "In fact…" Something Halia had said reminded him of a certain passage in Oleth's journal he'd been puzzling over a lot of late. He flipped back through the pages of the journal. "Read this."

Halia took the page from him. "This is written in the ancient Edenian language. Did you do the translation?" Caelum nodded. "I thought the language was extinct."

Caelum shrugged. "I'm probably the only one alive who ever cared to learn it."

"Well, I suppose it's a good thing you did," said Halia. She furrowed her brow as she read through the passage.

The earth trembled, and night turned to day as the beast was born. Not of flesh, but of wrath. Not of creation, but of destruction.

"This speaks of the birth of the creature," she said thoughtfully. "Is there any more written about it?"

"Painfully little," he replied. "Most of the information written about the Unbound has been written recently, and the authors treat them as myths. Very little documentation comes from before the time of the great church schism, but those older documents seem to describe the Unbound through first or third-person accounts." He growled in frustration. "I used to assume this passage was metaphorical, yet I experienced the trembling of the earth, and I saw an incredible flash of light. If the first line is literal, perhaps the others are as well."

"Which would suggest that the Unbound is no natural creature…"

"Then where did it come from?" Caelum's heart beat faster. He pulled his chair around the table to sit beside Halia, his voice growing more energetic as he spoke. "Everything I've studied suggests the Unbound are purely vicious, intent on nothing but destruction. Yet you claim the Creator would not create something evil. Could that mean this monster is, as you say, simply a distortion of something else, something good?"

"I suppose that is possible, but a distortion of what?" She shook her head. "There isn't anything I've heard of that even comes close to the description of this monster."

He grimaced. He didn't want the idea to be a dead end. "Here, look at this passage." He flipped forward a few pages.

He watched Halia's eyes move as she read, intent on each word. When she finished, she looked up at Caelum. "A lot of this poem is missing."

Caelum nodded. "I know. The parchment this poem was originally transcribed from was too faded to make out completely. It has always been astounding to me how little has been recorded about the Unbound, particularly now that we know it is all true!"

She sighed and closed the book, sliding it to Caelum. "Perhaps you're right. This is all practically gibberish to me. I wish I could make more sense of it." She tilted her head slightly as she stared down at the closed book. "What is that?" she asked, pointing to the symbol on the front of the book.

"It's an enneagram. Er, a nine-pointed star."

Halia gave him a tight smile. "I know that, but what does it *mean*?"

She asked the question in such a way that Caelum was sure she had more than simple curiosity. He shrugged. "I've never associated it with a specific meaning. Why do you ask?"

Now, she gave him a knowing smirk, and he wondered how much he'd been underestimating her. "I've seen it before," she said casually. "Just today in fact."

"Today?" Caelum could hardly contain his enthusiasm. "And it was just like this one?"

"Mm-hm," she said, nodding.

"Where?" he practically demanded.

Halia's smile lost its smugness as she caught his excitement. "Come with me."

Chapter 16

In these trying times, I find it necessary that a record be kept of all that transpires henceforth. That is why I, Oleth Zandarion, have committed to accompanying these brave men on their quest. I will hold to this oath whatever the cost, to whatever end.

-Journal of Oleth Zandarion
Translation by Caelum Karasin
E.A. 967

Caelum got up and followed Halia out of the grand library and into the streets of the city. She led them to the main road, turning left where the road led upward, toward the highest point of the city, where the temple, palace, and barracks were located. He had not been up this way since he had been expelled from the guard and wasn't thrilled about the idea of facing the inevitable awkward stares and hushed conversations from the men he once served alongside.

There was a flurry of activity as they neared the barracks, where soldiers were finishing preparations for their looming large-scale operation. Through the bustle, Caelum spotted Daric amidst the crowd and called out to him. "Daric!"

His friend looked up from tightening the saddle straps on his horse and smiled. "What are you doing up here, did you come to see me off?" he asked as he joined them, grasping arms with Caelum.

"Not exactly. Halia brought me here to see something important." Caelum looked around at the soldiers packing and whispered. "Is there any way I can talk you out of going on this mission?"

Daric sighed. "Caelum you know I have to go. Somebody has to do something about the Unbound, and it's so close to home—"

"Daric you and the others won't be able to stop it."

Daric breathed his frustration. "I know it's risky, but we have to—"

"It's suicide!"

"Stop being such a coward!" Daric shouted, then lowered his voice. "If it weren't for you, I would still be there in the valley with Sonya," Daric reminded him. "I trusted you before when you said the Knights of Radiance were the only ones who could stop the Unbound, but you were wrong, Caelum. I'm not going to stand by and do nothing once again just because you say that my efforts will be in vain. Maybe you are content to stay here and sit all day trying to come up with a better plan while people are dying, but I am going to fight this thing with everything I have, even if it seems hopeless!" He lifted his chin in resolve. "Even if I go to my death."

Caelum stood silently, stunned by his friend's words. As painful as it was to hear, Daric was right. Caelum had always convinced himself that he was simply practical, but perhaps that was just an excuse. He was afraid. Everyone around them was staring; their raised voices had attracted more attention than Caelum realized or wanted. Daric's jaw moved, about to say something else, but a horn sounded the call for the men to leave. Instead, Daric just shook his head.

"Goodbye Caelum," he sighed, and he turned and walked away.

Coward…

Halia gently touched Caelum's shoulder, pulling him out of his daze.

"Are you all right?" she asked.

"I'll be fine," he lied. He could tell she didn't believe him, but thankfully she let it go.

"Then let me show you what I've seen."

Halia led him up to the palace, a place where Caelum still felt uncomfortable. As he knew would be the case, every guardsman they passed while walking the hallways avoided looking at him. He was certain they'd all heard of his dishonorable expulsion and didn't want to associate with him.

And they aren't the only ones, Caelum thought. *Even Daric thinks I'm a coward.*

Halia turned a corner that led down a narrow stairwell to the dungeons.

"What are we doing here?" he asked.

Halia arched an eyebrow. "Just be patient, I will show you."

At the bottom of the steps, they entered a small chamber lit by two torches mounted beside a large iron door leading further into the dungeon. A single soldier sat writing behind a desk, Winfallan by the look of him. Caelum didn't recognize the man when he looked up, but then again, he only knew a few guardsmen outside the Elite Guard.

The soldier eyed Caelum curiously before looking at Halia. "Here to see the prisoners again, priestess?"

"That's right, Dagin. I brought a friend to assist me."

Dagin grunted and rose from his seat, fumbling for the key at his belt as he walked over to the locked iron door and opened it.

"Holler when you're finished," he said, closing the door behind them.

The flickering torchlight cast eerie shadows along the stone walls around them as Caelum followed Halia deeper into the dungeons, prisoners glaring at them as they passed.

"So, what brings a priestess to the Edenian dungeon?" Caelum asked, trying to forget about Daric's scolding and instead focus on the reason he was here.

"When I arrived in Edenia City, I was told my father had retreated into the wilderness for prayer and meditation," she said. "I had expected to aid him in his day-to-day priestly duties, but in his absence, I have sought other ways in which to serve. It is not uncommon for priests and priestesses to interact with those who have been imprisoned for their crimes, to show them that the Creator still cares for them." She looked at the prisoners with compassion. "I want to help them in any way that I can."

Caelum didn't understand why anyone would show so much kindness to criminals. "It seems to me like they got what they deserved," he said. He thought back to the day they retrieved the bodies of their fallen comrades. Everyone but Halia had been ready to leave Daxton's body right where it lay. She was a strange woman.

"That may be," she conceded, "and yet these people are all still wonderfully crafted works of the Creator, and they bear within them the radiance of His goodness, which make their lives, and every human life, precious."

Caelum looked around at the menacing sneers on the faces he passed. He certainly couldn't see this so-called "radiance" she spoke of. He wandered a little too close to one of the cells, and a glob of spit hit his coat.

"Agh!" he said, hurrying past the cell. His face twisted in disgust as he wiped off the spit.

"Best to stay in the center of the walkway," Halia advised. Caelum moved closer to her and away from the cells, where the one who had spit at him snickered. Caelum couldn't wait to get out of this place.

Halia stopped in front of the farthest cell, where a man sat shirtless, his legs crossed upon the floor, eyes closed. He had a bald head and a long, black beard. His skin was a golden shade Caelum had never seen before, and his upper body was covered in strange tattoos. On his chest, over his heart, a tattoo depicted the same nine-pointed star on the cover of Oleth's journal.

"Who is he?" Caelum asked, and was surprised when the man in the cell answered

"I am Naranjo." His voice had a strange accent, unlike anything Caelum had heard among the recruits from across Edenia. The prisoner rose to his feet and grabbed the bars of his cell to stare at Caelum. "Who are you?"

The man hardly came up to his shoulders, but his intimidating glare made Caelum's heart skip a beat before he responded. "I… my name is Caelum. I am a scholar."

Naranjo grunted and turned to speak to Halia, flicking his head back toward Caelum. "Why did you bring this man?"

Caelum noted Halia was standing back, away from the cell, well out of reach of Naranjo. He gulped and took a step back himself and are beyond him as he did so.

"He is a friend of mine," Halia said. "We would like to ask you something." She turned to Caelum to explain. "Naranjo is Razzan. He was with the group of Razzans your old unit was sent to apprehend before my arrival. He was captured and brought here." Halia averted her eyes and her voice softened. "He is scheduled for execution tomorrow morning."

Naranjo spat. "We were outnumbered ten to one, and we still made them pay in blood."

Caelum frowned. He had not heard how the mission had gone after the incident on the cliff. He hoped everyone was all right, but by the way Naranjo talked, it sounded like they might have suffered heavy casualties. Naranjo wore a lazy smile, taking pleasure in Caelum's concern.

Caelum clenched his jaw and took a step toward Naranjo. He was in no mood to be provoked. "Enough. Tell me what that symbol on your chest represents, the nine-pointed star," he demanded.

"And why should I do that?" Naranjo said.

"Because my people will die if you don't, and so will yours."

Naranjo burst out laughing. "Oh, that's rich. Your people will die whether I tell you or not, that I can assure you." He walked back to the center of his cell and sat, crossing his legs and closing his eyes, just as they had seen him when they arrived.

The Razzan knew something, Caelum was sure of it. Something important. "You have information I need." Caelum stood up straight. "I have information you seek. Perhaps we can come to an agreement."

Naranjo opened one eye and looked at Caelum curiously. "I'm listening."

Caelum continued, "You came into our lands, violating the peace between our peoples, because you were looking for something. You and your men failed to find it, and now you are trapped here." He hoped his hunch was correct. "I can tell you the location of that which you seek, and what it can do."

Naranjo narrowed his eyes, then shook his head. "Information means nothing to me while I am locked in a cell."

Caelum hesitated before he spoke again. How far was he willing to go to see this through? This man might know something useful, but he could just as easily be another dead end in his pursuit for answers. Yet he was the only lead Caelum had to go on, and he knew if he did nothing, people would die, including his best friend. Thinking of Daric recalled the pain of their last conversation. He pushed it aside and looked Naranjo in the eyes. He knew what he had to do.

"And if you were to be free of this prison?" he asked quietly.

Naranjo smiled wickedly. "Now we are getting somewhere, Edenian."

Halia yanked Caelum aside, out of Naranjo's hearing. "What are you doing?" she whispered.

"Halia, if we don't stop the Unbound, it will destroy everything," he replied. "We *have* to find out what he knows."

"You were wrong before, and it cost my brother his life," Halia reminded him.

Caelum nodded. "I know. That is why we must do whatever is necessary to find the answers we need."

Halia gritted her teeth in disapproval. "You're talking about breaking this man out of prison. That's treason. We could be executed."

Caelum could not back down. "If we aren't able to find the Enkeli then we are all dead anyway."

"You seek the Enkeli?" Naranjo spoke from his place on the floor in his cell, where Caelum and Halia had believed he was out of earshot. "Not only can I tell you of these things, but if you release me, I can take you to see the Enkeli myself."

Caelum and Halia shared a long look before Halia covered her face with her hand, shaking her head. She pulled Caelum farther aside, this time careful to make sure Naranjo would not overhear. "This is madness," she whispered. "How would we even get him out of here?"

"The garrison will be practically empty since they have dispatched most of the soldiers to fight the Unbound," Caelum said, thinking aloud. "There shouldn't be too many guards to worry about. They may have even left already."

Halia paced away from him, then turned back. Five steps each way as she considered, muttering to herself. He waited as she thought, and finally, she stopped next to him. "I don't think this is a good idea, Caelum."

It wasn't the answer he hoped she'd come to. "Halia, this man may be our best chance to finally get some answers."

"Then let us go to the king! Surely he will see reason and release him in exchange for information—"

"And what if he doesn't? I certainly have little influence, and your father is nowhere to be found, so you cannot convince him to speak for us. If we so much as suggest the release of a Razzan spy with Edenian blood on his hands, we are likely to be imprisoned ourselves. Then Naranjo will be executed, as scheduled, and our opportunity lost forever." Halia bit her lip, considering, and he pressed on. "The way I see it, you have two choices. Either report me to the guards now or help me free the Razzan."

She placed her hands on her hips. "That's not fair, Caelum."

"I know it isn't," he replied, "but you were seen with me when we came in here. If I escape with Naranjo, you are immediately suspect. And I need this man."

"Caelum, I've only met you today. How…" she began. "How can I be sure that I can trust you?"

"You can't," he admitted, "but you told me earlier that the Creator may have used our tragedies to bring us together for this very purpose. If you are afraid to trust me, trust your own intuition."

Halia stood silently in the flickering torchlight. After a moment she met his eyes. "I'll help you," she said.

Caelum smiled. "Thank you, Halia."

She took a deep breath and looked back down the row of prisoners. "I can't believe we are going to do this…."

He couldn't either. Instead, he said, "Wait here for me."

"We're doing this right now?" she blurted.

Caelum nodded. "I'll be right back," he said, leaving a bewildered Halia behind as he walked back to the door Dagin had let them in through earlier. It was now or never. Whatever the consequences from this decision, it couldn't be worse than the consequences of inaction.

He banged on the iron with his fist. "Hey Dagin, I'm heading out to fetch the priestess something to eat. Can you let me out of here?"

Caelum heard the big man's chair screech as he backed it away from his desk, and his keys jingling as he fumbled at the lock. "Gonna be a long time yet, is she?"

Caelum feigned exasperation. "Has to say a prayer for every single prisoner. Some of the nastier ones seem like they would prefer to see the headsmen than the priestess."

Dagin chuckled as he opened the door, and Caelum moved in a flash, wrapping one arm around the man's neck, locking it into place with the other. Dagin clawed at Caelum's arm, trying unsuccessfully to free himself; when that didn't work, he frantically pounded at Caelum's torso with his elbows. Caelum clenched his teeth, ignoring the pain as he counted steadily.

Nine... ten.

Dagin went slack in Caelum's arms, and Caelum released him slowly onto the floor. He picked up the man's keys, then grabbed Dagin by one arm and slung him over his shoulders. He was impressed at his own strength, and he supposed his time in the Elite Guard had been good for something, at least. He grabbed a pair of shackles hanging near the door and headed back to Naranjo's cell.

Halia gasped when she saw Caelum return carrying a limp Dagin. "Did you hurt him?" she asked.

"Well," he admitted, "he is going to wake up with a headache. Maybe a bad one." Caelum winced—Dagin hadn't deserved that—but at least he hadn't done anything worse. "Other than that, he should be ok."

"I'm impressed, Edenian," said Naranjo in his deep, accented voice.

"We aren't out of here yet," Caelum replied, opening the cell door with Dagin's keys. Naranjo walked out wearing an arrogant smile, which Caelum found annoying. "Help me get the guard into your cell."

"You're going to leave him locked up?" Halia asked, eyes wide.

"You are going to leave him alive?" echoed Naranjo.

He glared at the Razzan. "Yes," he snapped. He answered Halia more gently. "Don't worry, he will be out in a few hours, after his shift ends and the new guardsman comes down here. That should give us plenty of time to get out of the city."

Caelum and Naranjo lifted Dagin and laid him out on the cot. Caelum took off his red scholar's coat. "Put this on," he told Naranjo.

Caelum was quite a bit taller than the Razzan, so the coat dragged on the floor behind Naranjo's feet, even with the hood up.

"I feel like a fool wearing this," he said.

Caelum had no sympathy for the scout. "Keep the hood up and everyone will think you're me. You may have noticed on the way in that the guards are avoiding me," he said to Halia. "You two should have no problem sneaking out of the palace."

"What will you do?" Halia asked with a worried look.

"I'll follow behind you after a little while. We can meet outside the Scholar's Guild living quarters, then hide in my room until we are ready to leave."

Halia shook her head. "Too many people at the Scholar's Guild will see through Naranjo's disguise. Some of them might even recognize that he is Razzan."

She was right, and Caelum couldn't believe his own stupidity at the suggestion. They couldn't meet at the Scholar's Guild.

"Do you have another idea?" he asked.

She smiled, amused. "Why yes, yes I do. Meet us behind the temple. There are hidden back ways only by the temple servants. We can hide there."

Caelum nodded. "Watch for me." He turned to the Razzan. "Naranjo, give me your hands." Caelum held up the shackles he had taken from the guard room. Naranjo took a step back and shook his head.

"I will not wear those," he growled.

"Yes, you will," Caelum said firmly. He wasn't about to send the priestess off alone with a killer. "I will take them off once I join you at the temple. Unless you would prefer to stay in your cell, awaiting the headsman?" The Razzan wore a dour expression, but reluctantly held out his arms. Caelum secured them, then helped Naranjo hide the chains in the baggy sleeves of his scholar's coat. "Now get going before the guard wakes up," he said. Halia nodded, and she and Naranjo hurried out of the dungeon, Caelum's coat dragging on the ground behind the Razzan. Nobody would notice. He hoped.

Dagin was already beginning to stir, so Caelum set to work strapping him down by tearing up the single bed sheet left for prisoners. He also cut one short to tie up his mouth, trying to be as gentle as he could. He felt awful about doing this to him, but he had no choice.

Dagin awoke and began to struggle against his restraints, turning red with the effort.

"I'm sorry, Dagin," Caelum said, pathetic as it sounded. The man just continued to rage against his bindings.

About a half an hour after Halia and Naranjo left the dungeon, Caelum decided it was time he follow. He didn't know exactly when the next guardsman would show up to relieve Dagin, but he would rather not find out.

He was right about the palace being relatively empty and made it outside without incident, then headed through the courtyard toward the Temple of the Creator. The soldiers crowding the space earlier had already left, and it was eerily silent. There were no pilgrims or parishioners at the temple gates, either. The temple building was magnificent with its pure white stone spires reaching high into the heavens, the golden hammer emblem embedded in the stone above massive oaken doors shining brilliantly in the noonday sun. He had seen the building many times before, but never had he set foot inside.

Caelum made his way around to the back of the temple, where Halia was waiting for him. She ushered him inside into a small hallway lined with doors that he assumed all led to living quarters. She opened the third door on the right to reveal Naranjo, sitting on a plain chair, thumbing through a book on the tenets of the faith. He was still wearing Caelum's red scholar's coat. The rest of the room was quite bare, aside from a simple mattress on a flimsy bedframe and a small chest, atop of which stood two other thick books. Halia closed the door behind them.

"Glad to see you finally made it, Edenian," said Naranjo.

"Me too." Caelum replied. "We don't have a lot of time. Once the guards know that you are missing, they are sure to put the city on lockdown." Caelum hoped that wouldn't be for a good while yet. "Halia, is there any chance we can use that same wagon you rode in on your way here to sneak Naranjo out of the city?"

"That shouldn't be a problem," she replied.

"Good." That was one less thing for him to worry about. "I will go into the market to get all the supplies we will need for our journey, you two wait—"

"It has been taken care of, Edenian," Naranjo said, gesturing at three large packs laid out on the small pallet beside him. "The priestess has seen to it."

Halia blushed. "I think we have all that we need. We can leave now if you want to."

Caelum looked quickly through the packs. "Nice work Halia," he said with a smile. Halia was clearly a more experienced traveler than he initially thought. Caelum beckoned to the Razzan with one hand. "Now, give me back my coat and let's go."

"Happily," said Naranjo. He waited for Caelum to undo his shackles, then handed Caelum his coat and instead donned a set of acolyte robes among the gear Halia had obtained, pulling up the hood to hide his face. Caelum grabbed both his and Halia's packs, Naranjo carried the third, and they were off. Halia led them through a maze of small corridors, their footsteps echoing through the cold marble hallways until they reached the stables. An older boy in acolyte robes was tending to the horses, his shoulder-length hair obscuring a missing ear on his left side. Caelum couldn't tell whether from an injury or a deformity at birth, but he suspected the latter. Though strictly forbidden by Edenian law, it wasn't uncommon for a child born with a deformity to be abandoned upon the steps of a church. The acolyte's eyes widened when the three of them entered, and he hurried over to greet them.

"Priestess Halia, how may I serve you?" the boy asked, his voice cracking as he did so.

"Niles, I feel stifled by my time in the city," Halia said wearily. "I wish to be refreshed by exploring the surrounding countryside, to gaze upon the natural beauty of the Creator's design. Will you be so kind as to ready my wagon?"

She's a pretty good liar, for a priestess, Caelum thought to himself.

Niles nodded with a nervous enthusiasm. "Y-yes, of course Priestess. I suppose this is your driver—" Niles held his hand out to Naranjo in greeting. "Jori, wasn't it?" The Razzan ignored him. Niles withdrew his hand and wiped it on his robe. "Right. Well. Shall I inform Garret of your departure? Or perhaps Kyprus? He will surely want to accompany you—"

"That will not be necessary, Niles."

The stable boy looked confused by the breach of protocol. "But, priestess, you can't mean to leave the city without an escort?"

"Of course not," she said with a laugh that Caelum would have believed authentic if he hadn't known she was lying. She gestured to him. "Caelum shall be my escort. He is a former member of the Edenian Elite Guard."

Niles looked up and down at Caelum doubtfully, raising one eyebrow as he did so. "He doesn't even have a weapon."

"My goodness, you are correct, Niles," Halia said with a gasp. "You may also fetch Caelum a sword. Perhaps you know where my father has kept my brother's ceremonial blade?"

"Yes, Priestess, he has it hung in his chambers, but—"

"After you ready our wagon, fetch Caelum the sword. Thank you, Niles." Her tone left no room for argument. Niles hesitated for just a moment, then he nodded and with slight bounce he ran off to take care of his tasks.

Caelum was taken aback by Halia's commanding demeanor. *She is the Archpriest's daughter, all right,* he thought to himself, and his head spun. *The Archpriest's daughter...* He had been so foc[...]d on the Unbound, focused on the fact that Halia was Ca[...]'s sister, that the reality of his current situation hadn't ful[...] sunk in. Freeing Naranjo had been an act of treason ag[...]st the crown, but by entangling Halia in this mess, he was likely to bring the wrath of the church down upon himself as well. *Well, they can't cut my head off twice!* He didn't think that would stop them from trying, however, should he fail.

Halia was looking at him curiously. "What's gotten into you? You look like you swallowed a bug."

Caelum shook his head. "No, it's not that your highness, or… er, my Lady Priestess, or, um…" He scratched his head.

She sighed. "Just call me Halia."

Though Naranjo's face was hidden in the hood, his voice was suspicious. "Halia, you are not a typical priestess, are you?" he asked.

"Yes, and no," she replied. "My father is… he is the Archpriest of Edenia."

"Ah," said Naranjo. "And this Edenian is merely a peasant of no importance. I believe I understand."

"Hey!" said Caelum. "I am a *scholar*, which is quite an impressive achieve—"

Halia shushed him, whispering harshly, "Stop acting like a fool and try to look like a proper escort. Niles is coming, and we have to be convincing!"

Caelum scowled at the Razzan. "Fine," he said, crossing his arms.

Halia grinned. "See? Now you look more like an escort."

Niles returned and looked uncomfortable carrying the sword and sheath. He handed it to Caelum, eyeing him skeptically as the scholar buckled it on under his coat. The sword hilt was golden and designed to look just like the golden hammer emblem of the Church of the Creator. Caelum drew the blade and a metallic ring reverberated through the stable.

Naranjo whistled through his teeth. "That is quite the blade," he whispered.

Caelum gulped. He had never held anything like this before. As he examined the craftsmanship, he became more aware of just how incredible a gift this was, even if it was only temporary. Etched in the blade were words written in the ancient language of Edenia. *Kral nau tirse, Vosik nau ilyem*— Forged for peace, Primed for War. He sheathed the sword and noticed Niles frowning at him.

"Are you sure you don't want me to fetch Garret, my lady?" asked the stable boy. Caelum glared at him, and Niles flinched. Under normal circumstances, Caelum would applaud Niles's precaution. Today, however, he found it quite bothersome. And slightly offensive.

"I'm certain, Niles, thank you," said Halia. "You may return to your work."

Niles looked Caelum up and down one last time before going back to grooming the horses. They found the wagon waiting for them outside, hitched to two horses. Naranjo, with his hood up, jumped into the back and out of sight. Caelum helped Halia up to sit in back also.

Halia paused a moment at the back of the wagon. "You do know how to drive a wagon, don't you?" she asked.

"Of course," he lied. How hard could it be?

He walked to the front and hopped up to the driver's seat, flicking the reins and clicking his tongue in imitation of the way he remembered his father doing it. The cart lurched forward, and Caelum heard a heavy thump and a curse from the back of the wagon.

"Sorry!" he shouted, coaxing the horses into a smoother pace as they continued down into the lower city.

The streets were practically empty now that the soldiers had departed, a stark contrast to how things had been when the Knights of Radiance paraded out of the city the first time. Fear was setting into the people's minds with the most recent news about the Unbound. They could now see what Caelum had known from the beginning: that this threat was serious. Caelum felt uncomfortable riding through the eerie silence.

It was mid-afternoon by the time they reached the gate leading out of the city. It was manned by a single guardsman, who was waving at them to stop. Caelum recognized the man by his bald head and well-trimmed beard.

"Hey Romley," he said as he waved in response, bringing the wagon to halt. "Is there a problem?"

Romley shook his head. "Nah Caelum, just doing my job. What are you doing driving one of the temple's wagons?"

"I've been hired to escort a priestess to Almanis Valley to help with the relief effort, since I am headed there myself anyway."

The guard nodded. "Mind if I have a look in the back? We've been on stricter orders lately, what with everything that's been happening."

"Go right ahead." Caelum's nerves turned in his stomach, and he hoped it didn't show on his face. As Romley walked around the wagon, Caelum peeked in the back and saw Naranjo hide a knife in his sleeve. *Where did he get that?*

When Romley saw Halia, he bowed slightly. "Hello priestess," he said. "Sorry to bother you, but orders are orders."

Halia smiled at him. "I commend your dedication. I assume we pass your inspection?"

"Of course, priestess," he said, then he tilted his head to peer behind her at Naranjo. Romley frowned. "You there, what's your name?"

Naranjo didn't say anything. He just sat there, and Caelum could see him readying the dagger in his sleeve.

Romley continued, with growing suspicion, "Isn't it a little warm to be wearing a hood in the shade of a wagon?" He stepped forward, preparing to climb into the wagon.

Caelum desperately tried to think of some way to diffuse the situation and prevent Naranjo from hurting Romley without blowing their cover. "He's a mute," Caelum blurted, "and… uhm… his face is ugly. So he wears a hood… because he's ugly. *Really* ugly." Caelum winced at his own pathetic lie. Romley didn't seem convinced. He reached out to pull back Naranjo's hood.

"He was a victim of the moon plague when he was a boy," Halia said quietly, much more convincingly than Caelum. Her sympathy for the lie she was inventing felt almost tangible, as if she were reliving an actual experience. "He lost his ability to speak and suffered horrible scarring upon his face."

Romley cringed and took a step back. "He… he isn't catching, is he?"

"Of course not," Halia reassured, though Romley didn't look convinced. "I am sorry to have troubled you. I should have mentioned his condition earlier. Would it be all right if we continued on our way?"

"Yes, priestess," answered Romley, now desperate to be anywhere else, "and the Creator's blessing upon your journey." Romley hurriedly bowed to Halia and backed away, reluctant to stand any closer to the wagon than necessary. Caelum watched as Naranjo's knife disappeared back up his sleeve. Then Caelum started the horses, much more smoothly than his first attempt, and drove through the gates out of the city.

They were silent until the city walls had shrunk behind them, reminding Caelum of one of Daric's small carvings. Soon they would reach the crossroads, where Daric and the guard would have turned southwest, toward home.

"So," said Halia, chuckling. "His face is ugly?"

"It was the best I could do!" Caelum said defensively. Halia kept laughing. "It worked, didn't it?"

"Only because of the priestess," said Naranjo from beneath his hood, sounding equally amused.

Caelum scowled over his shoulder before turning back to the road. "I had to do something before you murdered the man."

Halia's laughter trailed off. "What do you mean?" she asked, sensing the sudden tension.

Caelum pulled the wagon to the side of the road, turning to glare back at Naranjo. "I don't know how you came by that knife, but you need to hand it over right now."

"You fault me for wishing to protect myself?" the Razzan asked.

"I did not break you out of the dungeon so that you can kill my people," Caelum growled. "Hand it over now, or you will be back in the dungeon before the day is through."

As they locked gazes, Caelum feared their dispute would come to blows. Finally, Naranjo relaxed and sat back with a grin. "Fine, Edenian." He flicked his knife lazily into the air. It landed with a clank next to Caelum.

"Thank you."

Alarm bells chimed in the distance from Edenia City. "I

guess they are onto us," Caelum said. "Time we get moving again. Naranjo, where do we find the Enkeli?" he asked, fearing he already knew what the man would say.

"We continue north," he said. "To Razza."

Chapter 17

The Edenian province of Crisantia is known for two things: Crisantian Ale and the incredible wall separating Edenia from their rival nation to the north, Razza. For years Crisantia was subject to numerous raids by Razzan bandits. One of the first acts of Malthier Mantell as the newly appointed Duke of Crisantia was brokering a peace treaty between these two nations. Per the conditions of the treaty, a colossal wall was erected along the border of Razza and Edenia, disallowing any and all interactions between their peoples.

-A History of Edenia and Its People
Headmaster Barius
E.A. 627

Razza.

Caelum didn't know a lot about Edenia's neighbor to the north; not many did anymore. The two nations had been at war for as long as anyone had recorded, that is, until the Peace was signed and an enormous wall had been constructed, cutting off all contact between Razza and Edenia. Could Razza really hold the key to defeating the Unbound?

After the crossroads, they rumbled along the northern road for nearly an hour, none of them saying a word. Caelum had been deep in thought, plagued by questions. Had he done the right thing breaking Naranjo out of the dungeon? Would the Razzan's information be valuable? Even if it was, would there be time for him to reach Daric and the rest of the soldiers before they took on the Unbound? *I guess it's time to find out what he knows.*

"Naranjo, we've delivered on our end of the bargain," Caelum said over his shoulder. "It's your turn. What can you tell us about that symbol on your chest?"

Naranjo inhaled deeply. "We are a long way from Razza. I would hardly say you've delivered on your end." Caelum heard the Razzan shift in the wagon behind him, and he glanced back to see Halia pinning the man with a stare. "But I will tell you." The Razzan pulled back his robe to reveal the tattoo on his chest, and Caelum slowed the cart to a stop to get a better look. "The nine-pointed star is a sacred symbol. Each of its nine points represents one of the nine gods."

"The nine gods?" Halia asked curiously, leaning closer to Naranjo's tattoo. "I've never heard of such a religion."

"What do these 'nine gods' have to do with the Enkeli?" asked Caelum, trying to stay on topic.

The Razzan continued, "The Enkeli is one of the gods. The first, in fact."

The first, Caelum thought to himself. *The gift of the first. This... this might be what I've been looking for!* "And you've seen this Enkeli?" he asked.

Naranjo laughed and close his robe. "Um, well... no. Not exactly."

"Not exactly? You told us you could take us to it!" Caelum shouted, frustrated. He had gone so long without any sort of breakthrough, and it seemed like he was finally getting close. As had happened so many times before, however, it looked like he was at another dead end. That alone was enough to put him in a sour mood, but this time he had committed *treason* to pursue a useless lead. "You lied to me," he whispered with cold fury.

"Hold on, Edenian," Naranjo said, extending a hand toward Caelum. "I said I haven't *seen* it. I *can*, however, take you to it. The Enkeli holds a position of high honor amongst my people, but I'm sure our sages will grant you an audience. After all, you bring news of another of the nine."

Caelum froze at the Razzan's words and the implications they presented. *Another of the nine?* If Naranjo believed the Unbound to be one of his nine gods, then he could never find out the true nature of his and Halia's quest. Caelum was thankful that they hadn't mentioned it around the man. If he found out they were looking for a way to destroy one of his gods, he would most certainly refuse to aid them any further, and probably stick a knife in their ribs as a parting gesture. Caelum would have to be careful with what he said around the man.

Another thought troubled Caelum. If the Unbound was one of these nine gods, and the Enkeli another, were they traveling toward another Unbound? And, if so, how could Naranjo and his people survive its fury? There was still so much he didn't know.

"What else can you tell us of these nine gods?" Caelum asked. "Where are the other seven?"

"The nine gods are shrouded in mystery, revealing themselves to us only at the proper time. None beside the Enkeli have been seen for centuries, and the eighth and ninth have never been revealed, as far as I know." Naranjo's face lit up in a grin. "To think that another of the nine would reveal itself in my lifetime. You must describe it to me. Which of the nine is it?"

"Well I…" Caelum began, facing his own turn to come clean. "I haven't actually seen it, either."

This time Naranjo's expression darkened. "You have deceived me Edenian." Naranjo growled.

"Not any more than you have deceived us," Caelum replied. "And though I haven't seen it, I have seen what it can *do*. This thing wields fire, leaving a burning trail anywhere it goes."

Naranjo wore a thoughtful frown. "Fire…" He nodded, content with Caelum's information, scarce as it was. "This is good news, Edenian. The sages will be eager to learn this."

Caelum was puzzled. "Fire? Does that mean something?"

"Maybe, maybe not. It is for the sages to decide."

"Who are these sages?" Halia asked.

Naranjo answered as if giving a familiar lecture. "The sages are to my people what you, priestess, appear to be for yours. They guide us in the ways of the nine gods."

This sparked a theological debate between Halia and Naranjo that lasted for several hours. Caelum was lost in his own thoughts, trying to piece together Naranjo's information with everything he already knew about the Unbound.

The last light of day was fading when they stopped to make camp for the night, choosing a spot that provided the cover of trees and plentiful grazing for the horses. They decided against making a fire, since it was possible that they were being pursued, though Caelum believed it unlikely. There were too few of the guard still in Edenia, and too many possible routes for them to have taken. They sat in a small circle snacking on dried meat and cheese, along with stale bread that Caelum thought might crack his teeth, but he was hungry, so he forced it down with a swig from his canteen. Halia nibbled on a piece of bread and stared at it, perplexed.

"When I sent that acolyte to buy supplies, I gave him more than enough coin to afford fresh bread."

Naranjo chortled. "Sounds like he went looking for a bargain so he could pocket a little extra. Smart boy." Halia grimaced, then examined her piece of cheese, probably checking for mold.

"We will reach the border in a few days. We can resupply there before crossing the Crisantian Wall." said Caelum, which recalled a question. "Naranjo, how did you and your men get past the wall? Is there some secret pass? Maybe an abandoned guard tower we can take advantage of, or something?"

Naranjo shook his head. "No. We climbed."

Caelum sighed heavily. "Of course you did."

"How could you have climbed?" Halia asked in disbelief. "That wall is almost a hundred spans high, and it is sheer stone!"

Naranjo shrugged and spread his hands. "Mostly sheer. There are small cracks where stone meets stone, and there are too few guards to patrol all parts of the wall at all times."

"That's insane," she continued. "There is no way we can make that climb."

"One of us will climb the wall and toss down rope. You climb rope. I do not see a problem." Naranjo looked at Caelum and Halia with a puzzled expression, waiting for their response.

Caelum hated the idea. He didn't care to climb ever again after his last, but he had no alternative, and they *had* to get to Razza. He needed to find the Enkeli. "Then let's get some sleep," he said. "We have a long road ahead of us. I'll take first watch."

Halia and Naranjo didn't argue with him, and they both fell asleep quickly, exhausted from the day's journey. The evening air was warm, so Caelum lay atop his bedroll, bunching up his red scholar's coat to use as a pillow. He was tired, but he didn't trust Naranjo enough to just doze off. He feared he would awaken to find the man gone, or perhaps he wouldn't awaken at all due to the man slitting his throat as he slept. Caelum fought off sleep until just a couple of hours before dawn, when Halia awoke and took his place. Though Caelum was concerned she trusted the Razzan too much, he was too tired to worry any longer. He awoke the next morning, alive, though still feeling sluggish, and found Naranjo and Halia packed and ready to go.

"Good morning, Caelum!" Halia said cheerfully.

She somehow looked remarkably bright and orderly, her golden hair brushed and braided to perfection, despite spending a night outside on the ground. Caelum looked as disheveled as he felt. He pulled a twig out of his tousled blond curls. "Mornin'," he yawned as he donned his rumpled coat.

"You sleep like the dead, Edenian," Naranjo said. He leaned against the wagon with his arms crossed. "The priestess said to let you rest, even though I told her you were a fool for taking a double watch."

"Thanks," Caelum said dryly, packing his things.

Halia and Naranjo got in the back of the wagon, and Caelum took his place on the driver's seat. His backside was still sore from spending all day yesterday driving, and he wasn't looking forward to bouncing along the northern road for hours again today. Regardless, he flicked the reins and they started the second leg of their journey. Storm clouds on the horizon threatened rain, which found them the next morning. Caelum suffered through the downpour until evening, too stubborn to let one of the others drive. He was already soaked; the others might as well stay dry in the cover of the wagon. When evening came, they started a fire, and Caelum hung his clothes to dry. Naranjo cooked a stew that was surprisingly good, and Caelum was tired enough to let the Razzan have the first watch.

He awoke feeling refreshed. The northern countryside of Edenia was beautiful this early in the spring, especially after the rain. The snow-capped peaks of the Almanis Mountains towered over them to the east. The plains to the west were an ocean of green and gold that stretched as far as he could see. It was a pleasant ride, and the day passed uneventfully until, in the late afternoon, they drew closer to Pastol, the town closest to the Crisantian Wall. The terrain here was rockier as they entered the foothills of the mountains. A cold wind blew, and Caelum wrapped his crimson scholar's coat tighter around him to ward off the chill.

Pastol was a small town, populated mostly by families of soldiers stationed at the wall or by resilient businessmen who thought to make a profit from those soldiers' boredom. Nobody ever came here, except the occasional supply wagon from the capital, so Caelum drove into the barren town amidst curious stares and excited whispers.

He stopped the wagon near what he assumed was the local tavern, judging by its size, though there was no sign out front. The front door swung open, and Caelum caught the scent of meat roasting, confirming his hunch and making his stomach growl. A dark-haired woman in her middle years exited in a hurry, but she paused when she spotted the wagon, staring curiously. Caelum peeked back to whisper to Halia and Naranjo. "Everyone is staring at us. I didn't think of it before, but they're going to want to know what we're doing here, and I don't want to rouse suspicion."

"Let me handle it," Halia said from the back of the wagon.

"What are you going to do?" Caelum asked.

Instead of answering, Halia got up from her seat in the wagon. Caelum hopped down and ran to the back of the wagon to help Halia step down, as a proper driver would. "Thank you," she said, and walked over to address the small crowd gathering around the newcomers.

"The Creator's blessings upon you all," she said, and the crowd quieted, drawing closer around her. "My name is Halia, priestess of the Creator, and I have come to offer prayers for any who wish to receive them." People in the crowd murmured excitedly, then came forward, clamoring to speak with Halia, many bringing their small children. Halia smiled at each of them as they approached. Even though she had probably done this same kind of thing hundreds of times, Caelum was impressed by her natural charisma and genuine kindness that brought comfort to those who stood around her. The people mostly asked prayers for their loved ones who served in the guard, or for healthy children, or for aging parents. A young man with red hair approached them. Red hair was extremely uncommon in these parts or anywhere else in Edenia apart from the western border, suggesting the boy had ancestral ties to the people of the Western Wildlands.

"Excuse me, priestess," he said respectfully, bowing to Halia. "My father has been missin' for three days. Some people are sayin' he ran off with a young woman who's gone missin', but he would never do that." The young man lowered his eyes. "I'm worried about him, and Mother has hardly eaten since he's been gone. Would you pray with me for his safe return?"

"Of course," she said, "what is your name?"

"My name is Enri, m'lady."

"Then, Enri, let us pray." Caelum was fascinated by the whole experience, and as he listened to each prayer Halia said he forgot the reason they were there in the first place, until Naranjo grabbed his shoulder.

"Let's go, Edenian."

"Right," said Caelum, and the two of them went inside the tavern.

The building was all but empty, as it was too early in the day for most of the men to have finished their work. They were approached by a man Caelum assumed was the barkeep, judging by his portly build, bald head, and thick mustache.

"Not often we get visitors this far north," the man said cheerily. "What can I do for you?"

Naranjo kept his head down and face concealed by the hood of his acolyte robe as Caelum answered for both of them. "A table and two plates of whatever is giving off that wonderful smell from the kitchen would be a great place to start, Master…?"

"Nathim, if you will."

"Thank you, Master Nathim. One mug of ale as well."

Nathim dipped his head slightly. "Of course."

The barkeep led them to a table near the back of the room, and as soon as they were seated, he hurried off to see to their order.

"I hope that *one* mug of ale is for me, Edenian," Naranjo grunted once they were alone.

Caelum arched an eyebrow at the man. "An acolyte of the Creator with a mug of ale?" He snorted. "That would surely look suspicious."

Naranjo looked at him quizzically. "Your clergymen don't drink?"

"Of course not," Caelum laughed.

Naranjo sniffed. "You Edenians are insane."

In short order, a woman wearing a grease-stained apron emerged from the kitchen bearing a tray of food. She frowned as she put their plates on the table. "Don't you bring trouble here, sir," she said to Caelum.

Caelum stared back, feigning innocence. "Surely, I don't know what you mean, ma'am."

"Mm-hm," she said, narrowing her eyes at them. "That's what the last young man with a pretty smile said before runnin' off with my eldest daughter. You just attend to whatever business you have here and be on your way." The woman cleared the empty dishes off another table before walking briskly back into the kitchen, glaring at them as she did so.

The two men ate in silence. More people crowded into the common room as the evening wore on. Master Nathim came to check on them, and Caelum shot a gloating smile at Naranjo as the barkeep filled his mug of ale to the top. Eventually, Halia joined them, looking thoroughly exhausted. Caelum ordered another plate for her, adding a few extra copper coins for the serving woman, hoping she might stop gloweling at him. As they finished their meals, a group of musicians began playing a lively tune in the corner of the tavern. Villagers pushed tables and chairs to the side of the room to clear a space for dancing. Halia beamed, and she smiled at Caelum teasingly.

"Let's dance," she said.

Caelum's eyebrows nearly flew off his head. "Wha…? I mean, um," he bumbled, "but, you're a priestess! That hardly seems proper…"

Halia laughed and shook her head. "You think the Creator of all good things doesn't enjoy music?"

"Apparently he doesn't enjoy ale," Naranjo said bitterly.

Halia ignored him, offering Caelum her outstretched hand. "Come on."

Caelum stared at her hand like it like it might bite him. "Surely we don't have time for this…."

"Go right ahead, Edenian," said Naranjo, "it will take some time for me to make preparations."

Well he's no help. Halia looked at Caelum expectantly. "So, the truth is," he said, feeling like a fool, "I…don't know how to dance."

Halia arched an eyebrow. "You are making excuses." She pulled him to his feet. "Come on, I'll teach you."

Caelum's face felt as if it was turning as red as his coat, but he let Halia drag him to the dance floor. They held hands and she began leading him in some simple steps. They danced slowly at first, but as he became more comfortable, Halia added more steps. Soon, they matched the pace of the dancers around them. "I think I'm starting to get the hang of this!"

Halia smiled at him. "See, I knew you could handle it," she winked at him.

Caelum smiled back and decided to show off by twirling her like he saw some of the other men doing with their partners. Halia spun gracefully, but as she came back around, Caelum tripped over her feet and brought them both tumbling to the ground, him landing hard on top of Halia. He cursed himself and got up immediately. "Halia, are you all right?" he asked.

Halia sat up and stared at him a moment before bursting out laughing. Her white dress had smudges all over from the filthy tavern floor, and her usually perfect hair was tousled. Caelum, relieved that he hadn't hurt her, laughed along with her and helped her to her feet. "I'm sorry," he said.

Halia chuckled and blew a stray strand of hair out of her face. "Don't be. That's the most fun I have had in a long time." The song concluded, and the two of them walked back over to their table. Naranjo hadn't moved.

"A shame such an elegant partner was wasted upon a clumsy fool," the Razzan said.

"Nothing was wasted," said Halia, smiling to herself. She then ordered one of the innkeeper's special blueberry sweetcakes to share, which they all agreed wasn't that special after all. The musicians played a few more songs, and Caelum and Halia danced twice more, without incident this time since he refrained from attempting any more spins. After they finished dancing and had finished their food, Naranjo leaned in over their table. "If you are done with your revelry," he said, voice barely louder than a murmur, "there is something else I should tell you about our… task."

Something about the way Naranjo spoke made Caelum uncomfortable. "What do you mean? Is there something you haven't been telling us?"

Naranjo sighed, looking as if he were trying to find the right words. "My people… we do not cross over the wall on our own. We have… contacts… on this side of the wall, men who… well, you will see."

Caelum sneered. "You mean there are Edenians helping you to spy on us?" Halia looked heartbroken, but Caelum was furious. Edenian soldiers had *died* at the hands of Razzan spies, spies that were aided by the very people those soldiers fought to protect. How could anyone betray their own people like that? *Greed*, Caelum thought. The Razzans probably paid very well for their services. He felt sick.

"Yes, my contacts are Edenian smugglers," Naranjo replied without a hint of emotion. "I have already reached out to our guide, and we will meet with him at a designated spot tonight, when the moon falls below the mountains and the night is darkest."

Caelum shook his head, baffled. "You already reached out to him? When? I've been with you since we arrived! How could you have—"

Naranjo cut him off. "I have already put my people at risk by saying this much. I will tell you no more." Caelum stared at the Razzan furiously with his jaw clenched, breathing harshly through his nose to keep from shouting.

Halia placed her hand on Caelum's arm. "Let it go. What is important is that we make it over the wall and find the Enkeli."

Caelum took a deep breath, then slumped, putting his head in his hands. "What are we doing?" He shook his head. "Committing treason, working with an enemy of the realm, apparently working with a traitor to the realm as well… and we don't even know if we are going to find anything in Razza."

Halia patted his shoulder. "Do not despair, Caelum. Remember why we are here." Halia was careful not to say anything about the Unbound in front of Naranjo. "Your friend is counting on you, as are countless others. We *are* doing the right thing, I know it."

Caelum smiled at her weakly and took another drink. "Then we wait for the darkness."

Chapter 18

The former Duke of Crisantia, Lord Bardwright, was stripped of his title and executed for the high crime of treason, along with his two sons. Lord Bardwright's sons were found guilty of the rape and murder of then King Marcus' daughter, Princess Celise. Lord Bardwright and his sons vehemently denied the allegations, but the evidence against them was indisputable. Three separate letters penned in the princess' own hand were produced, describing some of the abuses she had suffered during her stay at the Bardwright manor, and witnesses came forward claiming to have heard directly from Princess Celise herself that she feared for her life. Upon examination of her body, the coroner found scars and other signs of abuse which corroborated descriptions in the princess' letters.

-A History of Edenia and Its People
Headmaster Barius
E.A. 627

Caelum had always considered himself to be a patient man, but tonight he just wanted to get things over with. After they finished their meal, he and his companions "retired" to their rented room upstairs in the tavern for the night, or so they told the barkeep. The small room they shared was lit only by the pale moonlight that shone through the single window on the far wall. Caelum sat across from Naranjo, who had nodded off and was sleeping peacefully, seemingly unconcerned about the task still ahead. Halia, on the other hand, had paced nonstop since the three of them came upstairs. She stopped for a second, biting her nails, and turned to whisper to Caelum. "How much longer?"

Caelum peered out the window. "It shouldn't be long now." The moon was just beginning to dip below the peaks. Minutes passed like hours, and Caelum passed the time by tapping his fingers along with the rhythmic *thud* of Halia's pacing. A thousand doubts swirled in his mind, tempting him to abandon this trek into Razza, and he struggled to overcome each one as it came, fueled by the knowledge that there was nothing else he could do to help against the threat of the Unbound. Only a sliver of the moon remained visible above the mountains, barely illuminating the sleeping town. The wide, unpaved streets were empty, except for the occasional patrol. "I suppose I could wake the Razzan."

"No need for that," grunted Naranjo. "I'm awake." Naranjo stood up and grabbed his pack, opening it and taking out a coiled rope. "Have you been watching the patrols?"

Caelum nodded. "One patrol just passed. In another few minutes, the second should pass, and then we will have our longest opportunity to sneak out unnoticed."

"Good," said Naranjo. "Best you get ready then."

Caelum and Halia grabbed their things, and the three of them waited for the second patrol to pass by. Once they were clear, Naranjo silently opened the window and tossed down one end of his rope. They were only on the second floor, low enough that Caelum wasn't too nervous about climbing down. The real climb was going to be later that night. Caelum shuddered at the thought before grabbing the rope and stepping out the window. He descended quickly and quietly, looking back up just as Halia began her graceful climb down the rope. When she reached the street, Naranjo tossed down his end of the rope before lowering himself out of the window, hanging onto the ledge while gently closing the window with his other hand. He descended effortlessly to the ground, then he grabbed the rope Caelum had re-coiled and placed it back in his pack.

"Follow me," he said, and the three of them made their way through the shadows north of the town toward the wall.

The streets of the town were empty, and though they took care to avoid the patrols, the guards were inattentive. Naranjo led them off the main rode and up a rocky path through a narrow gorge. Caelum had never seen the wall up close, and though he dreaded most of what was ahead of them, he was looking forward to seeing it. It was an incredible architectural feat, spanning the length of Edenia's northern border, winding its way through the mountainous landscape and sometimes seeming as if it were a part of the mountains themselves. Naranjo stopped suddenly, drawing Caelum out of his thoughts. "This is the place."

Caelum looked around, but there was nothing that differentiated this place from anywhere else along the rocky path. "Are you sure?"

"Well, what do we have here?" a voice asked from behind them and to the right. Caelum turned to see a man walk out from a small cleft in the side of the cliff wall that he had not noticed before. "This is something you don't see every day, even here at the edge of the world." The man was dressed in black from head to toe, even wearing a mask that covered his face.

Naranjo stepped forward. "Three to cross the wall. You will receive twice your usual payment once we are across."

"Double, you say?" The man spoke with a hint of mockery in his voice, though Caelum couldn't read much from his body language. "Well, why don't we get to it then?" The man said nothing else, but continued up the path, clearly expecting them to follow. Naranjo moved first, and Caelum cautiously set off after them.

"There is something about that man…" Halia whispered at his side. "I don't trust him."

Caelum sighed and shook his head. "I don't either. He is a criminal and a traitor to the realm. But then, so are we," he admitted. Halia frowned and said nothing.

The distant wall loomed ever closer as they followed their guide farther up the mountainous pass. Caelum stumbled on a loose stone in the darkness, nearly taking Halia down with him as he fell, landing hard on his backside. He could hardly see, but he knew that they couldn't risk any sort of light without being discovered. Halia extended her hand to him, which he graciously accepted, and they continued on their way.

After walking for nearly an hour, the party stopped at the foot of the wall, its shadow stretching high into the night sky. Their guide, whose name Caelum did not know—nor did he want to—unslung a pack from his shoulder and withdrew two oddly shaped metal bars, about a foot long and flat on one end. He also took out two other metal objects with jagged teeth, sitting on the ground and fastening them to his boot. Caelum watched as the man slung a long rope over his shoulder, then approached the wall and jammed the flat side of one of his metal bars high into the wall. The guide pulled himself up to repeat the process higher, digging his clawed boots into the wall as he went.

"How is he doing that?" Halia asked.

Caelum answered, "My guess is that they have somehow managed to carve out small cavities up the length of the wall, not easily detected by the naked eye, but designed to be used with those iron rods he has." He paused, watching. "I assume they have many such locations along the width of the wall." He frowned. "If that is the case, then maybe there has been more interaction between Edenia and Razza in the years since the Peace than we thought." Caelum found it odd the smuggler wasn't being more careful to keep his technique a secret.

After a few more minutes, Caelum heard the slap of the rope against the wall, meaning their guide must have reached the top. He stepped forward to climb first, but decided against it. He didn't particularly like the idea of letting the Razzan climb first, potentially allowing him to cut and run, but he liked the idea of leaving Halia alone with him, or sending her up first to be alone with the smuggler, even less. Instead, he motioned for Naranjo to go first. He wasn't sure if the man could even see him in the darkness, but Naranjo grabbed the rope and began climbing swiftly. Caelum waited a few moments after the man was out of sight before whispering to Halia, "You're next. I'll be right behind you." Halia nodded and nimbly ascended into the darkness. Caelum took a deep breath, assuring himself that this climb wasn't nearly so bad as those he had made previously, and he steadily made his way up the side of the wall.

He knew better than to look down as he climbed, yet he was compelled to look below him. He found that since he couldn't actually *see* the ground below, he wasn't struck by the usual wave of nausea and dizziness that normally gripped him. He grinned and continued toward the top, finally crawling up between two merlons to stand atop the great barrier. Up here Caelum had an unobstructed view of the stars, which provided enough light for him to make out his surroundings. It took him another moment to realize he was alone.

Halia and Naranjo should be here, along with our guide. Surely they couldn't have already started descending the other side...

A cold shiver ran down his spine as fear whispered possibilities of his companion's fates. *The smuggler must have betrayed us.* He quickly grabbed the hilt of his sword as if to draw, but froze when he felt cold steel rest lightly against his throat.

"Well now," said a familiar voice, and Caelum's heart sank. "First a coward, and now a traitor."

Caelum turned his head slowly and felt a warm trickle run down from where the unwavering blade was held at his neck. His eyes followed the length of the blade until he was staring wide eyed at the last person he expected to see. "Flex," he said through gritted teeth.

Flex stood before him wearing a green cloak lined with black fur over his standard guard uniform. Caelum could now make out the shapes of his companions in the shadows behind him, bound and gagged. Halia watched him and Flex worriedly, while Naranjo was sprawled on the ground with a good-sized lump on his head, unconscious or worse.

Flex forced Caelum down to his knees with the point of his sword. "I'm ashamed I didn't see you for what you really are sooner. Perhaps then Kurt might still be alive. Perhaps then I would be with my true comrades, fighting to protect my country from the greatest threat it has ever seen, rather than being stuck on this Creator-forsaken wall at the edge of nowhere." Flex looked down on Caelum with a mirthless grin. "I'm going to enjoy this."

Caelum braced himself as Flex drew back his fist to strike, and out of the corner of his eye, he thought he saw movement in the shadows. Flex saw it too, but only had time to curse before the smuggler slammed him against the side of a merlon, knocking Flex's sword out of his hand and sending it clattering against the flagstones. The smuggler grabbed Flex, then covered his nose and mouth with some sort of kerchief, but the disciplined soldier continued to fight, striking the larger smuggler with elbows to his gut. Caelum could tell watching the struggle that Flex was still favoring the arm he had broken at Blind Man's ridge. Flex's movements became more sluggish as whatever concoction the smuggler had soaked into his kerchief took effect, until finally he slumped down to the ground, completely limp.

Caelum rose to his feet, feeling foolish to have suspected the smuggler of betrayal, only to have the man save his life. He cleared his throat. "Forgive me for my behavior earlier. This whole ordeal has me on edge, and I'm afraid I distrusted you. It seems I have judged you poorly."

The smuggler only grunted, barely acknowledging him as he tore a long strip from Flex's cloak and bound his hands and feet. Caelum turned to check on Halia, who was still bound behind him, but then the smuggler spoke.

"Leave her be." Caelum peered over his shoulder and once again found himself facing the point of Flex's sword, this time in the hands of the smuggler.

Caelum dove back and away from the smuggler, drawing his sword and rolling to his feet. The man wasted no time in his pursuit, thrusting his blade at Caelum's middle. He parried the blow and sent an elbow to the man's face, breaking his nose and covering his face in blood. The man recoiled backward, holding his nose, his eyes wide. He had clearly underestimated Caelum, judging him by his scholar's coat and dismissing him as a warrior. He probably hadn't expected Caelum to even have a sword, as he had been wearing it on his belt beneath his scholar's coat, and they had only traveled together in darkness.

The man approached again, this time more slowly, planning his attack. Caelum held his guard high, blade pointed at the smuggler's eyes. He had no intention of waiting for the man to strike, instead pivoting to strike a blow of his own. He heard a muffled cry from Halia, causing him to turn his head just in time to see another shape behind him before something heavy hit him behind the knee, knocking him off his feet. Before he could recover, a heavy weight slammed on top of him, pinning him down. A crude hand covered his face with a peculiar smelling cloth, and he fell away from consciousness.

Chapter 19

We have no food. We have no water. I fear our journey may come to a premature end. Even should we accomplish what we set out to do, there will be no hope of ever returning to those we left behind. Yet that is inconsequential. Should we fail, then the homes we now long for will soon perish. Our lives are a small price to pay to prevent humanity's extinction.

-Journal of Oleth Zandarion
Translation by Caelum Karasin
E.A. 967

Caelum awoke to the sound of groaning wood. He was drenched in sweat and had a painful ache in his shoulders. His hands were shackled behind him and bound to an iron bar, part of the caged wagon in which he was captive. Naranjo was bound to his right, still unconscious from the blow to his head the night before. *Was it last night?* Caelum was unsure how long he had been unconscious. Halia was across from him, glistening sweat almost masking the tear streaks falling from her downcast eyes, and Flex was next to her, staring out into the distance, lost in his own thoughts.

Caelum looked outside the wagon at their surroundings. They were traveling through a desert, passing giant dunes that made it seem like they were aboard a ship in an ocean of sand, though the mountains were still visible to the south. The sky was a vibrant blue without a cloud in sight, allowing the sun to beat down harshly upon the wagon. He suddenly became aware of his painful thirst.

"They left you some water, there on the ground to your left." Halia smiled at him weakly. Her golden hair hung loose and messy around her face, and her normally pure white robe was stained with dirt and blood. Her eyes brimmed with tears. "I am so glad you are awake. I've been alone since we were taken." Caelum suddenly grew cold. A beautiful young woman left alone with two, or perhaps more, dangerous ruffians all night long…

"Did they hurt you?" Caelum asked, surprised at the vehemence in his voice. He was furious at himself for his failure to prevent their capture, and if she had been hurt, then these men, whoever they were, would pay dearly. He tested his bonds, but they were secured tightly.

Halia shook her head. "No. At least, no more than a few bruises from rough handling when they shoved me in this wagon. The blood is not mine. It belongs to the man whose nose you broke."

The tension left Caelum's chest, and he let out a deep sigh of relief. However, that they hadn't hurt her yet didn't mean that they would not later. He looked down at the bowl of water left for him. Much of it had spilled as the wagon jounced along, but there was enough left to ease his thirst. He had to bend down and lap it up, like a dog, but he was too thirsty to care about his captors' mind games. Water dripped from his chin as he sat back up to continue their conversation. "Halia, what happened since I was knocked out?"

Halia closed her eyes and sniffed. "The man who struck you from behind was the smuggler's partner. Our guide must have gone to fetch him right after he climbed the wall, before any of us made it to the top. By the time the two smugglers returned, Flex had already captured Naranjo and me, doing half of the dirty work for them." Halia's throat sounded dry, so she leaned over for a drink of water, lapping it up as Caelum had, before continuing. "After you and Flex were subdued, he bound you hand and foot. They tied a rope around each of us, one at a time, and lowered us down the Razzan side of the wall. They loaded us into this wagon and have been driving east since dawn. The two men you fought with on the wall stayed behind."

Caelum considered her words. The smuggler had been playing them from the start, certainly, but to what end? If it had been only Flex, Halia, and himself, he might have thought they were to be sold as slaves, but would the Razzans enslave one of their own? Naranjo had seemed so sure of the man, as if he had worked with him or his type in the past, but something must have changed since then. *But what?*

"You…" Flex spoke to him, voice thick with loathing. The man's slick black hair and sharp features gave him a sinister look when paired with his seething anger. "Does your treachery know no end?" he spat.

"Flex," Caelum began, "what I am doing is for the good of Edenia…"

"Liar!" the guardsman shouted. "You speak of the good of Edenia, but you disregard the virtues for which she stands: courage, wisdom, temperance, and justice. Your lack of courage cost my friend his life. You have broken countless laws, and your foolishness has led us all to our current hellish situation, yet you have the gall to speak to me of the good of the realm?" He sneered. "Then please," he mocked, "do enlighten me."

Every word Flex spoke felt like a physical blow to Caelum, but he took a deep breath and explained everything, from the nine-pointed star, to Naranjo's tattoo, and finally the Enkeli and the gift of the first.

Flex snorted. "That is all nonsense."

"He speaks the truth, Flex," said Halia.

"And you, Halia," Flex continued. "I can believe that Caelum is foolish enough to betray the realm, but I never expected this of you. How did he entangle you in all of this?"

Halia's expression hardened. "He didn't entangle me in anything. I chose to be here. That Unbound needs to be stopped, and if my brother couldn't do it, there must be a reason. We believe we are close to discovering that reason."

"Your brother?" Flex's expression turned pensive, then his eyes widened in astonishment. "You're Callus's little sister!"

Halia nodded once, her eyes never leaving Flex. "I am. And you can be sure that I will do whatever it takes to avenge his death." Flex was left speechless, retreating to his own thoughts for a time.

The wagon jerked to a stop, and the driver, a short, portly man, whose golden-toned skin marked him as Razzan, walked back to the prisoners, reaching in to pour water from the pouch at his side into each of the bowls laid before them. He did so carelessly, and Caelum winced every time water sloshed over the side, wasted upon the floor.

"Where are you taking us?" Caelum asked.

The driver didn't even glance at Caelum when he spoke. Instead he just tied his water skin to his belt, climbed back up to the wagon seat, and flicked the reigns. The wagon lurched into motion once more, and Caelum quickly leaned over to drink his water before any more could slosh over the side.

"It's useless," Halia said. "I have been trying to talk to the man for hours, but he hasn't responded even once." She struggled against her chains, trying to find a more comfortable position. "I suppose somebody who transports captive slaves must learn to become deaf to their cries."

"We'll find a way out of this mess." Caelum tried to sound reassuring, but he wasn't sure he believed it himself. Flex snorted at his false optimism, but Halia seemed to find some comfort in it.

The afternoon went on, and the temperature became merely hot, as opposed to hellish, for which Caelum was grateful. The driver stopped twice more for water, and during one of those stops, he also tossed a few chunks of bread into their prison, out of reach, so that they had to use their feet to bring the food within bending reach. As the setting sun turned to a deep red behind them, Halia spotted their likely destination in the distance.

"I see some sort of city," she said.

Caelum peered out through the bars of their cage. As they approached, he could make out what looked like a few large buildings enclosed by a wall—a fortress, perhaps— surrounded by thousands of tents. They crossed the first line of tents and continued onward, keeping to the main road that led to the fortress in the center of the camp. People bustling amongst the tents paid them little mind as they passed.

Apparently, a wagon full of slaves was nothing unusual in this place.

Naranjo stirred, bringing Caelum a welcome sense of relief. He believed Naranjo was their best chance at getting out of this mess alive and free, and he had been afraid the man might never wake. Naranjo groaned as he opened his eyes, blinking a few times before noticing his surroundings. His eyes narrowed when they found Flex. "You're the one who struck me."

"Apparently not hard enough," Flex challenged.

"Naranjo," Halia said gently, her voice placating, "do you know where we are?"

Naranjo looked around, frowning. "I do. We are at Zin Krafas, the holiest place in all Razza. It is unusual for there to be so many of my people here." Naranjo looked shaken, as if he knew more than what he had said.

"We were betrayed, Naranjo," said Caelum. "The man you said would help us has delivered us to this fate."

The Razzan still seemed to be in a daze. "I do not understand," he said. "It is not unusual for my people to take slaves, but we do not enslave our own."

Flex smiled bitterly. "It seems you don't know the brutality of your own people, savage."

Naranjo didn't bother to acknowledge the soldier. "I will speak to them," he promised Halia. "There has been a mistake."

Flex barked a bitter laugh. "I am surrounded by fools."

They continued toward the center of the camp, toward Zin Krafas, and they slowed to a stop at the gate to the fortress. The driver spoke a few words to the guard and was waved inside. In the courtyard, a man wearing a long black robe approached the back of the wagon. The driver hustled down from his seat to address the man, wiping his sleeve across his brow.

"Four more for our master, the Lord Harbinger," he said.

"Very good," answered the black-robed man, dropping a small pouch into the driver's hand.

The driver frowned at the pouch as he weighed it. When he opened it, pouring out its contents to clink into his hand, his face turned red in anger. "This is less than *half* of what we agreed."

"If you should like," said the black-robed man flatly, "I can inform the Harbinger of your displeasure."

The driver's face went from deep red to ashen almost instantly, he slipped the coins back in the purse quickly, his head bowed. "No… of course not," he rambled. "What I meant was that His Lordship has been most generous…" His babbling continued, but something else caught Caelum's attention. Naranjo's gaze was locked on the black-robed man, expression betraying his shock. Caelum nudged him with his knee, and the Razzan startled.

"What is it Naranjo? You look as if you know that man," whispered Caelum.

"I… I do not know him," Naranjo murmured. "But if what he says is true, if the Harbinger has truly appeared… This changes everything."

"Who is this Harbinger?" asked Halia.

"The Harbinger is the one who will lead my people to—" Naranjo stopped suddenly, catching himself from revealing more than he wanted. "No, it is not important. What is important is that I speak to one of my countrymen."

Caelum started to insist he tell them more, but the back door to their mobile prison swung open, squealing loudly. The driver unfastened their restraints one at a time, shoving them out of the wagon and linking them instead to a chain held by the black-robed man. His cart now empty, the driver took to his seat and drove off, clearly believing the man couldn't hear the obscenities he mumbled under his breath about being cheated.

The black-robed man stared after him coolly as the wagon disappeared outside the gate. As he turned his smug gaze back to Caelum and his companions, Naranjo spoke up. "That man may be too foolish to have realized, but I am not Edenian, and therefore do not appreciate being handled as if I were cattle." He said haughtily. "I had merely been traveling with these two," he gestured to Caelum and Halia, "but I need them no longer."

"What are you doing, Naranjo?" Halia demanded, shaken that Naranjo could abandon them so easily. Caelum had never really trusted the man, and though he was a little disappointed, he was not surprised. Neither was Flex, who clearly expected the worst from all three of them.

Naranjo ignored her and continued talking to the other Razzan. "I harbor no animosity toward you for this misunderstanding. If you will release me, I will go on my—"

"Quiet, fool," ordered the black-robed man.

Naranjo's mouth clicked shut before opening again in rage. "How dare you—"

A knife was at Naranjo's throat before he could finish his sentence. The black-robed man leaned in close. "I will not hesitate to cut your throat if you so much as speak another word," he promised lazily. For a moment it looked as if

Naranjo was about to protest, but then he bowed his head, and the black-robed man tugged on the chain, leading them all inside Zin Krafas.

He led them through a bare limestone hallway and down a long staircase into the dungeon. Light from a single torch illuminated the entrance, leaving the rest of the room cloaked in shadow. The black-robed man withdrew a key and opened an empty cell, forcing them inside, locking the door behind them with a metallic click. Without another word, he left.

Nobody said anything. Caelum could feel himself beginning to panic. He had to think of something, but there was nothing he could do. They were in a foreign land, imprisoned with no hope of escape. Even Naranjo was speechless. Caelum leaned his back against the bars of their cell and let himself slide to the floor, dropping his head into his hands. Halia eventually broke the silence.

"You weren't really going to abandon us, were you Naranjo?"

Flex chuckled darkly. "Of course he was. He is a Razzan. His people have no honor."

"If you recall," said Naranjo, "it was one of your people who knocked you all out and took you captive." Flex scowled and retreated to a corner of the cell, though they were all still bound to the same chain. Naranjo sighed, "But he is right that I would have left you there. As I said, the arrival of the Harbinger changes everything."

Halia looked hurt by the Razzan's confession. Caelum too had thought that she and Naranjo had begun to form a kind of friendship. Naranjo looked pensive but unrepentant, and Caelum wondered about this Harbinger. Who was he that the mere mention of his name changed everything?

"Who is the Harbinger?" Caelum asked aloud, but Naranjo shot him a look that made it clear that he would offer no answers.

Instead, Caelum decided to have a look around. Their cell was small, but not so small as his study back home had been. As his eyes adjusted to the darkness, he could make out a bit more of their surroundings. There were other cells, all of them empty. He guessed the dungeon might be able to hold around one hundred prisoners at any given time. Some of the cells contained a bench, or a pile of hay, but Caelum couldn't make out much more. The cell adjacent to theirs seemed to have been recently occupied, judging from the smell and the puddle in the corner reflecting the torchlight. A rat skittered across the floor in front of Caelum, and he jumped back and let out a startled scream, landing on top of Flex.

"Ow! Get off me!"

"Sorry…" he said.

"You should have caught that rat," Flex berated. "Creator only knows if they intend to feed us."

Caelum's stomach churned at that thought. He hadn't eaten since the tavern in Pastol. "They've kept us alive this long. I doubt they would let us die of starvation."

As if on cue, another black-robed man entered the dungeon bearing a tray, which he slid into their cell. There were four bowls filled with some kind of porridge. Caelum picked one up and tasted it, then thought perhaps he would have preferred the rat after all. Flex and Halia also picked up their bowls, but Naranjo was lost in his own thoughts.

"What do you intend to do with us?" Flex demanded of the black-robed man, but he just walked away silently, as the other had done.

"They will not answer you." A low voice from one of the cells startled Caelum, and all four of them turned to stare deeper into the darkness. He had thought the cells were empty, but now he could just make out a form rising into the hulking shape of a man, taller than anyone he had ever seen, with an emaciated body and broad shoulders. "They do not speak to the prisoners," the giant rumbled. "They only bring food and water, until they come for you. Then you will leave and never return. So it has been." The stranger's voice was heavy with sorrow and weariness, and, Caelum thought, pain.

"Who are you?" he asked, at the same time Flex spoke, "What do you mean until they come for us?"

The stranger took an audible breath before he replied. "Every day they bring prisoners, and at every sunset the prisoners are taken away. I do not know why or where to. The last group was taken shortly before your arrival." The stranger coughed wetly. "As for who I am," he said, "they call me Enkeli."

Chapter 20

When the darkness was blackest, a glimmer of hope was restored through the ones who came before. The Enkeli.

-*Journal of Oleth Zandarion*
Translation by Caelum Karasin
E.A. 967

"Father, you cannot deny it now. That was another one of *our* people that they brought in today." Azara faced the king, fists planted on her hips. The golden beads she wore in her many slender braids clicked together as she shook her head in frustration. "It is time we uncover what the sages are concealing within Zin Krafas."

The king smiled dismissively, which infuriated Azara. He sat upon his golden throne, brought from the ruling city of Dendarah, and placed in a large tent set aside specifically for those who wished an audience with the king. Azara thought the whole thing was ridiculous. Shouldn't a daughter be able to speak to her own father in the privacy of their own tents? Instead, her father was flanked by two of his royal Guardians, each wearing armor polished to a shine and bearing long spears. All royal Guardians and members of the royal family wore gold scale armor. It gave them a serpentine look, to match her family's emblem. She herself wore a slim fitted dress that mimicked the style, along with an elaborate golden belt and necklace—though if she were to go into battle, she would don proper armor.

Her brother, Azamel, stood at her side. They were twins and had grown up very close, but now that Father was grooming him to eventually take over as king of Razza, he had become more distant. Both her father and brother were resplendent in their royal armor, and both bore the symbol of the Nafretiri family's authority: a gleaming blade of opalescent sheen, gifted to her ancestors by the gods. Seven such blades were in her family's possession, though only she, her brother, and her father ever wielded them.

"Azara, you know full well that the authority of the Harbinger exceeds even my own," said her father. "It is not your place to question his methods."

"But Father—"

The king cut her off with his upheld hand. "Azara, you will speak of it no more." She ground her teeth together to keep silent. She bowed slightly, then was escorted out of the tent by Azamel. Once outside, she turned her fury upon her brother.

"Why don't you support me in front of Father? You know that it is madness for the Harbinger to enslave our own people!"

"Azara, you must calm down," he said. "If father were to go against the will of the Harbinger, it would spark civil war amongst our people. Surely you must see that."

"Of course I do," she said, "but I will *not* see my own people enslaved."

Azamel squared his shoulders and stood a little taller, just as their father did before a lecture. "Regardless of how you may feel, it is the will of the Harbinger. I'm sure he has a good reason for doing as he does. For all we know that man you saw is a criminal."

Azara hesitated at her brother's words. The Razzan she saw imprisoned had been wearing the robe of an Edenian acolyte. Perhaps he was a convert to their religion, and that was reason enough for the Harbinger to make him a slave. Perhaps there were reasons for the others she had seen as well.

"See?" said Azamel with a condescending grin. "You are guided too much by your passions, Azara. You just need to take the time to think things through."

Azara scowled. "Don't lecture me, Azamel."

Azamel spread his hands wide. "I'm just trying to help."

She folded her arms. "If you really want to help, back me up next time I talk to father."

"Next time?" Azamel narrowed his eyes, his suspicion growing. "What do you intend to do?"

Azara smiled mischievously and winked at him. "Just have my back."

"They call me Enkeli."

We've found him. Caelum shared a triumphant grin with Halia while Flex tilted his head in piqued interest, but Naranjo launched to his feet.

"No!" he shouted, slamming his fists against the bars. "I refuse to believe that! If it were true, if you are the Enkeli, why would our sages have you locked up and wasting away in this dungeon?" Naranjo's knuckles were pale from gripping the bars in front of him. Caelum had the sense that a wrong word could send the man into a violent rage.

"I do not know," said the Enkeli.

Caelum wished it wasn't so dark. He couldn't make out very many details of the Enkeli's appearance in the flickering torchlight. *I can't believe we found him!*

In his excitement Caelum blurted out the question that had burned in his mind since he first heard the Knights of Radiance had fallen. "Can you tell us about the gift of the first?"

Caelum could hear the Enkeli's labored breathing across the dungeon. "The gift of the first…?" he began. "I—" The Enkeli's words cut off as he was overtaken by a sudden fit of coughing.

"Are you ill?" asked Halia, grasping the bars of their cell. "You don't sound well."

"I am—" He coughed once more. "I am fine," he rumbled, his voice deep as distant thunder. "The gift you speak of… stirs in me a memory, though one I cannot firmly grasp."

"What, you mean you don't know?" asked Caelum, his spirit sinking.

"I may have once known," the Enkeli replied. He raised his hand to his head, wincing as he did. "But there is so much I do not remember." Caelum noticed through the dim light that the giant man's head was marred by an incredible scar from his brow to his jawbone. He shuddered at what might have caused it. "Perhaps if you tell me more about this gift, I might remember."

Caelum laughed bitterly and slumped onto the cold floor. "I wish that I could."

He had traveled so far and done so many things in the hope of speaking to the Enkeli, only to find himself imprisoned and likely on the way to his death. Finding the Enkeli here in this dungeon had offered a spark of hope, but that spark had now been snuffed. He leaned his head back against the prison bars and closed his eyes. Light footsteps sounded from the stairs above, and another black-robed sage emerged. This sage was smaller than the others they had seen, and he moved with a fluidity in sharp contrast to the rigidity of their previous jailers. The sage approached their cell cautiously, then spoke.

"Naranjo, is that you?" she asked, pulling the hood of the black robe back. Caelum was surprised the sage was a young woman, but even more surprised that she spoke at all. The Enkeli had said the guards never spoke, and their own experience had supported his claim. The woman's skin was a rich golden shade that seemed to glow in the torchlight, her braided hair, black as a raven, fell past her shoulders. Her eyes were lined with kohl, giving them an exotic shape. Caelum had never seen a woman so striking.

Naranjo's eyes widened; and he looked as if another surprise might cause him to faint. "Princess Azara, what are you doing here?"

"Just out for a stroll," said Azara, grinning wickedly. "More importantly, what are *you* doing here? I knew the sages had brought in a Razzan slave, but I didn't expect it to be you, Naranjo. Is it true you converted to the foreigner's religion?" she gestured to Naranjo's grimy, formerly white acolyte's robe.

Naranjo stared in confusion before he glanced down and caught her meaning. "Of course not. These garments were nothing more than a disguise."

Azara looked dubious. "Then why have you been imprisoned here?"

"I don't know," he said with his eyes downcast. Azara frowned.

"Umm...." Caelum interrupted, "who are you?"

Azara turned and eyed Caelum and the others curiously, as if only just noticing them. She didn't seem like she was going to answer him, but Naranjo answered for her.

"She is the Princess Azara, and she shouldn't be here," he answered, then turned back to the princess. "Azara, you need to leave before you are discovered."

Azara sniffed. "Just because you once served as my Guardian doesn't mean you have any right to tell me what to do."

"But Princess," Naranjo continued sternly, "only sages are permitted entry to Zin Krafas, and even a princess can be executed for trespassing on sacred ground. There is still time for you to leave without anyone the wiser. You must..." Naranjo's voice trailed off as the form of another black-robed sage stood silhouetted in the doorway at the top of the stairs. Azara turned and looked at the sage.

"Why have you imprisoned this man?" Azara demanded. "He has done nothing wrong." The man just stood motionless, and Azara scowled. "I will leave, but not before you release him." The sage didn't give any sign that he heard her. She turned back to Naranjo. "I will not allow —"

"Look out!" thundered a deep voice from across the dungeon, and Caelum had just enough time to see light glint off of steel in the sage's hand before he whipped it forward, sending a dagger flying straight toward Azara's back. Naranjo shot his thick-muscled forearm through the bars of their cell to shield a shocked Azara, and Caelum heard the soft, wet noise of the dagger embedding into his flesh. Naranjo roared in pain. Azara grasped Naranjo's arm, ripping the dagger free and flinging it back at the attacker. The dagger struck him in the chest below his collarbone, knocking him backward and sending a second dagger clutched in his hands clattering to the stone floor.

The room was silent but for Azara's heavy breathing and Naranjo's muffled grunts. Halia pulled his arm back into the prison, binding the wound with an almost-clean section torn from her underdress.

"I just killed a sage." Azara sounded more surprised than remorseful.

"If you hadn't," said Flex, emerging from his shadowy corner of their cell, "it would be you lying in a pool of your own blood." The girl continued to stare at the dead sage.

"Princess," groaned Naranjo, clutching his freshly-bound arm, "if you leave now, you may yet avoid detection. I will take responsibility for—"

"I will not!" snapped Azara. "These sages have imprisoned our own people, and then they *dare* to assault a member of the royal family. You would have me scuttle away, pretending nothing is out of the ordinary?"

Naranjo grimaced—Caelum wasn't sure whether from her words or his wound. He suspected both. "Princess, the Harbinger—"

Azara crossed her arms. "I do not care for this so-called Harbinger."

Naranjo's eyes shot open wide. "Princess, your words border upon heresy!"

Fire blazed in the princess's eyes. "If they are heresy, so be it. The Harbinger has been among our people mere months. These are *my* people the Harbinger leads, and I will not stand by and watch as they are enslaved, whether by his orders or not."

"But—"

"Not another word from you Naranjo." Azara waited to be sure he acquiesced, then nodded once. "Now, I am getting you out of here." She walked over to the sage's corpse, careful to avoid stepping in the pool of blood. She bent over to search the man. Caelum heard the clinking of keys, and Azara rose and walked back to their cell, unlocking the door. Caelum and his companions were still chained together, and Azara quickly undid the bindings around Naranjo's wrists, then turned to go.

"What about us?" asked Caelum.

Azara raised one eyebrow. "What about you?"

"Are you just going to leave us here?"

"Yes," she said simply, and she pulled the black hood of her disguise over her face. Azara moved to the corpse of the sage she had killed, removing its robe and giving it to Naranjo, who donned it in place of his previous disguise as the two made for the exit.

Azara stopped suddenly. "I almost forgot." She grabbed a torch from the wall and walked farther into the darkness of the dungeon, stopping before the other occupied cell. "I must thank you for your warning. Without it, I would surely have perished. Perhaps I can put in a good word for you with my father. He will…" Azara's voice trailed off as the Enkeli rose from his crouched position. The giant man towered over her, almost eight feet tall. His pale skin was covered in grime, and he wore only a tattered cloth around his waist. In addition to the hideous scar marring the right side of his head were many smaller scars across his body. Two protrusions that looked to Caelum like broken spearheads rose from the Enkeli's back.

Naranjo cursed. "This cannot be," he said.

Azara looked curiously at the pitiful giant. "What manner of creature are you?"

"I am called Enkeli," he rumbled in a deep voice, "and you need not thank me for doing that which is right."

Azara's eyes looked as if they might pop. She took in the condition of the Enkeli once more, and her body shook with rage. "Not only do the sages enslave our own people, but they torture our very gods!" she roared, withdrawing the cell keys once more, furiously wrenching the door open.

"Princess, we cannot be sure that this creature—"

"Be silent!" she snapped and knelt before the Enkeli, unfastening the bonds around its ankles. "Why has this been done to you?"

"I do not know," rumbled the Enkeli, "but you should not bother with me. More of the sages will arrive soon, and even should we escape, we will not be able to leave this place unnoticed. Not with me."

"Why can't either of you just be grateful that I am rescuing you, rather than try to talk me out of it?" Azara finished unshackling the Enkeli. "Now let's go."

"If you insist in following this course of action," said the Enkeli, "then I must ask one more thing of you."

Azara paused and looked dubiously at the Enkeli. "What might that be?"

The Enkeli coughed violently before he was able to speak. "You must also free the others."

Azara looked back at Caelun and his companions with distaste. "You can't be serious," she said. The Enkeli nodded once. "Fine," she said tersely, "but once we are free of Zin

Krafas they are on their own. I will not be responsible for them."

The Enkeli rubbed at the old scabs from where the shackles had chafed against his skin. "Very well."

Caelum couldn't contain his relief when Azara agreed to the Enkeli's terms. He hadn't failed yet, not entirely. If they could get out of here alive, he could speak at length with the Enkeli and perhaps discover some tidbits of knowledge that could help against the Unbound. Azara walked back to their cell and opened the door, muttering to herself as she released each of them from their chains.

"This is all well and good," said Flex, "but I don't suppose that we will be allowed to simply walk out of this fortress unchallenged."

Azara narrowed her eyes. "I'm not stupid, Edenian."

"Then you have a plan?" he asked. Caelum thought he saw Azara blush, though it was hard to tell in the dim lighting.

"I… need a moment," she said.

Flex chuckled, earning a sharp look from the princess. "Perhaps we could use more disguises," he suggested. "Where did you come by the black robe you are wearing?"

"I made it, thinking it might be useful sometime," she said breezily.

Flex looked at the robe in approval. "The noblewomen of Edenia do not typically trouble themselves to learn such skills. I am impressed."

She scowled again. "I am not an Edenian noblewoman."

"No," Flex agreed, "you are not."

She turned her back on the soldier, as though perturbed by his existence. "We don't have a lot of time. I will take one other with me to scout out our escape. The rest of you will wait here until we return, hopefully with a way out." She paused. "Who among you is the best warrior?"

Caelum looked around at his companions. Naranjo was in no condition to fight, and Flex was still favoring his right arm, broken during that fateful climb. The Enkeli certainly couldn't go—he would immediately attract attention from anyone they might encounter. That left him and Halia.

"You go, Caelum," said Halia. "I'm better trained to tend wounds than swing a sword. I'm worried the Enkeli is worse off than he admits."

Azara cast a doubtful look at Caelum. "Aren't you a little scrawny for a warrior?"

Caelum was about to reply with some choice words of his own, but Flex spoke up. "The scholar is not incompetent in combat."

Caelum's burst of anger at Azara's snarky comment fizzled out immediately at the unanticipated praise he had just received from Flex. He felt like his jaw might hit the floor. Flex was sparse in his compliments, and Caelum was certain that this was the nicest thing he had ever heard the man say about *anyone*.

Flex's words also seemed to satisfy Azara, who nodded once and spoke to Caelum. "Close your mouth, Edenian, and grab that sage's robe. We have to move."

Naranjo had already removed the dead sage's robe, for which Caelum was thankful. Caelum took off his scholar's coat and threw the black robe on over his clothes. The robe was wet with blood, but it blended in with the black fabric and was barely noticeable. At least, he hoped it was barely noticeable.

Caelum knew that they had small chance of escaping, but as he followed Azara up the stairs and out of the dungeon, he was happy to have been given *any* chance at freedom, any chance of finding a way to help his friends back home. Azara peeked into the hallway at the top of the stairs, giving Caelum the all clear and motioning for him to follow.

"Where are we going?" asked Caelum.

"I don't know exactly," the princess admitted. "We are scouting for an opportunity."

"Might I suggest we stop by the kitchens?" he offered.

Azara gave him a dull look. "I don't care if they didn't feed you in your cell, Edenian, we have no time for a snack."

Caelum's stomach grumbled loudly, but he shook his head. "That's... that's not what I meant. This fortress could hold an army, and an army needs a lot of food. There must be a steady stream of deliveries, offering a possible way out. We could sneak out in barrels or something."

Azara stood staring at Caelum for a moment. "Perhaps you aren't completely useless," she admitted grudgingly. "We will make for the kitchens."

Caelum wasn't sure whether to be pleased she agreed with him or peeved at her choice of words, but he nodded. "So, which way to the kitchens?"

She looked left and right before heading to the left. "This way." Though she concealed it well, Caelum could tell she had no idea where the kitchens were, but they had to start looking somewhere, so he followed, tasking himself with memorizing the path so they could find their way back to the dungeon.

The further into Zin Krafas they walked, the more black-robed sages they passed. Nobody spoke, which worked in their favor. Azara kept a steady pace, not pausing at any crossroad, and after a short time, Caelum caught a scent of something that set his mouth watering. *I guess she knew where she was going after all.* He grew more nervous with every painful minute that ticked by, certain that if they dawdled, they would be discovered.

They began to see fewer and fewer black robes, and soon they were alone again. Caelum's nose told them they were close. They rounded a corner and followed the corridor into a large dining hall. It was currently unoccupied; Caelum guessed dinner would have been over about an hour ago. At one end of the dining hall was the kitchen, and again Caelum didn't see a single soul. *This is too good to be true.* He and Azara made their way into the kitchen when a voice sounded behind them.

"You there, what are you doing?"

A single black-robed figure had entered from a doorway across the dining hall. Caelum and Azara froze, turning slowly to face the man. They had hoped to avoid any sort of confrontation. Caelum was fairly certain there were no female sages, so Azara would not be able to bluff without blowing their cover. Caelum's Edenian accent would give him away to anyone with half a brain. The two of them just stood still, and Caelum thought desperately for a way out of their predicament, but he had nothing. The man was on the other side of the dining hall, and if they tried to attack, he would easily be able to escape and raise an alarm. Caelum knew too much time had passed since the man had first spoken, and still they could only stand there, staring.

"Ah," the sage said finally, "more of you silent ones, eh? I suppose you work in the kitchen and have not yet been informed. The Harbinger has arrived, and there will be another calling ceremony tonight. You are to cease your duties and attend the ceremony at once.' The man stood waiting, clearly expecting them to follow. Caelum started toward the man, preparing to wrap him in a swift headlock until he blacked out, when a steady stream of other black-robed sages made their way through the dining hall, toward where Caelum assumed the ceremony was to be held.

Caelum had no choice but to follow the rest of the crowd. Azara fell into place behind him, and they went back into the labyrinth of plain stone hallways. Caelum still did his best to try to map their path, but the crowd and the length of their journey made the task more difficult.

After a short while, the line of sages slowed, entering a small door in single file. Caelum and Azara found themselves in an enormous underground amphitheater, filled nearly to bursting with people, almost all of whom were wearing the same black robes. Benches lined the curved edge of the room in rows that descended far down below them. At the bottom was a platform, upon which were two wooden posts with several chains attached. Caelum noticed the others who had entered before them were filing in to stand behind the last row of benches, as all the seats had been filled. Caelum took a similar position, making sure to place himself right next to the exit. Azara stood beside him. Hopefully they would have an opportunity to duck out unnoticed during the ceremony.

A single sage walked onto the platform and raised one hand, the gesture bringing the room to a sudden silence, and he spoke. "The will of the gods has been revealed through the words of the Harbinger. Let those who would serve faithfully step forward now."

Caelum watched as a cluster of men seated near the front of the room stood and approached the platform. They were the only people in the room who weren't wearing the black robes.

The speaker addressed the crowds once more. "Bring forth also the faithless, that they might find redemption."

A clamor arose near the platform as several prisoners were led from a passageway on the lowest level, bound as Caelum and his companions had been. Azara stiffened next to him, and Caelum realized not all the prisoners were Edenian. The speaker addressed the prisoners. "You are wretched beings. Your very existence offends the gods, and yet the Harbinger, by his mercy, offers you salvation. Kneel before your savior, he who is chosen by the gods!"

A man emerged from a tunnel at the very back of the room, behind the platform. The Harbinger's black robe was similar to those worn by the sages, yet he also wore a magnificent silver cloak that seemed to glow in the torchlight. He strode up the steps onto the platform and stood next to the speaker. The Harbinger stood at least a foot taller than the other man, and his height paired with his lean figure gave him an imposing, wraith-like appearance. Goosebumps prickled Caelum's skin as the Harbinger turned to the prisoners. The whole room was silent in anticipation.

"I am a vessel of the gods, and I speak for them now," the Harbinger said, his bright voice ringing clear through the amphitheater. "They offer you a choice. You may give your life to me, willfully forsaking what little freedom you have in determining your own pathetic fates and becoming a slave to my will and to the will of the nine gods. Or, you may die. Choose now."

One of the prisoners, a red-headed brute of a man, stepped forward. Caelum stifled a gasp. *That red hair,* he thought to himself. *He looks just like that young man from Pastol.* The resemblance was uncanny. It had to be the missing father. *What is going on here?*

The red-haired man sneered, then grunted and spat at the Harbinger, staring challengingly up at him. "I ain't givin' you nothin'."

The Harbinger calmly withdrew a handkerchief and wiped the spit from his arm. "Bring him to me," he commanded, regal in his bearing.

Two of the guards unchained the defiant prisoner, and he struggled against them. He managed to knock one of his captors down and deliver a flurry of punches to his face before he was subdued by more of the black-robed men. They dragged him up to the platform and stood him between the two wooden posts. They spread his arms wide and chained one to each post, then they shackled his feet to the floor.

"Let me go!" The red-haired man struggled against his bindings to no avail. The Harbinger ignored his futile efforts and spoke to those he had called faithful.

"You who seek the blessing of the gods, do so knowing that you willingly sacrifice your own destiny to my will and to that of the nine gods." The Harbinger paused to give them a chance to reconsider, but they all stood their ground. "Very well," he said, beckoning the nearest of the faithful. "Come, my son, and receive my blessing."

Caelum risked a glance at Azara while the man made his way up to the platform. She was sweating more than the heat demanded, and her eyes were locked on the Harbinger. The "faithful" one on stage was stripped from the waist up and bound between the posts in the same way as the prisoner before him, the two men bound back to back. The black-robed guards tied three more ropes around both men, one at their waists and the other two around each shoulder. The Harbinger watched in silence as his disciples finished their tasks; when they had retreated off the platform, he approached the two bound men, facing the prisoner. The man had ceased struggling, anger falling away to terror. "Please," he begged, "just let me go. I have a family."

The black-robed speaker who had opened the ceremony knelt before the Harbinger, presenting a long wooden box. Caelum had a feeling that they needed to leave. Now. All eyes in the room were transfixed upon the happenings on the platform, paying no attention to him and Azara. The Harbinger reached down and opened the box, revealing an opalescent blade that seemed almost afire. Azara gasped, drawing the attention of a nearby sage and ruining their opportunity to escape unnoticed. The sage frowned at her. Azara was quick to recognize her mistake, immediately replacing her shocked expression with a mask of the calm observer. The slip cost them, however, as the sage continued curiously looking over his shoulder.

Caelum focused his attention on the ceremony below, not wanting to draw any more unwanted attention. The speaker, still kneeling, offered some sort of prayer as the Harbinger held the iridescent blade above his head.

"...until the sun fades and the moon falls," the speaker finished, and the Harbinger lowered the blade until he held it straight out in front of his chest, chanting softly, but Caelum couldn't make out the words.

When the chanting stopped, the Harbinger whirled with the speed of an arrow and plunged the tip of his sword through the chest of the prisoner, just far enough to pierce the back of his faithful. Both men howled in pain. Caelum watched in horror as the Harbinger carved downward through the two men, their agonized screams filling the chamber. A strange aura of light surrounded the willing participant, flickering before it flowed through the blade and into the sword. Caelum's wide eyes were fixed on the blade, which now glowed eerily. As the Harbinger curved his blade and carved upward, the prisoner's screams faded to a gurgle, his innards falling onto the floor. The strange light passed from the sword into the red-haired prisoner just as the Harbinger curved his blade downward once more, passing it through the prisoner's heart and slicing down to his belly before he finally removed the blade. The prisoner was dead, and the light was gone.

Caelum felt like he was going to be sick. What sort of twisted, fanatical cult was this? Azara stood next to him, looking as though she had swallowed her tongue. The curious sage looked at them both now, and Caelum tried to hide his repulsion.

Sages on the platform untied the bodies, unceremoniously tossing the mutilated corpse of the prisoner off the platform. The other man still lived. His back was bloody and bore a serpentine gash. Other sages cleaned and bound his wound, then offered him a black robe. As the man donned his newly acquired robe, a deafening cheer erupted from every sage gathered. Many of the prisoners cried, pleading desperately to serve the Harbinger, professing their faith in the gods so long as it spared them the fate of the red-haired man. The Harbinger smiled wickedly down at them.

"So pious, suddenly," he mocked. "If only the gods could accept you all." He flicked his blade down, flinging drops of blood onto the platform.

Caelum grew cold. Of course, they wouldn't all be spared. Whatever demented ritual this was demanded a sacrifice for every "blessing." Only a handful of prisoners would have the choice at life at all, and Caelum wasn't sure if the kind of life offered wouldn't be worse than death, even so gruesome a death as he had just witnessed.

One of the gathered "faithful" proved the lie to his name, attempting to back out of the ritual after witnessing firsthand the horrific details of the dark ceremony. He was sacrificed next.

Caelum watched in terror as the ritual was repeated over and over. They had to leave, and soon. The Enkeli had told them that prisoners were taken away and that he never saw them again. This was why. The sage eying them was now looking forward, watching the ritual, so Caelum tugged at Azara's elbow and slipped out of the room, looking over his shoulder as she followed him down the corridor and away from the hell they had left behind. After they had gone a safe distance, he pulled Azara aside, fighting back the bile that threatened to empty his stomach. Azara was shivering.

"They slaughtered them…" She looked at him, tears welling in her eyes. "I didn't know," she said, and her lip quivered. "I swear, I didn't know…"

"I believe you," he said. "But we need to leave, now. We can force our way out the front if we have to, but we can't wait any longer." He sighed. "At least if we go now most of the sages here will be occupied with the…" He swallowed. "With the ritual."

Azara still looked ill. "I, um, I think I know a way out." She started down the hallway, and he heard her mutter, "You aren't going to like it."

Chapter 21

It was easy in those times to blame others for the hardships we faced. "We didn't bring this calamity upon us, they did!" we commonly heard in our communities. Yet what did it matter? We all suffered. Only together could the world be put right. Yet our people's misconceived presumption of innocence has been proven false, for on this day we encountered a new enemy from our own tribe, and in them lies a darkness as black as any evil from old.

-Journal of Oleth Zandarion
Translation by Caelum Karasin
E.A. 967

Azara was right, he didn't like the plan. Caelum hurried back to the dungeon, retracing his steps through the labyrinth of deserted hallways beneath Zin Krafas. He doubted he was taking the fastest route back to his companions, but his memory was sharp, and he knew this route would at least get him there. He doubted the others would be enthused to learn what he and Azara wanted them to do. *But what choice do we have?* he wondered. Every second they remained trapped in this place put them all at greater risk, increasing their chance of sharing the same fate as the poor people butchered for the Harbinger's deranged ritual. He had weighed their options, and he knew Azara's plan was their best shot.

Caelum reached the doorway that led into the dungeons and descended the flight of stairs, finding his companions just as he had left them. Halia was crouched near Naranjo, tending to the man's wound. The Enkeli was near her, and it looked as if Halia had seen to some of his injuries as well. Flex sat alone in the corner of the cell, clearly apart from the other three. All four looked up at him when he entered, and Caelum quickly lowered his hood so they knew it was him.

"You're back!" said Halia, rising to her feet with a smile.

Naranjo used his good arm to prop himself up into a sitting position, frowning when he saw Caelum alone. "Where's Azara?" he asked, words carrying more than a hint of a threat.

"She's fine," Caelum responded quickly, hoping to defuse the situation before the Razzan strangled him. "She's waiting for us above. We have to go, and quickly." Halia helped Naranjo to his feet, and Flex and the Enkeli rose to follow as well. Caelum held up a hand to stop them. This was the part he had been dreading.

"Before we go, there are some things I need to tell you," he said, wincing. He had to prepare them somewhat for the horror they were going to witness. "There is a ritual taking place as we speak, a ritual involving human sacrifice." Halia and Naranjo looked appalled. The Enkeli bowed his head, and Flex sneered as if he expected nothing less from the Razzans. "That's not all," he continued. "Our best way out of this place will require you all to… hide among the dead." Caelum lowered his head, unable to meet their eyes. "That means you will have to look as if you have suffered the same wounds as those who have been sacrificed…" His voice trailed off as he turned to look at the corpse of the sage Azara had killed earlier. The others followed his gaze and began to understand. Nobody spoke for a moment.

Flex broke the silence. "Then we have no time to waste."

"Right…" said Caelum, still uncomfortable. "You will need to cover yourself with…" He gulped. "With gore, focusing on your torso and back."

Flex knelt beside the body and smeared his shirt with blood from the pool on the floor. Naranjo followed after, and Halia and the Enkeli reluctantly did the same. In short order the four of them looked like a scene out of a nightmare, and Caelum hoped the disguises would be convincing enough for their plan to work.

Caelum led the group out of the dungeon to the place he and Azara had designated for their meeting. He wasn't sure how much time they had before the ritual would end, but once it did, their window of opportunity would close.

"This place…" said Halia. "It feels completely deserted."

Caelum shook his head. "I wish that were the case. Azara and I could barely fit into the room where the ritual is being held. There must have been thousands of sages."

"I didn't realize there were so many Razzan sages," she said.

"There weren't," Naranjo said. "It sounds as though, since the Harbinger arrived, their numbers have grown exponentially."

"And now we know why," Caelum added darkly. Naranjo was silent. "At least they're all occupied with the ritual. If only the guards at the front had been invited as well."

"That would be too easy," Halia said with a wink.

Caelum laughed half-heartedly. She was such an odd sight, cheerful and beautiful, yet covered in blood. She shouldn't be here, yet he had gotten her into this mess. *Creator please, let me get her out of here safely*, he prayed silently, though the act of praying felt strange, even on Halia's behalf. He would never forgive himself if something happened to her.

At the bottom of another long stairway, he froze. Azara was there, but she wasn't alone. A black-robed sage held her by her hair, tilting her head back and holding a dagger to her throat. It was the same man that had been suspicious of them during the ritual.

"There you are," he chuckled haughtily. "We have been waiting for you." The sage looked surprised when the rest of Caelum's companions came down the stairs after him in their bloody attire. "What is this?" he asked, less confident now. The man clearly hadn't expected to be so outnumbered, and their gory appearance must have been even more unsettling. "Don't come any closer!" he shouted, his grip tightening on his knife. They were far enough away from the ritual not to be heard, but Caelum feared that if they didn't find a way out of this situation soon, more sages might appear. Caelum didn't know what to do. Azara was afraid, though she was doing her best to try to hide it. He shouldn't have left her alone.

"Please," said Naranjo, "if you need a hostage, take me inste—"

Caelum felt a rush of wind at his back, and suddenly the Enkeli was in front of them, holding the sage's wrist in his hand, squeezing until the knife clattered on the floor.

"There has been enough blood shed this day," the Enkeli said in his deep voice.

The sage stared at the Enkeli wide-eyed. Azara grabbed the sage's arm and twisted so that he was tossed over her hip, falling face first to the ground, unconscious.

The Enkeli sighed. "I suppose that was necessary."

"But this isn't," Azara said angrily. She flipped the unconscious sage over with a nudge of her foot and knelt over him, picking up his knife and laying it across his throat.

"Azara!" snapped Naranjo.

Azara paused to look at her former Guardian. "He was going to kill me."

"He is no threat to you now," said Naranjo, "and he is still a sage, chosen to serve the gods. Leave him be."

"How can you say that?" she demanded. "There is no excuse for what these sages are doing!"

"Perhaps," said Naranjo, "but I ask that you wait until we know for sure."

Azara lowered her knife and handed it hilt-first to Naranjo, then rose to her feet, grumbling. Caelum grabbed the body of the sage and dragged it to a nearby empty room. Hopefully nobody would find it until they were long gone.

"We need to hurry," he said after he was rid of the man. "Who knows how long it will be before another sage wonders where this one went off to?"

"So what is this plan the two of you have devised?" asked Flex. Caelum could still sense the resentment every time Flex spoke to him.

"The ritual taking place now is barbaric, and people are being slaughtered." Caelum wished there was something that they could do for those poor souls, but he wasn't sure that he could even get his own group out of the fortress alive. "They are slaughtering them, then they just toss the bodies down off their platform." He had never seen such a casual disregard for the sanctity of life. "Other sages load the bodies onto carts and wheel them through a tunnel that Azara believes leads to a back exit."

"This tunnel," said Flex. "What makes you so sure that it will be an exit?" Caelum let Azara answer this time.

"They have to dispose of the bodies. Judging by what we witnessed, this isn't the first time they performed this ritual. They must have disposed of hundreds, if not thousands of corpses. My people would have noticed bodies taken out the front gate of Zin Krafas, yet we have seen nothing of the sort." She took a deep breath through her nose. "And it doesn't smell like they have a bunch of corpses rotting down here, so they must take them out of the fortress another way." Flex nodded, seemingly satisfied.

Caelum continued his briefing. "Azara and I will use our disguises to join the sages loading the corpses and load you all into one of the carts near the entrance at the end of this passage. Then we will cart you to wherever they dump the bodies." His companions looked at him with expressions of grim resignation. "Everyone ready?" They nodded. "Then let's go."

The auditorium was not far. Azara and Caelum walked at the front, the others following behind from a short distance, far enough away that Caelum and Azara could potentially deal with anyone they might come across before their cover was blown. But they didn't encounter anyone, and soon the sounds of the ritual could be heard from down the hallway.

The two of them walked confidently out of the entryway into the bottom level of the auditorium, back into the horror of the ritual. There were a handful of prisoners remaining to be sacrificed, and the metallic scent of blood nearly overwhelmed Caelum. Thousands of sages stared down at the platform beside them, where the Harbinger continued carving his victims and followers. To their left was the tunnel where sages pulled the carts that had been filled, the tunnel they hoped would lead them to freedom. Caelum scanned the room, looking for an opportunity. Two sages loaded the latest discarded victim into a cart that seemed about half full compared with the others.

That will do.

He walked over to the cart and grabbed it, steering it toward the tunnel as if it were full, arcing wide so he would go right past the entryway where his companions waited for him. The two sages loading carts didn't seem to mind; they simply went to fetch an empty cart for the next bodies. As Caelum passed the archway, he shifted the cart to the right, popping off the left side wheel with a loud *snap*. Caelum lost control of the wagon and it tipped, spilling the bodies out the side and into the passageway. Azara was heading to him with a new, empty cart. He spared a glance over his shoulder at the sages in the room, but nobody paid any attention to the carts and the men working them. Caelum smiled inside his hood.

Azara and Caelum loaded the spilled bodies, plus a few extras, into the new cart. The plan nearly fell apart when they tried to load the Enkeli, who was almost too heavy for Caelum to lift, even with Azara's help. Once everyone was in, Caelum continued toward the tunnel with Azara helping to pull the cart.

He breathed a sigh of relief when they entered the tunnel, already forgotten by those behind in the auditorium. They weren't clear yet, but Caelum was growing more confident in their chances of success. The tunnel stretched farther than he could see, sloping slightly upward. Caelum knew tunnels such as these were included in the construction of fortresses as a means of entry or exit during a siege, often with hidden doorways on the outside that made the entrance nearly impossible to find.

Caelum felt terrible for his companions. He couldn't imagine the discomfort, both physical and mental, they must feel being surrounded by dead bodies, yet it was necessary for a while longer. They passed sages bringing empty carts back to the auditorium. Caelum hoped those carts wouldn't see use again soon. He wondered how often the ritual was performed. Did everyone who wore a black robe go through the ritual? There were thousands of sages, and if each one demanded a sacrifice…

"There's the exit," murmured Azara.

Caelum saw light pouring from an opening ahead of them. Outside, he could see the now familiar Razzan desert landscape, as well as the Elys Mountains looming in the distance. It was funny to think that his home lay just on the other side.

Caelum wheeled the cart through the exit, emerging from the mouth of a cave into the scorching desert heat. Ahead of them were five black-robed sages preparing enormous pyres laden with hundreds of bodies. One of the sages beckoned for Caelum and Azara to bring the cart over. Caelum shared a look with Azara. They hadn't thought through this part. What were they going to do now?

They began to pull the cart toward the man, slowly in order to allow them some time to think. They definitely could not outrun the sages, not with the injured in their party. He didn't think he and Azara could take on all five of the men at once, not if they had concealed daggers like the sage in the dungeon. Azara had kept the pair they had taken from the man, but Caelum was unarmed. They would have to unload some of the bodies covering his companions and hope that some of them were in a condition to fight. Even then, he wasn't sure of their chances. They needed to catch the sages off guard.

Caelum stopped the cart near the closest pyre, trying not to focus on the mangled corpses stacked upon it. Two of the sages approached to help unload the bodies. Caelum grabbed one of the bodies, and Azara helped him lift it out and place it on the pyre. Flex had been under that one, and Caelum could now see the man lying with his eyes wide open and glazed, trying to look like a corpse staring into nothing. He knew Flex was watching everything peripherally. The two sages helping them unload took a body that had been covering Halia. Caelum and Azara took another body that was covering Flex's lower half, fully revealing him. One of the other sages grabbed Flex's arm, thinking him another body for the pyre, and didn't even have time to react before Flex dealt him a quick jab to his throat. The other sage reached into his robes for his daggers, but Flex shoved the first sage hard into the second, sending them both to the ground. Caelum and Azara pinned the fallen sages, but the men thrashed violently, stronger than Caelum expected. It was all he could do to prevent the sage from strangling him or pulling out his daggers. At the edge of his vision, Caelum saw another sage draw his daggers and flick his wrist. Caelum shifted his weight and flipped the sage he was wrestling to intercept the thrown dagger. The dagger struck the sage between his shoulder blades, and Caelum could feel the man's strength fading. He shoved the now dead weight off himself and regained his feet. The three remaining sages closed in from all sides, not realizing that more of their companions waited in the cart.

The Enkeli burst out from under the bodies, grabbing the nearest sage and hurling him violently into a nearby boulder to crumple lifelessly to the ground. The other two were caught off guard, giving Azara the opportunity to fling one of her daggers into a distracted sage's neck. Caelum ran to tackle the other sage, but not before the enemy hurled a dagger of his own at the Enkeli. Caelum heard the *thunk* of the dagger finding flesh before he crashed into the man, knocking them both onto one of the unlit pyres. Azara came from behind him and plunged her dagger into the sage's neck, sending a spray of warm blood into Caelum's face. He wiped it on his sleeve and stood up, panting. He turned around and his heart nearly stopped. The Enkeli was on the ground, a dagger embedded in his torso.

Caelum ran to the Enkeli's side, despair threatening to overtake him. They couldn't lose him now, not after all they had been through to find him. Not when he had yet to tell them what they needed to know.

The Enkeli was still breathing, grimacing as he reached toward the wound in his gut. Halia grabbed his hand, stopping him short of touching the dagger's hilt.

"Let me do it," she said gently. The Enkeli lowered his hand, closing his eyes as he waited. Halia gripped the hilt firmly in both hands and pulled it straight out in a single motion, hastily pressing on the wound with a cloth Flex handed to her, salvaged from somewhere.

"It didn't strike anything vital," said Halia, "but he is losing a lot of blood, and I'm worried about infection. He needs water, clean bandages, and a healer."

"We must return to my people," said Azara.

"So your people can imprison us again?" asked Flex, shaking his head. "No thank you."

"And where will you go instead?" Azara challenged. "You plan to walk back to Edenia through the Razzan desert, without any supplies?"

"We'll take our chances," he replied.

"Flex," Halia interrupted. "We are going to go with Azara."

Flex tilted his head as he looked at her, as if she were out of her mind.

"We came here seeking answers," Halia continued, "and the Enkeli can lead us to them, I know it." She looked at him pleadingly. "You saw what was happening in that place, something bigger than our previous conflicts, individual or national, a larger evil than what has separated us in the past. It's all linked Flex, I know it. The Unbound, the Enkeli, that horrible ritual. The Enkeli holds the key. We can't leave without him." Azara watched the exchange with interest, and Caelum kept out of it to avoid angering Flex.

Flex stared at Halia for a long moment. "So be it," Flex agreed.

Caelum cleared the rest of the corpses from their cart, using tattered pieces of clothing to wipe out the gore as best he could. Naranjo still lay in the cart, ashen from the blood loss of his own wound. They picked up the Enkeli and laid him in the cart beside Naranjo. The rest of them would walk, taking turns pulling the cart until they got close to the Razzan camp, at which point the Edenians would hide until Azara brought back help to sneak them into her tent.

The sun was setting. Caelum was exhausted from everything he had been through, and his muscles ached from pulling the cart. During the escape, he hadn't had much time to process, but now, questions consumed him. Why would the Razzan sages have the Enkeli imprisoned, when he was supposedly one of their gods? What was the horrific ritual the Harbinger performed, and who exactly is the Harbinger? And the biggest question burning within him: did the Enkeli know anything that would help them find a way to stop the Unbound? Caelum glanced back at the wounded Enkeli in the wagon. He didn't look good. Caelum tightened his grip on the cart and pulled more vigorously. They had to make it to the camp in time to save him.

"Azara," said Halia, pushing the cart from behind, "what was the purpose of that ritual your sages were performing? Is that a normal part of your religion?"

Azara shook her head dazedly. "I… I do not know. I have never heard of such a ritual, and the sages do not allow non-sages to enter Zin Krafas. They must burn the bodies at night to hide the smoke."

"You are a princess of your people," Halia insisted. "Surely you can and must put a stop to—"

Azara rounded on Halia. "Do not presume to tell me what I *must* do," she said, cutting off Halia. "The Harbinger and the sages have gone too far, and I *will* deal with them as I see fit."

"I didn't mean to offend," said Halia.

"I did," Azara responded. "Now don't talk to me."

Halia frowned but remained silent.

Evening came, and they trudged along through the darkness, their path lit only by the moon and the stars. Azara seemed to know where they were going, so Caelum wasn't concerned about losing their way. The desert was pleasantly cool at night, for which Caelum was grateful. After a while, he could make out the glow of the fires from the camp surrounding Zin Krafas.

"Wait here," said Azara. "We can't risk going any closer as we are. If you are discovered, you will die," she said bluntly.

Caelum frowned. "That's encouraging," he said sarcastically.

Azara glowered. "Just settle down and rest while I get help," she said, and ran off into the darkness toward the Razzan camp.

About an hour later, Azara returned on horseback. Several mounted men and a large covered wagon, driven by a man practically as big as the horses who pulled it, followed.

"Your Highness," said one of the men riding closest to Azara as they approached. "You neglected to tell me that these people were Edenian." The man wore a dark look, and Caelum suddenly wished he had a sword at his hip.

"They aren't *all* Edenian," she said. "Besides, Jahzen, what difference does it make?"

Jahzen sighed, "Your father won't like this…."

"My father wouldn't like a lot of things that I have done," said Azara. "Fortunately, he doesn't know about them." She smiled mischievously. "Just like he will never know about this."

Chapter 22

A true Razzan helps his brothers.
A true Razzan burns with passion.
A true Razzan knows only the strong survive.
A true Razzan gives life, and takes it.
A true Razzan lets others see of himself
only what he wants them to see.
A true Razzan is learned.
A true Razzan knows words are a powerful weapon.
A true Razzan will never be forgotten.
A true Razzan is slave to no man.

-Razzan Creed
Author Unknown
Date Unknown

It looked like Jahzen's eyebrows were in danger of climbing right off his head when Azara told him about the Enkeli. Caelum still wasn't sure how to refer to the Enkeli. Was the giant human, or something else? His sheer size and strength certainly didn't seem human, and the strange protuberances on its back seemed like a deformity. Caelum and Flex helped the Enkeli into the covered wagon, and Naranjo followed, looking as if he was on the verge of collapse but refusing to accept help from anyone. The Edenians crammed into the wagon with their wounded companions, and they were off. They rode into the encampment without incident, stopping only once when they were challenged by the guards on duty outside of the royal suites, which were massive tents that could have swallowed Caelum's own home back in Almanis Valley.

Thoughts of home filled his mind: days of teaching the children of the valley in the schoolhouse, nights he spent alone in his study with a good book. Memories of Sonya's famous honeycakes, laughing around the table with Daric, usually at Caelum's expense. All those things were threatened by the Unbound, and it was possible the beast had already laid waste to his home. Even now, Daric rode with an army to face that monster, no more prepared than the defeated Knights of Radiance had been. Caelum stared down at the bleeding form of the Enkeli, his last best chance of finding a way to stop the Unbound.

Hang in there…

They passed through the gate and stopped in front of what he assumed was Azara's suite. They donned hooded cloaks to walk the short distance to the entrance of one of the large tents, led by Azara. Inside was a space large enough for twenty people to fit comfortably. The tent was lit by two golden candelabras. Rugs and cushions of gold and every shade of purple lay about the room. A small table set in the middle of the tent was filled with fruits, cheese, and foods Caelum didn't even recognize, which made his stomach growl.

"Lay them over here," Azara told Jahzen and his men, who bore the two wounded companions on stretchers. They set the men down on a series of pillows Azara had hurriedly arranged like a bed.

"I have already sent for Izac," said Jahzen. "He will be here to tend to them shortly."

"Thank you, Jahzen," Azara said.

He looked as if he wanted to say more, but instead saluted, fist to palm, and ducked out of the tent.

"Well," said Azara to the Edenians, "I'm sure you all are as hungry as I am, so go ahead and eat."

Caelum, Flex, and Halia didn't need much convincing. They sat cross legged around the table and dug in. Caelum started with the familiar foods before asking about some of the other things on the table.

"Azara, what is this?" he asked, pointing to a tray of unfamiliar white meat.

"Snake," she said, as though it was obvious, and Caelum slowly drew his hand away from the platter. Flex, on the other hand, had already devoured one serving of the reptile and was helping himself to another. Flex was not a big man, but he had an appetite that could rival Daric's.

"Thank you, Azara," said Halia, who looked like she had hardly touched the food. "You have done so much for us."

"I didn't do it for you, I did it for him," she said, gesturing toward the Enkeli lying near them. "At least..." she sighed. "At least that's how it started. But I couldn't have left you to the Harbinger. I hated that man before, but he is even more monstrous than I imagined."

The tent flap opened, and in came a frail, gray haired man bearing a round case. His eyes widened at the sight of the Edenians around the table, but he quickly regained his composure and bowed to Azara, who rose to greet him.

"Izac, thank the gods. Speaking of the gods, one of them is dying." She led him over to the Enkeli and the physician nearly jumped out of his skin when he saw the giant, then put a hand to his chest to calm himself.

"Princess, surely this cannot be…."

"It is, and his life is in your hands, Izac.

The man gulped audibly and knelt beside the Enkeli, opening his case and getting to work. Halia went to the physician and offered to help, but the man was clearly uncomfortable about working with Edenians, so she came back to the table. Azara walked to the tent flap.

"You all wait here," she said.

"Where are you going?" asked Caelum.

"To talk with my father."

Azara's head spun. Too much had happened this day, and it felt as if her world was caving in around her. She had known the Harbinger was up to something, but now, knowing the details, she was frightened. What she had witnessed was inexcusable cruelty. No man who could perform such horrible acts should be given power, especially unbridled power over *her* people. She had to tell her father about the Harbinger's treachery, and he would know what they would need to do to stop him. It would likely mean civil war between those loyal to the crown and those loyal to the sages, but even that would be better than subjecting her people to the whims of a madman. As she approached her father's suite, a guardsman held up a gauntleted hand, signaling for her to halt.

"Princess Azara, your father, the king, is retired for the evening. If you would like, I can inform him of your visit when he—"

She cut him off. "I don't have time to wait. This is an emergency. You will have to wake him." She crossed her arms, waiting impatiently while the guard fumbled for words. After a moment, he gave up, bowing slightly and entering the tent. A few moments later he returned, holding the flap open for Azara to enter.

She was met by one of her father's servants, who led her to his dressing room, which was unusual. The king was inside, along with another servant dressing him in his armor.

"Azara, I can't say I enjoy being disturbed from my rest in the early hours of the morning."

"I'm sorry, Father," she said.

He waved his hand dismissively. "Don't be. In fact, it is good for me to rise well before the sun on this day. I have received word from the Harbinger. Today, we march on Edenia."

Azara couldn't mask her surprise. She had known this day was coming, but she couldn't believe it had come so soon. The prophecies spoke of a man who would appear around the time of the gods' return. This man would be a link between her people and the gods, and would lead them in a war with the heathens of Edenia. This was why her people followed the Harbinger. Azara personally thought going to war with Edenia was foolish. Her people had prospered for centuries without any serious conflict with their neighbors to the south, and they could continue to do so in peace. She never voiced her concerns to anyone, of course, because that would be treason, just like what she was about to say. She winced and bowed her head.

"That is actually what I have come to talk to you about, Father."

"Get on with it, then," said the king.

"Yes, Father," she said, as her father's manservant fussed over a tear in the king's tunic, forcing him to remove it while the servant fetched a new one. "Yesterday, after we spoke, I went to...." The words died on her tongue as her father turned to grab the fresh tunic. There, on his back, stretched an ugly serpentine scar, a symbol that would forever haunt her soul.

He knows.

Her father donned his fresh tunic and looked back at her over his shoulders. "You went where?" he asked.

"I went to... the desert, to clear my head," she lied. "I thought about the things I had said." Her mind was frantic. Her father *knew* what the Harbinger was doing, and he did nothing. Not only did he know, but he had actually participated in the ritual. *This can't be happening.* "I want you to know that I have changed my mind, and that I trust you, and I trust the will of the Harbinger."

Her father smiled at her, and it sent shivers down her spine. "That is good to hear, Azara. Now, I have much to do to prepare for our departure. Azamel has already left, along with the Harbinger's own detachment, to serve as our vanguard. I suggest you go ready yourself, as well."

"I will do that, thank you, Father," she said, and left with a bow.

What was she going to do now? Her father knew of the atrocities committed by the Harbinger, and he followed anyway. Did Azamel know as well?

No, she thought, *not Azamel.*

She had always looked up to her twin brother. Azamel and Azara had done everything together growing up, and he had always supported her when she needed him. She had acquired a reputation as a bit of a troublemaker when she was younger, and Azamel had always been there to bail her out after she inevitably was caught in her schemes. As a grown man Azamel had proved himself to be an honorable leader who cared deeply for the men and women under his command, just as he had cared for his rebellious twin sister. There was no way he would knowingly serve a corrupt Harbinger.

She wished he were here now, to help her navigate her perilous position. The Harbinger's agents would be looking for the escaped prisoners, and she had brought them here, right under her father's nose. If he found out they were here, he would have them sent back to the prison or executed. Even the Enkeli, she knew, despite the fact that he was supposed to be their god, whom both her people *and* the Harbinger were supposed to serve.

He wouldn't go so far as to execute his own daughter, would he? she wondered with a shiver. She found the captain of her Guardians waiting for her in the torchlight. "Jahzen, have the men roused and ready for anything, and meet me in my tent in one hour."

Jahzen always looked grim, but his expression was even darker than usual. "Trouble, Princess?"

"Oh yes," said Azara, "even worse than I feared."

"He's waking up," said Halia.

Izac the physician had left some time ago, and Halia had taken his place at the Enkeli's side. The sky was lightening. Flex was asleep, taking what rest he could. Caelum wished he could have done the same, but he was too worried about the Enkeli, hungering for the answers he might hold regarding the Unbound. He rushed to Halia's side, his hope flaring to life in him anew.

"Where... am I?" rumbled the Enkeli.

"You are safe in Azara's camp," said Halia, laying a reassuring hand on his shoulder. "You have been hurt, and I know you are still in a lot of pain." The Enkeli winced as he turned his head, proving her right.

"Water... please," he said. Caelum filled the ladle with water, holding it while the wounded giant took a drink. "Thank you."

Caelum set the ladle back on the table. "If you don't mind my asking, umm, sir." He felt awkward not knowing how he ought to address the creature. "Can you tell us your name?"

The Enkeli grew thoughtful. "My name? Nobody has called me anything but Enkeli for quite some time." He took a deep breath and smiled warmly. "My name is Simainen. Some used to call me Sim."

"It is very nice to meet you, Sim," said Halia, returning his smile.

"Sim," said Caelum, "I know you have trouble remembering what happened to you, but is there anything at all that you recall that might help us in our quest?"

"Caelum!" scolded Halia with a disapproving glare. "He is hurt, and he just woke up. Give him time to rest before you start interrogating him!"

"It's all right, little one," said Simainen. He looked at Caelum and blinked slowly. "I do not remember much, and the things I can recall remain hazy. I remember coming to this land for a purpose, but what that purpose might have been I cannot say. All I know is that I have failed. I was brutally beaten upon my arrival and taken to the cell where you found me. There I was imprisoned, and men would mock me and hurt me. Everything I once had was taken from me, and, as it also seems, everything I once knew." Simainen brought his hand up to touch the horrible scar upon the right side of his head.

"Do you remember how you got that scar?" asked Caelum.

"I only remember the pain, not the circumstances," he replied.

"What about those protrusions on your back?" asked Halia. The Enkeli's face went pale, and they decided not to press him about them.

"This is savage, what was done to you," said Flex, walking over from across the room.

"For once, I agree with you, Edenian," said Naranjo. Caelum hadn't realized the scout was awake. His arm had been seen to and his color was returning, along with his appetite. Halia brought the Razzan some food that he guzzled immediately, speaking in between bites. "The Enkeli is the first of the nine gods. It is disgraceful that some of my people have mistreated you so, but know that it was unbeknownst to many."

"Fear not, warrior," said Sim. "I do not hold the many responsible for the sins of the few." He paused and scratched his head, "Although, what you say baffles me. I believe I would remember if I was a god…"

"You may not be a god," said Flex, "but I saw the way you moved and the way you fought. It was incredible." Sim smiled half-heartedly.

"I know you wished to avoid the violence," said Halia, grabbing his hand, "but you *were* incredible. And you saved us." His smile grew more genuine.

The tent flap opened and Azara stepped through, dressed in black leather covered in golden scales. The armor gave her a snake-like appearance, complemented by the golden serpent emblazoned on her black cloak. She wore a sword on her hip, and was followed by Jahzen, who was also dressed for battle.

"We have a situation," she said unceremoniously.

"Well, that's not vague," said Flex, crossing his arms.

She glared at him. "My people are preparing to invade Edenia. They will march today. Does that make things clearer?"

The three Edenians stared at her in shock. Flex was the first to recover. "I have to return and warn them!" As he rose to leave, Azara stopped him with an outstretched arm.

"If you walk out of this tent, you will be killed on sight. How is that going to help either of our peoples?" Flex stared at her, considering.

"Let's hear her out," said Caelum. "It sounds like she has more to say." Flex shot him an annoyed look, then returned to where he had been sitting.

Azara continued, "You know I have no love for the Harbinger, and this war is his desire, not mine." She let out a deep breath before continuing. "Unfortunately, we have another problem."

"An impending war isn't enough?" said Caelum. He regretted saying it even before the dark look he received from Azara.

"My father bears the scars from the ritual."

Nobody said a word as the implications of Azara's revelation settled in. Clearly the king not only knew what was happening inside Zin Krafas, but he supported it, meaning Azara wouldn't be able to persuade him to stop the atrocities nor dissuade him from the war.

"So what are we going to do?" asked Flex. "We can't just sit here and do nothing."

"Believe me, Edenian, I don't want you here any more than you want to be here," she said. "In this, however, we have a common goal: stop this foolish war between our peoples. In order to do this, I need you to help me assassinate the Harbinger."

"Assassinate him?!" exclaimed Caelum. "That's insane!" He already had one impossible task ahead of him; he didn't need another.

"It is the only way to stop this war," Azara said with conviction. "With the Harbinger out of the picture, his movement will lose its credibility."

"Why do you need us for this?" asked Flex.

Azara turned to face him. "I need you to be the ones to do it, and to take responsibility for his death. If I or my warriors were to kill the Harbinger, it would spark chaos among my people. If an Edenian kills him, it will be a sign of his weakness."

"How do we know that us killing the man won't just encourage a war for vengeance?" Flex pressed.

"I can't say that that is not a possibility," Azara admitted. "However, a war for vengeance is much easier to prevent than a war of religious fanaticism. Besides, what do you have to lose?"

"Azara, what you speak of is treason," said Naranjo. "Treason, and blasphemy!"

"It is also the right thing to do," she said, reprimanding Naranjo with a cool stare. "What do you say, Edenians?" she said, turning back to them. "Will you assist me in saving thousands of lives from a misguided war?"

Caelum wasn't sure how to respond. He had no love for the Harbinger, but neither was he an assassin. Also, despite

Azara's reassurances, he felt like they were being used. Killing the Harbinger would change the war, but he doubted it would stop it. He did, however, see another possibility. The Harbinger was supposed to lead the Razzans to war against Edenia, while also forging a bond between the Razzans and their god, the Unbound. If they were able to eliminate the Unbound before that could happen, the Harbinger would be discredited, and his following would weaken. Unfortunately, suggesting that they slay Azara's god didn't seem like a good idea, so he kept his mouth shut.

"Azara," said the Enkeli in his deep voice. He stared at Azara, frowning. "Where did you get that?" He pointed at the sword she wore on her hip.

"This?" she said, drawing the sword from its sheath.

Caelum gaped as she did so. The sword shone iridescent in the candlelight, and it looked as though it had been carved from a single block of some precious stone. It was a beautiful blade, and Caelum had seen one just like it—in the hands of the Harbinger as he sliced through the bodies of dozens of helpless prisoners, as if they had been made of wax.

"It has been in my family for generations," explained Azara. "Years ago, my ancestors met the gods in the desert and were gifted with seven blades identical to the one I hold now. They are symbols of the Nafretiri family's right to rule."

"And now the Harbinger possesses one as well," said Caelum.

Azara's face darkened. "My father must have given it to him. Before this, only my father, my brother, and I ever used the blades. Father must have given him one of the other four. It is a disgrace for him to allow that monster to use our sacred birthright."

"Your ancestors met only one of their gods in the desert," said Sim, looking distant, "but I did not give them the blades."

Azara stared incredulously at the Enkeli. "Are you saying it was *you*? But that was almost two hundred years ago!"

"Yes, that does sound about right," rumbled Sim. "They attacked me, took my blades, along with the rest of my possessions, and they locked me in that cell."

Azara looked horrified. She unbuckled her sword belt and cast away the sword and sheath onto the ground as if they were poisonous snakes. "My… my whole life is a lie!" she looked as if she had eaten something rotten. "My family earned its right to rule because of the blessings of the gods, but we never received a blessing at all…" she said bitterly, collapsing to her knees. Jahzen knelt beside her.

"Princess…."

"Don't call me that!" she snapped.

"Very well then, Azara," he said. "Whether or not your family was chosen to lead by the gods, our people need *you*." He put a comforting hand on her shoulder. "You are the only one that can save our people from the net the Harbinger has lured us into."

"You're right," she said, standing. "Whatever wrong my family has done, and whatever harm the Harbinger intends to do, I will make it right." She looked to the Edenians. "Will you help me, for the sake of both our peoples?"

"We will," said Flex, without hesitation.

Azara nodded. "Thank you," she said, rising to her feet. "The Harbinger departed for Edenia over an hour ago, along with the vanguard of the invasion force, led by my brother Azamel. I will leave with my own forces as soon as we are ready, and it will appear as if I am merely eager to share in the glory of being the first to strike against Edenia. We will depart in a quarter of an hour. I will not speak with you again until we are well on our way to your homeland." She turned and left the tent, Jahzen following behind her.

Caelum walked over to where Azara had discarded her sword and picked it up. He brought it over to where the Enkeli lay, offering it to him.

"This is a magnificent blade," said Simainen, "but it was never mine to wield." He extended his arm, pushing the blade back toward Caelum. "You asked me before about a gift. Let this blade be my gift to you, Caelum. Use it well to preserve life, rather than simply to take it."

Caelum didn't know what to say. "You… you're giving this to me?"

Sim nodded. "I want you to have it."

Caelum stared down at the blade in his hands, slowly removing it from its sheathe. It was lighter than he had expected, and even more magnificent up close. He had never seen anything like it. Simainen had been in possession of the sword before he lost his memory. This blade, along with the others like it, had to be what Caelum had come to Razza seeking. The gift of the first, given now to him.

"Caelum," said Halia, "is that blade…"

"Yes," he said, joy welling up inside of him. "Yes, I think this is what we have been searching for!"

"What are you two talking about?" asked Flex, sounding annoyed.

"It's…" Caelum began, stopping when he spotted Naranjo listening in. "I think it's the key to saving Edenia."

"I think you have delusions of grandeur," Flex said, rolling his eyes as he walked away.

"I can't bear to see an Edenian holding that sword," grumbled Naranjo.

"It was mine to give, Naranjo," said Sim.

"Of course, my lord Enkeli," said Naranjo, dropping the matter entirely.

Azara had fresh clothing sent for each of them, and Caelum was glad to get out of the grimy garb he had been wearing since Pastol. He kept only his crimson scholar's coat, buckling his new blade around his waist. Jahzen returned later to usher them secretly to the wagon that would bear them all to Edenia, Simainen included. Despite his injuries, the giant was better off making the trip with them. If he were discovered in the Razzan camp, he would be thrown back into the dungeon at Zin Krafas. That is, if he weren't executed on the spot.

Shortly after they were all loaded into the wagon, Azara's detachment of soldiers began the long march to Edenia. Caelum was surprised when he noticed they were heading south, toward the Elys Mountains, rather than west, toward Pastol and the border wall to Edenia. Flex noticed as well.

"Shouldn't we be heading west?" he asked.

"West?" Naranjo chuckled. "If we wanted to knock on Edenia's front door and give them time to prepare for an attack," he said wryly. "No, we go in the back way. The Elys Mountains are near impossible to pass, but we have been preparing for this for a long time. Our engineers have dug us a tunnel right through the mountains." He grinned. "We'll be in Edenia before the end of the day." He laughed at their incredulous faces. "Surprise!"

Chapter 23

Almanis Valley is sometimes referred to as the fourth province of Edenia, but this common assertion is inaccurate. Though the territory is technically a part of the province of Edenia, the people of the valley more closely resemble frontier settlers than they do other citizens of the empire. The area remains largely unpopulated, as few settlements have been established far beyond the Nauru Pass leading to the capital. Most of these settlers have never traveled outside of the valley, and rarely do they have any contact with their governing nation.

-A History of Edenia and Its People
Headmaster Barius
E.A. 627

"They should be back by now." Bradford slammed his fist down onto the table. They had been playing this deadly game of cat and mouse with the Unbound for too long, and he had lost too many good men. He sat around a table in his command tent with Lissa, Dennix, and his other remaining officer,

Mitchell Dirkson. A map of the surrounding area was spread out before them, with markings representing their three campsites and the outlined paths between them.

"They could have had to go to ground," said Dennix. "Maybe they haven't had an opportunity to make their way back here yet."

Bradford shook his head. "Nobody could survive in hiding that long with the beast hunting them." He squeezed the bridge of his nose between two fingers. "Maybe there is a chance that some of them made it, but we have to assume the worst. Either that beast is making its way to one of our camps, or it is heading south toward Almanis Village. We don't have enough men to keep this chase going for much longer." He looked at his officers. They each looked as worn and ragged as he felt. "Nobody believed we could make it this far, yet here we are. We have done the impossible, and for that we can be proud." He had asked so much of them already. "We will make one last ride, baiting the beast to follow us as far north as we can take it. We will buy the crown a few more days to bring reinforcements."

Nobody said anything. They had all been prepared for this eventuality, but it was never easy to stare death in the face. The silence broke when a man entered the tent, one of Bradford's scouts, sent out earlier to track the beast's movements.

"Sir," said the scout.

"Benson," Bradford greeted with a smile. "Am I glad to see you. What do you have for us?"

Benson cleared his throat. "The Unbound is headed right for us, sir. If we don't get moving, it will be on us in under an hour."

Bradford sighed. "Well, there's nothing else for it, then," he said, turning to address his officers. "Prepare to ride. Leave behind anything that might slow us down." He turned to Lissa. "Any of the wounded that can ride will have to do so. Those that cannot will need to be loaded into wagons." She nodded her understanding. They all had their assignments. "Let's get to it," he said.

Nothing motivates a group to hustle quite like an invincible monster coming to mercilessly devour everyone. The camp was mounted and ready to depart in a matter of minutes. There had been three separate camps when Bradford put this plan into motion. They were leaving the third camp. Each camp had been set up to form a triangle spreading the length of the northern region of Almanis Valley, where they had stationed riders to lead the Unbound on an endless chase between them, rotating in fresh men and horses at designated checkpoints. He was surprised that the plan had worked for as long as it did, but it was successful in large part due to his men's ability to adapt, learning the monster's behavior and inventing new ways to confound the beast. Their efforts had come at a high price, and Bradford had lost over eighty percent of the men who began this hopeless marathon. They were supposed to have made an exchange with the remainder of group two, almost three days ago, but they never showed up. It was possible there were still some of his men alive at camp one, but there was no way for him to know. He couldn't spare a scout to check.

They rode north at a much slower pace than Bradford would have liked. Too many wounded. He almost believed he could feel every step the Unbound was gaining on him. *I've been out here so long I'm beginning to go mad.* Lissa rode beside him, and she reached over to grab his hand.

"Thank you for everything you have done, Jeremiah" she said.

Bradford chuckled somberly. "All I have done is lead these men to their deaths."

She squeezed his hand. "That's not true. You bought us time. Time for the villagers to flee this horror. Time for my Lily to reach safety." She smiled. "My daughter will live because of our sacrifice, and for that I am grateful."

Bradford felt a lump form in his throat. If only he had been able to provide a way for Lissa to watch her daughter grow up, to see her wed and start a family. If only he had thought of some way to stop this threat once and for all, rather than simply delaying its inevitable path of destruction. He might have bought the villagers and the kingdom some time, but so far nothing they had done had brought them any closer to defeating the Unbound.

He couldn't help but keep track of the time as they rode. He watched the sun, gauging how much ground he thought the Unbound had gained on them. *It shouldn't be long now.*

Another hour passed. And another. Still, there was no sign of the Unbound. Bradford sent Benson ahead into the foothills of the Elys Mountains to find a viewpoint from where he could locate the beast. Bradford feared the Unbound had turned south. It had an uncanny ability to sense human life, and larger populations seemed to have a stronger pull. Benson returned a short time later, horse and rider both looking exhausted.

"Sir," said Benson, "the Unbound is still heading north." Bradford let out a sigh of relief. "But I should say it is heading north*west*. It isn't on our trail anymore."

"What do you mean?" asked Bradford, confused.

"I mean something else seems to have caught its attention."

That didn't make sense. There were no other settlements in these parts that hadn't either been evacuated or destroyed. Nothing besides human life had ever drawn the beast before, but who would be this far north in the valley?

"Very good, Benson. We'll rest here for a little while." Benson saluted and went to take care of his horse. The poor beasts had been through lot lately, working just as hard as their riders. Lissa approached Bradford from behind.

"Jeremiah, do you think it could be the reinforcements we've been waiting for?" she asked.

He hated that he couldn't nod and smile, telling her that it certainly was and that everything would be ok now. Instead he shook his head. "Any reinforcements from Edenia will have to come from the south, or I suppose possibly the west, if they were willing to attempt a trek through the wilder routes of the mountains. This is something else." He stared solemnly to the north. "And I am going to find out what."

Daric looked down in heartache upon his homeland. They were making their way through the Nauru pass into the Almanis Valley, and the landscape that was once a lush green ocean of trees was now a black wasteland throughout the northern half of the forest. He couldn't believe the damage the Unbound had wrought, yet he couldn't help but feel relieved that Almanis Village remained untouched. Sonya was safe, at least for the time being. Daric wondered if he would ever see her again. The men around him whispered to one another, finally coming face to face with the reality of what lay ahead of them.

Daric wished Caelum were with him. He knew more than anyone about the Unbound, and Daric would have felt a lot more comfortable if he were around. He wished things hadn't ended so badly between them back in the capital. *You called him a coward.* He hadn't meant it; he had merely been speaking out of his own fear. He knew he was likely to die here, and now he wished his friend were by his side once more, so he could apologize before the end.

"Daric," said a voice from behind him. Lord Mantell approached atop his dark stallion. He was a big man, taller than Daric but not quite as broad. Daric had never seen the man without his outlandish silver cloak.

"Sir," said Daric.

"Ride with me, son." Daric tugged on the reigns to bring his gelding beside his commanding officer. "How are you feeling? It must be hard to come home to this kind of devastation."

Daric bowed his head. "It is, sir. I'm just glad that I have the chance to do something about it."

Lord Mantell clapped him on the shoulder. "I admire your enthusiasm, and your courage. There are men here twice your age who have ridden with me on countless campaigns, frightened out of their wits to face the threat ahead of us."

Daric tightened his lips. "They fear for good reason," he said. "I am afraid as well. My friend Caelum studied the Unbound for a long time, and he believes that our quest is doomed to fail."

Lord Mantell shook his head. "Your friend exaggerates. The threat is real, but we have the entire might of Edenia with us. The greatest warriors in the realm, yourself included. We will not fail."

Daric smiled half-heartedly. "You're right, sir."

"Of course I am," Lord Mantell said, chuckling. "Say, Daric," he continued, "I understand that you miss your companion from Almanis, but know that you are not without friends here."

"Thank you, sir," said Daric.

Lord Mantell nodded. "I want you to have something." He shifted in his saddle to reach a bundle tied behind him. He unrolled the blanket covering to reveal a sword in an ornate sheathe. "This has been passed down in my family for centuries, carried into battle by my father, and his father before him. It has never tasted defeat."

"Sir," Daric stammered, "I cannot accept this."

"You can, and you will," said Lord Mantell. "I am growing old, and I do not have an heir to bequeath the sword to, so I would like to give it to you. I sense greatness in you, Daric, and I know you will use it well. Now, why don't you take a look at the blade."

Daric reached out to grab the hilt, drawing it from the sheathe with a metallic ring. The blade shone in the noonday sun, strangely iridescent and appearing to have been carved out of a single stone, though Daric had never seen a stone quite like this. An opal, perhaps, but the stone would have had to be enormous.

"The blade is stronger than Edenian steel, and will never dull," said Lord Mantell.

"This… this is incredible." Daric could not stop marveling at the blade. "I don't know what to say."

"You don't have to say anything," said Lord Mantell. "Just cut out the heart of the Unbound and free Edenia from its grip of terror.

Daric grinned. "Yes, sir."

* * *

"What's it doing, Captain?" asked Dennix, who was crouching beside him. They hid amongst some boulders within the foothills of the Elys Mountains, staring up the slope at the strangest thing Bradford had seen since... well he had seen some strange things lately. But this was not what he expected to find when he ventured north to investigate the Unbound's curious behavior.

He watched for another minute before he admitted, "I don't know, Dennix."

The beast was there, up the mountain just within their field of view, yet it had taken no notice of the two ragged men. Instead, the beast was raging against... the mountain. It thrashed wildly, slamming itself against the rocky cliffside, spewing flame and melting rock, bellowing its terrible roar.

"It's gone insane," said the boy.

No, not a boy anymore.

Dennix had been through hell these last weeks. All the men had, and not one of them had remained unscathed. Dennix had been a handsome lad, once. Now his hair was gone, singed in an exchange with the creature, and his scalp and neck were scarred from a nasty burn. "I don't think it is insane, at least not any more than it started."

Bradford shielded his eyes from the setting sun and tried to focus on the beast. In his previous encounters with the Unbound he had never had time to watch the creature. It looked like a monstrous lizard, and it emanated an ethereal red glow from its entire body. It was a long creature with four legs, each with razor sharp claws that could cut through steel, and a tail as long again as its body. Occasionally the beast's body would erupt in flames, and, of course, it could project the deadly fire from its maw. The melted rock was a testament to its intensity. Bradford was probably the person with the most first-hand experience with the Unbound, and yet he had no knowledge of any weakness the creature might have. It never slept, and it didn't seem to need food, only devouring his men to satisfy its savage bloodlust. The only reason Bradford hadn't completely given into despair was the fact that people were counting on him. His men, Lissa, all the people of Almanis. Perhaps if he could hold on for just another day, the army of Edenia would arrive.

After they watched for a few minutes longer, Bradford noticed something. The Unbound was steadily following the rocky face of the mountain, inching its way eastward.

Bradford narrowed his eyes. "There is something behind that wall."

Dennix and Bradford continued to watch the creature, stealthily trailing the beast, careful to keep their distance, lest they accidently draw its attention. The Unbound continued along the side of the mountain, oblivious to its watchers.

"It's looking for something, Dennix," Bradford realized. "Judging by the path it's taken so far, that something is heading east, through the mountain."

"Could there be some kind of settlement *in* the mountain, sir?"

"Maybe…" Bradford wasn't aware of any passageways through the mountain, and none of the locals had said anything about it, either. "If we're quick about it, we might be able to get ahead of the creature and find whatever it is first."

Dennix glanced down at the captain's severed leg before catching himself.

Bradford growled. "I'll be fine."

In truth, he was in immense pain. Every step was agony, but of the few of his men who had survived since that first encounter, he was in relatively good shape. Lissa had helped him fit a wooden leg to his stump, and he was still able to walk with the help of his crutch.

They followed the path Bradford anticipated the beast would take, the sounds of its roar and crazed ramming of the cliffside fading as they went. The sun was beginning to set behind them, and Bradford started to worry it would be too dark for them to continue searching for... whatever it was. As the light faded behind them, he saw something peripherally. He looked more closely and tapped Dennix on the shoulder.

"Dennix, look up there! Someone has started a fire."

"They don't know what's coming for them," said Dennix. "We have to warn them!" Dennix started forward, but Bradford grabbed his shoulder.

"Wait, son." Dennix stared at him, perplexed. "I have a bad feeling about this. I think we should tread carefully, see what we are getting into."

"But captain, we don't have much time..."

"I know, I know," he said. "Just trust me on this, Dennix."

The man stared at him a beat before nodding. "I trust you captain."

They crept further up the mountainside, keeping to the shadows. Bradford had thought what he had spotted was a campfire, but the light was moving closer to them. Torchlight, then. They watched as two figures appeared on a ridge ahead of them, heading down the path. He ducked into the cover of a nearby boulder and pulled Dennix to his side.

Even in the light of the torches they held, Bradford could make out little about the strangers. They wore hooded black cloaks and spoke not a word as they approached.

"Dennix, wait here," he whispered, turning toward the man. "I am going to…."

He wasn't there.

"Ho, there!" exclaimed Dennix, walking down to meet the newcomers. "You men are in danger. The—" Dennix stopped suddenly. "Ugh…"

Dennix fell to his knees, clutching a dagger protruding from his gut. Bradford heard a whir and a second dagger sank into the boy's shoulder, knocking him onto his back. Bradford had to bite his fist to keep from shouting. Each of the black cloaked men had thrown a blade, and they now approached the downed soldier to retrieve them.

Bradford roared as he leapt from his concealment, crashing into the first of the black-robed men and knocking them both to the ground. He slammed the fist-sized stone he held down into the other man's face, crushing his skull. The second attacker drew another concealed dagger from his robes, preparing to strike. Bradford tried to scramble to his feet, but his wooden leg came loose, and he stumbled to the ground. He gritted his teeth and braced for the cold steel he knew would pierce his back.

Sorry, Lissa.

Steel clanked on the ground. Bradford turned and saw the second black-robed man bathed in flame. Dennix lay at his feet, clutching the torch that the first man had dropped, holding it against the second assailant's robes. Bradford kicked the burning man, knocking him to the ground and away from Dennix. Bradford had heard that burning was a terrible way to die, and he had felt the agony of burning flesh himself, yet the black-robed man didn't make a sound as he writhed and died.

He crawled over to Dennix's side and examined his wounds. He had a dagger in his belly, and one in his shoulder. He was breathing heavily, but his face was contorted in pain.

"Hal… there is no easy way to do this. I am going to have to remove these blades." The boy didn't respond. Bradford cursed and lay his forearm across Dennix's chest, then he gripped the hilt of the dagger in the young man's shoulder with his other hand, pulling it free in one swift motion. Dennix screamed but Bradford held him down. He held the dagger in the flaming torch beside them, waiting until the blade was red hot, then pressed it down onto the wounded shoulder. Dennix cried out again, but there was nothing else Bradford could do to help the boy. If this didn't work, he would die.

The now familiar smell of sizzling flesh filled the air. Bradford braced Dennix again as he removed the second dagger, using the hot blade again to seal the wound. Dennix passed out from the pain this time, but he was still breathing. Bradford used the last of the water in his waterskin to rinse the newly sealed wounds, then tore off some of the black robe from their attacker to wrap them.

Dennix died shortly after.

Bradford had thought himself numb to death after all the men he had lost since he had volunteered to come back to Almanis Valley, but losing Dennix brought all the pain he had been repressing for so long crashing down upon him, and he wept. He had never felt so powerless in his life. Powerless to stop the Unbound, and powerless to save this poor boy's life. He covered the body as best he could with stones he gathered nearby, then said a prayer for the fallen soldier and continued up the path.

Chapter 24

A time will come when the nine will disappear from the land, and the fear of the gods will be all but forgotten. But this time is only temporary. For they shall once again walk among us, and with them will come one from another land who will restore the link between god and man. And he shall be the harbinger of a new age, where those who dwelt long in the desert shall reclaim that which belongs to them. An age of heroes. An age of war.

-Razzan Prophecy
Author Unknown
Date Unknown

Bradford stood in front of a cave leading deep into the mountain. Whatever the Unbound was trying to reach would emerge from here, he was sure of it. He could hear the monster's roar in the distance, gradually growing louder as it drew closer. The night was dark, but still clear enough that Bradford had been able to find his path in the moonlight. The cave was another story. He wished he had the light from one of the torches those black-robed men had been carrying, but he didn't want to risk drawing attention to himself, so he had snuffed them and left them behind. Instead, he placed one hand along the wall of the cave and fumbled his way forward in the darkness.

He moved carefully until he was far enough inside the cave to be safe from the Unbound's inevitable arrival, as the opening would be too small for the beast to pass through. He could still see the entrance, but he would be far enough inside that the creature's projected flames wouldn't reach him. At least, he thought they wouldn't.

Between the roars of the Unbound and the periodic tremors it caused in its frenzy, Bradford thought he could hear another faint echo from deeper within the cave. *Footsteps.* He thought. *A lot of footsteps.* He grimaced. It wasn't just footsteps. It was the synchronized marching of an army, hundreds if not thousands of soldiers, and he doubted they were Edenian. North of these mountains was the country of Razza, and Razzans had no love for Edenia. If this passage through the mountain extended all the way to Razza… well things were about to get much worse. *I didn't think that was possible.*

Bradford couldn't see the hand in front of his own face, but he dropped to his hands and knees and felt around the floor of the cave, seeking any place where he might be able to safely hide from the coming soldiers. He didn't have much time; they would be here soon. He clenched his teeth in frustration. It seemed as if his life of late had been nothing but running and hiding. He found a small alcove that would provide some cover as the army marched past, but if any of them happened to glance back in his direction, he would most certainly be spotted. *No time to find anything better,* he thought as the glow of flickering torchlight appeared from farther within the cave. *Here they come.* He could hear voices of the oncoming soldiers.

Bradford pressed himself back into the alcove, making himself as small as he could, as he heard row after row of armor-clad warriors pass his hiding place.

A sudden, thunderous roar from the cave entrance shook the cavern, and Bradford screamed as a blinding light and searing heat filled the tunnel. Flames reached into the cave, dangerously close to Bradford. When he could open his eyes, he looked back toward the mouth of the cave and saw the unnatural red glow of the Unbound, hate filled eyes glaring at him from just outside. Chaos erupted inside the cave as the soldiers let out surprised shouts of their own. Bradford risked a peek from his alcove at the newcomers, those who had drawn the beast to this place, and his spirit sank. He had never seen a Razzan himself, but he knew enough about them to recognize that these soldiers were indeed from Razza, and there were thousands of them. This was an invading force. The Razzans had been startled enough by the Unbound to break rank, but their leader was already gathering them back into formation, and the soldiers' fear of the creature was gradually transforming into guarded awe. What Bradford found most disturbing was the fact that the Razzans did not seem surprised to find the beast waiting for them. Bradford hated the Unbound for the horror it had caused since it had first appeared, but he was glad now to have it standing between this invading force and his homeland.

A man robed in black, similar to the two who had attacked him earlier, joined the commander at the head of the army. "Brothers," he said in his strange accent, addressing the soldiers. "Behold one of the nine!" The men cheered.

One of the nine? Bradford wondered. He strained to listen as the black-robed man continued to speak.

"We have long awaited this day, and it is finally upon us. Edenia shall fall!" Cheering erupted again. "But first, the god must test our resolve!"

The… god? thought Bradford. He didn't like what he was hearing.

Joyful cheers turned into confused mumbling among the soldiers, and their commander held up his hand to silence them. The commander wore scaled golden armor that had a serpentine look to it, and a black cloak with a golden serpent emblem. He spoke softly with the black-robed man, but Bradford couldn't hear what they said. It looked like some sort of disagreement, but they seemed to settle it, and the black-robed man continued.

"As you can see before you, the gods possess terrible power. Yet the Harbinger has spoken to the gods and has discerned their will. The truly faithful of Razza have nothing to fear from them. Behold!"

The speaker turned and walked toward the cave entrance, toward the Unbound. The creature continued to roar, clawing at the small opening in an attempt to reach his prey.

The fool, thought Bradford. He had spent enough time with this creature to know it was no god, that it existed solely to end human life.

The man continued forward confidently, never wavering in the face of the beast. He walked within range of the monster's flames, but the beast didn't use its fire. The man continued forward, approaching the mouth of the cave and passing outside next to the creature, and still the beast didn't attack. It simply continued its frenzied clawing at the cave opening, trying to force its way inside. Finally, the man reached up and lay a hand upon the Unbound, turning to face the soldiers within the cave. A cold dread gripped Bradford. After standing next to the creature for a few moments, the man reentered the cave and walked back to his men, completely unharmed.

This can't be happening…

The black-robed man arrived back at the head of his army. "You see? Those loyal to the nine gods need not be afraid!" He faced the army's commander wearing an arrogant smile. "Lord Azamel, would you prove your devotion to the nine? If so, then step forward and lead your men to stand beside our god." The hint of challenge in his voice was not lost on Bradford. "That is, unless you fear that our god may not find you worthy?"

The commander, Azamel, stared coolly at the black-robed man for some time, and Bradford could sense the conflict in the young man. He was clearly afraid of the Unbound, but after the black-robed man's display of bravado, he wouldn't be able to refuse without looking like a coward.

Azamel turned to address his troops. "This will be a great day for our people. Every one of you men has served me faithfully, served Razza faithfully, and served the nine faithfully. There is nothing to fear."

Azamel turned in his mount to the mouth of the cave and trotted slowly toward the Unbound. Behind him soldiers resumed their march, though only those wearing the gold serpent emblem that Azamel also wore on his black cloak. Others who remained behind wore an emblem resembling a nine-pointed star.

Two separate legions then.

The beast continued its maniacal roaring as the commander approached with his legion. Azamel flicked his reigns, urging his mount for more speed—Bradford suspected it was to create more space between him and his men. He could almost admire the man for it, riding first into danger to protect the soldiers under his command, if the commander wasn't also riding to invade Bradford's homeland.

With a mighty roar, the Unbound released its fiery fury, incinerating Azamel and those nearest behind him. Those farther behind were not so fortunate. In such close quarters, the heat from the blast intensified and caused as much damage again as the flames themselves had done. Hundreds of wails echoed through the cave, cries of pain from the men who had survived the initial blast but were now dying agonizing deaths from their burns. Those of Azamel's men who remained unharmed scattered in a state of panic, fleeing back into the cave toward their comrades.

The black-robed man issued a command to the soldiers who had lingered behind with him, those wearing the emblem of a nine-pointed star. They readied their spears and formed a barrier stretching the width of the tunnel, preventing Azamel's soldiers from retreating any farther into the cave.

"Those who refuse the god's judgement will instead face mine," said the black-robed man, smiling maliciously. His soldiers pressed forward.

Pandemonium spread through the cave. Most of the men who had marched with Azamel chose to try their luck against the soldiers of the nine-pointed star, and they died on their spears. Some dared approach the Unbound, but those too met their fiery end. When the chaos died down, not a man among Azamel's soldiers was left alive.

The black-robed man leading the remaining legion raised his hand and wordlessly signaled for them to march. Bradford held his breath, fearing to even breathe as hundreds of Razzan soldiers passed hardly more than an arm's reach away from his poor excuse for a hiding spot. *If someone so much as glances this way…*

But no one did. Instead Bradford watched as the entire legion marched safely through the mouth of the cave. Their leader stooped to pick up what appeared to be a blade, then continued on with the rest of them, everyone filing out past the Unbound without incurring the beast's wrath.

How? he thought to himself. *What is different this time?*

The Unbound had calmed somewhat, but it still clawed at the cave entrance, trying to wriggle its way deeper into the mountain. Bradford wasn't sure if the beast was after him, or if there were more invaders deeper inside. Either way, he didn't like it.

The star-marked legion, now outside of the cave, looked like they were setting camp. Bradford needed to get out of this place and somehow warn the garrison in Edenia City of the invasion, but he was trapped. He leaned back in the darkness. For now, he would just have to wait.

Chapter 25

I see its fire in the distance. We are getting close. Where once we were the hunted, now we are the hunters. It is coming. Creator have mercy on us.

*-Journal of Oleth Zandarion
Translation by Caelum Karasin
E.A. 967*

"There it was again," said Caelum. He rode in a wagon crammed between Naranjo and Simainen, sitting in near total darkness. The only light came from the few torches spread among the riders outside.

"I didn't hear anything," whispered Halia from across the wagon.

"Everyone be quiet," snapped Azara from outside the wagon. The wagon stopped suddenly, and so did the rest of the riders. They waited in silence. A faint sound echoed in the darkness, a deep and menacing rumble. Had he been in the woods at home, Caelum might have thought it was a bear.

"That doesn't sound like a god. That sounds like a monster," quipped Halia.

"And what should a god sound like priestess?" Naranjo retorted. "How many gods have you spoken with?"

"Just one."

"Ah yes, your Creator, who you claim is always with you. Call your god then, and have him say something that we may all hear what a true god sounds like."

Halia scowled. "It doesn't work like that!"

Azara cleared her throat outside the canvas, reprimanding them for their noise.

Caelum leaned back as far as he could in the wagon. It had been a long day of travel, and those two had argued the finer points of theology for much of the trip. Simainen had listened intently to their discussion, though he hadn't said a word until he heard the roar in the distance.

They had left before sunrise, riding ahead of the main Razzan force, attempting to catch up to Azara's brother and the Harbinger's legion. Caelum guessed it was now evening, but though they'd been in the cave for a long time, he wasn't sure exactly how long. Azara's soldiers knew they were there; Azara had revealed that the Edenians were traveling with them once they had reached the cave. After the initial surprise wore off, they accepted the Edenians' presence. Azara hadn't told them about Simainen, nor about the real reason they were riding hard to catch up with the vanguard. Azara intended to have the Edenians kill the Harbinger.

And nobody has told Azara our true purpose.

Caelum shuddered as he heard another faint roar in the distance and thought about what awaited them in Edenia. He had an uneasy feeling about why the beast was so near in the first place. Naranjo had spoken about some connection the Harbinger had with the Unbound, or their "god" as he called it. Caelum hoped that wasn't true.

He drew the blade that Simainen had given him. It glimmered in the flickering torchlight, and Caelum wondered if it was in fact the weapon that could slay the Unbound. It certainly looked spectacular, but looking at it reminded him of its sister blade, used by the Harbinger for his dark ritual. A wave of nausea swept over him as he recalled that horrific sight. Azara had said that these blades were unique to the royal family of Razza. Simainen had revealed that they were in fact stolen from him hundreds of years ago.

Caelum wished Simainen could remember more of his past. The Enkeli had the answers Caelum sought, he knew it, but the poor creature was in a dreadful state. He bore more scars than Caelum would have thought a person could endure, including that nasty gash on his head, which Caelum assumed was related to his memory loss. Not to mention the wounds he had suffered during the escape from Zin Krafas. Simainen did seem to be recovering well, thanks both to the help of the physician Izac and Halia's careful ministrations.

Hours passed after Azara's warning of silence. Halia leaned against Caelum's chest and fell asleep. Flex and Naranjo nodded off as well. Caelum was too anxious about what lay before them to sleep.

"I would like to know more about you, Caelum," Simainen rumbled, and Caelum realized the Enkeli was awake as well. "Tell me about yourself."

Caelum didn't really feel like talking, but he owed the Enkeli not to be rude. "What do you want to know?"

Simainen paused a moment, face hidden in the darkness. "Do you have any family?"

Caelum leaned his head back. "My parents died when I was young. I was adopted by another family in Almanis Village. They had a boy about my age, Daric. We are as close as brothers."

"I'm sorry about your parents, Caelum," said Simainen.

"It's all right, it was a long time ago."

"Hmm," murmured the Enkeli. "If you don't mind me asking, how did they die?"

Caelum chuckled and shook his head. "You are rather forward, aren't you?"

"I understand if you would rather not talk about—"

"No, no it's fine," said Caelum. "My father was a merchant, and he traveled frequently. He took my mother and me with him on his last trek to Edenia, but on the way, our caravan was caught in a landslide. Our wagon flipped and was hanging half over the cliff. My father helped me escape, but my mother was injured and couldn't move." Caelum closed his eyes and lowered his head. The scene was still vivid in his mind "The horses were dragging the wagon down off the cliff. Father tried to cut them loose, but our driver was tangled in the reins." He swallowed against the lump in his throat, still raw after all these years. "He wouldn't cut the horses loose, and so all three of them fell to their deaths."

"Such a terrible tragedy," said Simainen, "though it was truly a heroic sacrifice your father made that day."

"So I've been told," Caelum scoffed.

Simainen cocked his head. "You don't think so?"

"I think it was foolish," Caelum answered. "He could have lived. My mother as well. The driver was dead either way."

"But your father couldn't have known that," said Simainen.

"But he should have!" Caelum exclaimed, shaking his head. "Everyone else remembers my father as a hero, but I remember him as a failure."

"You know," mused Simainen, "the two aren't mutually exclusive."

Caelum laughed bitterly. "My father, the hero who saved no-one."

"He saved you."

Caelum blinked against a sudden pressure in his eyes. "Yeah, I suppose he did…"

Simainen smiled. "And you saved me. And I saved Azara, who in turn saved us all. And even now you seek to save others, putting yourself at great risk." The rumble of the wagon and the Enkeli's deep breathing were the only sounds as Caelum considered Simainen's words. He thought the giant might have finally fallen asleep before he spoke again. "Might I add," he continued, "without coming across a pessimist, that there is a very good chance you will fail in your current endeavor?" Simainen looked at him intently, and despite the darkness, Caelum felt as though the giant were looking through him. "Does that make you a fool?"

Caelum closed his eyes and shook his finger. "I see the point you're trying to make, but this is different," he said.

"Is it? How so?"

"Because I don't have a choice," he said. "If I do nothing, thousands of people will die. If there is even a slight chance I might be able to do something about it…" Simainen was looking at him with a knowing smile and raised eyebrows. "Oh, don't look at me like that. My father risked more than his own life. He had a child who needed him, and my mother's life was at risk as well."

Simainen looked around and gestured at Caelum's companions. "From my understanding, it was your idea to come to Razza. Your friends wouldn't be here if you hadn't gotten them wrapped up in your quest for answers. And I have a hard time believing that there is nobody in your life that depends on you."

Caelum chuckled when Simainen referred to Flex as a friend. The man despised him. But the Enkeli did have a point. It was Caelum's fault that Halia and Flex were tangled up in this whole mess, and there were people back in Almanis who depended on him—his students.

Simainen folded his hands and leaned his head back. "You see, you are not so different from your father as you believed. Both of you were willing to put the good of others above your own well-being. Your father had a noble heart, and he has passed it on to you."

Caelum looked at his hands. "If only that were true," he said softly, thinking of Kurt. He had let a man die to save himself. There was nothing noble about that. Caelum wasn't sure if the Enkeli heard him, but Simainen said nothing. They continued in silence, and just when Caelum was beginning to think he would never see the light of day again, he heard a shout from one of the soldiers outside of the wagon.

"Lady Azara, light up ahead! I can see the end of the tunnel!"

"Very good," said Azara from atop her black horse, Viper. As the cave exit came into view, so did the light from a handful of torches outside the cave. Azara grinned. *Seems like we have finally caught up to my brother.* She brought Viper around to the back of the wagon that contained the Edenians and pulled back the cover enough to peer inside. "We are coming up on the vanguard of our army. Stay quiet and hidden until I speak with my brother. I will send Jahzen to you with instructions once I have more information."

She let the flap fall closed and rode to the head of the column. She was nervous. She needed Azamel on her side to accomplish what she intended, but even her brother's love for her might not be enough to convince him to aid her assassination attempt on the Harbinger. It was treason of the highest order, and without him witnessing the atrocities the Harbinger was committing on their people firsthand, she wasn't sure Azamel would believe her. Not to mention she had a history of… *embellishing* her recollections of certain events, when it served her. Something glinted in the torchlight ahead of her, and Azara stepped out of her saddle and guided Viper to get a closer look, holding her torch in her other hand. Another five steps and she screamed.

Jahzen was at her side in an instant, checking first to see that she was all right before turning to investigate the cause of her outburst. The body of a Razzan soldier lay staring at her through dead eyes, a gaping wound in his neck. Behind him another, and another. Jahzen's men pressed forward and found more bodies, all bearing her brother's serpent emblem upon their breast.

"What happened?" Azara demanded as she surveyed the gruesome scene before her. "Could the Edenians have foreseen the invasion?"

"Lady Azara," said Jahzen, careful to avoid stepping on the corpses. "There appears to have been some sort of fire. The bodies ahead are burnt."

"How could…" The thought died on her lips as she had a sudden dreadful thought. "My brother," she asked. "Is he…?"

Jahzen shook his head. "We didn't find his body, and there aren't enough bodies here to account for the entire legion." Jahzen turned to the mouth of the cave, watching two black-robed men enter from outside. "Perhaps they can tell us more."

It took every ounce of restraint she had to maintain her composure as the sages approached, though she did keep one hand upon her blade.

"Brethren," said Jahzen once they had arrived. "What sort of tragedy has occurred? We did not expect to engage the enemy for some time." The sages said nothing, instead gesturing outside, apparently wanting them to follow.

"We will get no answers from these fools," Azara growled. "Let's go."

She and Jahzen followed the sages out of the mountain, the rest of her entourage close behind them. The cool night breeze was a relief after so much time in the stale air of the cave. The night was cold, but clear, and the stars and full moon seemed like the noon day sun after so long in utter darkness. Her heart sank when she saw the small camp set up not a hundred yards from where they had emerged. *That can't be all the survivors*, she thought. When they arrived at the camp, she was greeted by another black-robed sage, this one spoke.

"Greetings, Princess Azara," he said with a shallow bow. "I expected you to arrive with the king."

"You expected wrong," she snapped. "What happened in there?"

"I assume you refer to the bodies in the cave?" The sage sighed. "A truly glorious tragedy."

"What are you talking about?" Azara wanted to scream. There was nothing glorious about what she had seen.

The sage's eyes were afire with zeal. "When we arrived, we witnessed the majesty of a god!" His voice rose and his words came faster. "In its presence, all faced judgement! Those with true devotion were granted passage, while the god's wrath purged our ranks of the unfaithful!"

"And my brother?" she asked with trepidation. "What happened to Azamel?"

The sage looked at her silently a moment, considering. "Your brother rides with what remains of the legions, accompanying the god and preparing for the assault on Edenia."

Azara breathed a sigh of relief. *He is safe.* "Tell me your name, sage."

The short man bowed again. "Of course, Your Highness," he said, wearing an arrogant smirk. "I am called Beljik."

"Princess Azara!" one of her soldiers called from behind them. She turned to see him and another of her soldiers walking down from the cave mouth. They were escorting a third man, Edenian by the look of him, his hands bound. "We found this man inside the cave, hiding near our fallen soldiers.

Azara didn't know what to make of the man. His appearance was haggard, like he hadn't slept or eaten in days. One of his legs was severed above the knee, and he wore a crude wooden peg in its place. He was unshaven, and his black-gray hair grew only on one side of his head, the other side burned away, she guessed, due to the nasty burn scar he bore on his face. A recent scar, she guessed, as his hair was still short on that side. Yet his worn-down appearance did not give him an air of weakness so much as it did ferocity.

"What are we waiting for?" asked Beljik, exasperated. "He's an Edenian spy. Kill him!" The sage looked as if he might carry out the deed himself, but Jahzen stepped forward to stop him. "Get out of my way!"

Jahzen didn't budge. "The prisoner was not brought to you sage, but to Princess Azara."

"You dare to challenge my authority? The Harbinger has placed me in command here!"

"Enough," Azara ordered, turning to face the little sage. "Beljik, I will see to the questioning of this prisoner, and I will deal with him as I choose." She stared him down. "If the Harbinger has a problem with that, then he can speak to me himself." She shivered at the thought. The Harbinger was likely with her brother and the vanguard, and she hoped to deal with him before he ever had a chance to hear about her insubordination here.

Beljik clenched his jaw and shot both Azara and Jahzen a vicious look, but he was clearly at a loss. His small detachment of men would not be able to stand up to hers if they challenged her with force.

It didn't stop him. Quick as a viper, Beljik dove for the prisoner, brandishing a dagger. Jahzen was quicker, and he punched the sage square in his face, knocking him out of his lunge and to the ground, nursing a broken nose. Blood seeped between his fingers. Jahzen drew his sword and held it pointed at Beljik's chest.

"Stay down, fool," said Jahzen coolly.

Azara was baffled by the sage's attack. Why was he so desperate to kill the prisoner? Even had he succeeded, Azara's men would have cut him down. Unless he was afraid of something worse than his own death. But what could that be?

Knowledge, she thought, and she turned back to the prisoner.

"You, Edenian," she said, then pointed toward Beljik. "Any idea why this man is so desperate to see you silenced?"

"You're his kin, aren't you?" The Edenian's voice was dry, so he cleared his throat before continuing. "The other commander, the one who also wore that symbol?" He inclined his head toward the golden serpent emblem Azara wore upon her black cloak.

"Yes…" she said warily. "He is my brother. Why?"

The Edenian let out a weary sigh. "Because that is the reason he wants me dead. Because I saw what they did to Azamel and his men."

Azara's heart sank in her chest.

"Lies!" spat Beljik, propping himself up from the ground. "The Edenian scum spews lies!"

Jahzen shoved him with his boot, knocking him back down. "Quiet," he ordered. The sage growled.

Azara struggled to find the words she needed to say. "What…" She gulped. "What happened to my brother?"

She could barely listen as the Edenian recounted the slaughter of Azamel and his men. She felt numb. Somehow, she ended up on her knees, she didn't remember falling. She was vaguely aware of shouts around her, of an attack from Beljik and his men upon her soldiers. Jahzen formed his men in a circle around her, holding off the assault, but everything happening seemed muted and hazy compared to the all-consuming void she felt within her.

He's gone.

She wasn't sure how much time had passed when Jahzen helped her to her feet. It was quiet, and men lay dead around them, most wearing the black robes of the sages. Not all.

"The initial attack took us by surprise," Jahzen said, "but once we were in formation, our losses were few." Azara nodded, but she was only half listening. Jahzen continued. "We lost twelve men. The sages fought viciously, and so we were unable to take any prisoners."

Azara looked at the dead surrounding them. Her countrymen, fighting against their fellow countrymen, and for what?

"Why would they do this?" she asked. "None of this makes any sense!" She felt the tears welling up in her eyes once again.

Jahzen averted his eyes and was silent a moment before speaking. "Perhaps the prisoner can tell us more."

She looked at their captive. He was standing where they had left him, looking as if he might collapse from exhaustion. She wiped the moisture from her eyes and approached the man. "You, what is your name?" she asked.

"Bradford," he said, "Jeremiah Bradford."

"And what are you doing out here, Jeremiah Bradford?"

He sighed. "Like I told your men, I came here tracking that beast that killed all of those soldiers in the cave. My men and I have been trying desperately to keep the creature away from the more populated areas of Edenia." He closed his eyes. "My companion was slain by two of the black-robed men, whose trail I followed to the cave. There I hid, and I waited, until your men found me and brought me out here."

Interesting. She wanted to hear more about the man's interactions with the god itself, but that was a discussion for another time. Azara pressed him. "Is there anything else that you can tell us about what happened in the cave?"

"Only this," said Bradford, meeting her eyes. "The black-robed man leading the army knew Azamel would perish when he approached the beast."

"Not a beast. You speak of a *god*," Jahzen interjected. Bradford shrugged.

How could the sage predict the god's actions? The thought made Azara uncomfortable. She was afraid that the sages did indeed possess some sort of piety that garnered favor with the gods.

No, that couldn't be it. She had seen the atrocities the sages had committed in the depths of Zin Krafas, and she refused to believe the gods would approve of such practices. Perhaps it had been deceived, or….

A sudden thought came to her.

"Jahzen," she said. Her captain answered with a salute. She continued, "I want you to strip down the fallen sages to the waist and examine their backs."

"Yes, Princess."

Azara knew the order sounded strange, but Jahzen carried it out without question. He was loyal to her, even more so to her than to her father. She watched as the men examined each of the sages in turn, and her suspicions were confirmed. Jahzen returned a short time later.

"Princess Azara, we have finished our examination. All of the men bore a similar scar upon their back, matching the description of the scars received from the ritual you described witnessing within Zin Krafas."

"Thank you, Captain," she said.

"We discovered something else, as well." Jahzen sounded uncertain.

"What is it?" she asked, curious about what it was that made him so uneasy.

"Some of the sages are… not Razzan."

"They're Edenian?" Azara didn't like the way the pieces were starting to come together. She knew the Harbinger had been committing treason, but now she feared that she was only beginning to understand just how deep his corruption was embedded into everything.

Jahzen nodded. "Indeed, Princess Azara."

"Then we waste no more time. We must catch up with the Harbinger's forces. Get the men ready to ride."

A gruff voice spoke up from behind her. "Aren't you forgetting about something?"

She turned to face the prisoner, whose presence she had forgotten. "If you have something to say, then spit it out."

"Those men you are chasing are following a monster. Your so-called 'god' is with them, and unless you know something I don't, it will simply do to you what it did to your brother and his men. You will all die."

"My brother was deceived and caught off guard," she retorted. "I will not be."

"No, instead you will be arrogant and careless," Bradford countered. "You don't know what—"

"That's enough," she cut him off. "Jahzen, take the prisoner away," she said as she mounted Viper. "It's time to ride."

"That sounds like battle." Caelum and the others were still packed into the wagon. Azara had ordered that they stay hidden now that they had caught up with some of the main force.

"I agree," said Naranjo. "Hariz what's going on out there?" the Razzan shouted to the guard outside their wagon. Hariz poked his head in from outside the wagon. He was one of the few who knew of the Enkeli.

"A skirmish," he said. "The sages attacked us over something, I am not sure what, but Captain Jahzen made quick work of them. The fight is already over."

"And the princess?" Naranjo demanded. "Is she all right?"

"She's fine," said Hariz, and Naranjo let out the breath he had been holding. Hariz peeked over his shoulder. "Looks like we are getting ready to march again." Naranjo sat back down.

Before they started moving, Caelum leaned out to talk to Hariz. "If there is no more need for secrecy, might we stretch our legs for a while? We've been sitting cramped in this wagon for a long time."

Hariz shrugged. "That should be fine, as long as you make it quick. Captain Jahzen has given the order to prepare to ride." Hariz held the wagon cover open for them, keeping a close eye out for anyone who might be able to peer inside. "You're good to go."

Caelum hopped down first, offering an arm to Halia as she climbed down after him. He offered a hand to Flex as well, but the Elite just snickered and jumped down next to them, favoring his injured arm. Caelum looked back toward Simainen. "I'm sure we can find a way to disguise you if you need to get out for a while."

Simainen, breathing heavily, waved him off. "You don't need to worry about me."

Caelum wasn't so sure. The Enkeli was in bad shape when they had found him, and the stab wound he had suffered had been treated but was far from healed. On top of that, Caelum hadn't seen the Enkeli take a break to relieve himself since they had left Razza, and that had to be uncomfortable.

"I will stay and look after him," said Naranjo. The Razzan had hardly left Simainen's side.

"We'll be back soon," Caelum said. Halia wandered off into the camp, escorted by Flex, and Caelum made for the nearest tree outside the Razzan perimeter.

None of the soldiers he passed paid him any mind. They were busy packing, watering and re-saddling horses, and taking care of any other last-minute needs before they set out on another long march. One soldier was leading a prisoner, which Caelum wouldn't have thought out of place if the man weren't so unusual. The prisoner didn't appear to be a sage, but rather some rough looking man who walked with a peg in place of one of his legs. The man was Edenian, probably a hermit if he lived this far north in the valley. As they passed, Caelum met the man's eyes and froze.

"Captain Bradford?" The other man looked as surprised as Caelum felt.

"You… the scholar. Caelum, wasn't it? What are you—"

"Quiet!" snapped the Razzan soldier, shoving the captain ahead.

Caelum followed after them. "If you would—"

"Nobody is to speak with the prisoner, especially not you, *Edenian*," the soldier insisted. "Now get out of here. If you have something to say, say it to Captain Jahzen." The soldier pushed past him and led Bradford away. Caelum stared after them.

What was Bradford doing out here? Caelum had heard that he and all the soldiers with him had been annihilated. Could he have run away? That didn't seem like the man Caelum knew, though to be honest, he hadn't known him for very long. Whatever the case, Bradford would know more about the

Unbound and about what had been happening in the valley since he had left. He needed to talk to the man.

Caelum hurried back the way he had come, back to the wagon. Flex was arriving back as well. Steeling himself, Caelum approached him.

"Flex," he said, "I need to talk to you."

"Go away," said Flex.

"Please," said Caelum. "I know you would rather have nothing to do with me, but this is important."

"Then say what it is you want me to hear," Flex growled, glaring impatiently.

Caelum looked around, then motioned with his head for Flex to follow him out of earshot of the wagon and any passersby. Flex sniffed and rolled his eyes, but he did follow.

"Flex, Captain Bradford is here."

"What?" Flex exclaimed, momentarily forgetting his condescending anger.

Caelum looked to see if anyone had noticed Flex's outburst and lowered his voice. "He is a prisoner here. I just saw him. I wasn't able to speak more than a few words with him; the guards were given orders not to let anyone talk to him. But there is no doubt, Bradford is here."

Flex put a hand through his hair and closed his eyes thoughtfully for a moment before answering. "We need to talk to Azara and hope she will let us speak with him."

"And what if she doesn't?" Caelum asked.

Flex's eyes hardened. "Then we will speak to him anyway."

Chapter 26

As a smith forms iron by his hammer, so does the Creator form the world by his will. When the Creator brought forth mankind, he bestowed upon them that which is of Himself: the power of will. Will to choose good above evil, life above death, love over hatred, courage over fear. The choice to live in the purpose, freedom, and beauty of our Creator. Or the choice to forsake Him.

-Book of The Creator
Author Unknown
Before the Alliance

Soon they were on the move again. Caelum would have expected more grumbling among the soldiers for having so short a rest after a long day's march, but these were Azara's personal escort, hardened and accustomed to the grueling hours in the saddle as well as the rash and unpredictable demands of their princess.

For Caelum and his companion in the wagon, the hours spent traveling were not grueling so much as terribly uncomfortable, especially because, in the excitement following his unexpected encounter with Captain Bradford, Caelum had forgotten to take care of the one task he had originally intended to accomplish. Only a few more hours until their next stop.

He and Flex had not had an opportunity to seek out Azara before being forced to set out once more, and now he thought the wait might drive him mad. He kept imagining what Bradford might tell him, his mind dwelling on the worst of the possibilities, fearing most that the Unbound had reached Almanis Village, destroying his home and the people he cared about. He closed his eyes, hoping to catch some sleep.

The wagon lurched to a stop, waking Caelum from his slumber. It was still dark out, but first light was beginning to dawn. Flex was first to climb out of the wagon, waiting only moments after Hariz gave the all clear. Caelum followed, and Halia joined them. The men around them looked weary but grateful for the chance to rest and have a warm meal, however bland it might be. There was a lingering winter chill in the spring air, and Caelum was once again thankful for his heavy scholar's coat. Halia wore Flex's cloak, while Flex himself wore only his tunic, not showing any signs of discomfort.

They found Azara alone, gazing over the rushing waters of the Sticks River. The river, which flowed down from the northern Elys Mountains into Lake Almanis, got its name from the yearly springtime tradition among the valley's inhabitants. At winter's end, during the Freshet Festival, Children from all over the valley would carve their name into a stick and paint it in vibrant colors. The sticks would then be gathered and dropped into the river, and prizes were awarded to those whose sticks were first to reach the lake. Caelum had never won as a child, but Daric had come in third. Thoughts of home and his friend brought with them a pang of worry, fueling his desire to speak with Bradford right away. Azara heard them approaching and turned to face the Edenians.

"What do you want?" Azara's emotionless tone seemed odd to Caelum, a heavy contrast to her usual fiery personality.

"Is... um," he stuttered. "What's wrong?"

Azara looked at them coolly. "I assume you haven't heard. My brother is dead."

Caelum felt for her, but he wasn't surprised. He had seen some of what was left in the cave. "The Unbound?" he asked, knowing the answer.

Azara nodded. "So says our prisoner."

"About the prisoner," Caelum began. "I know the man. If you would allow it, I would like to speak with him."

She shook her head. "Nobody is to speak with him."

Flex stepped forward to speak. "Azara, if you would please—"

"I said no." Her expression left no room for argument. Caelum and Flex shared a glance before they both gave a shallow bow.

"Very well," said Flex. Caelum and Flex turned to go, but Halia stayed behind with Azara.

When the two men were far enough away to avoid being overheard, Caelum asked in a hushed voice, "Do you think she suspects anything?"

Flex shrugged. "She may, but she is clearly distraught over her brother. I doubt she is thinking about us at all at this point." Flex stopped and looked around, checking to see if anybody was close enough to notice them. "Either way, let's make this quick."

They snuck outside the camp perimeter, keeping to the shadows as they circled the encampment, searching for Bradford. They spotted him near the eastern edge of the camp. He was seated on a log near a cook fire, his hands and feet bound and a gag around his mouth. Two Razzan soldiers sat nearby eating some kind of gruel. Flex and Caelum snuck around to a point where Bradford could see them, but the Razzans couldn't. Bradford noticed them quickly, careful not to react noticeably, and then Caelum and Flex sank farther back into the shadows.

Bradford began speaking incomprehensibly through his gag, eventually prompting his guards to remove it.

"I have to take a piss," he told them.

The guards grumbled a bit, but they untied the bonds at his feet and escorted him a little way outside the camp. Flex and Caelum were on them as soon as they were out of fire's light and in the cover of the trees. Flex knocked one over the head with a branch, while Caelum locked the other guard in a submissive choke hold until he passed out. They dragged the downed soldiers behind some brush and undid the captain's bonds.

"Hmph," grunted Bradford. "I thought these Razzans were about to finally put me out of my misery, but I had the misfortune of running into you two." Bradford massaged his wrists. "You boys want to tell me what the hell you are doing with a Razzan invasion force?"

"It's a long story," said Flex.

Caelum ran a hand over his hair. "They aren't going to be very happy when they find out what we've done here."

Bradford let out a short laugh. "They are going to have their hands full shortly. I doubt that they will miss you."

Caelum shook his head. "Captain, the Razzans worship the Unbound as a god. They think that it is going to lead them in the destruction of Edenia."

Bradford stroked his chin thoughtfully. "That explains a little bit of what I saw in the cave." He nodded. "Let's get out of here boys, we have a lot to talk about."

Azara watched the two Edenian men depart. Perhaps she had been too cold to them. What harm could there be in allowing them to speak to their new prisoner? She would have to reconsider it, but right now she needed time to think. It was another moment before Azara realized Halia had not followed the other Edenians. She stood there silently, watching Azara. "Is there something else you want?" she asked the priestess.

"I'm sorry," Halia answered. "I know what you must be going through."

Azara scowled. The last thing she needed was this woman's pity. "You know nothing. How can you? Azamel was my twin. We did everything together our whole lives. Now he is gone, and I am alone." The tears that began filling her eyes only made her angrier.

"Growing up in the priesthood wasn't easy," Halia began. "So much was expected of me. Any behavior my father considered 'childish' was met with swift punishment. I wasn't even allowed any friends outside of the temple, so my brother and I were very close." She smiled sadly. "I didn't get to say goodbye either."

Halia came to stand next to Azara, and but the princess couldn't meet the priestess's eyes. Instead the two of them gazed out into the darkness, the rushing river the only sound. Azara had always been taught that the people of Edenia were cruel, that they looked down upon her own people and wanted only to conquer. She wasn't so sure anymore. She felt like she could trust this woman, even share some of her grief.

"I wish this pain that I feel would just go away," Azara began, "but at the same time I feel it's an important piece of my brother that I don't want to lose."

"I feel the same," said Halia. "I didn't know what to do with my pain at first, and I was overwhelmed with my sorrow." Halia clenched her fists at her side, and her voice firmed. "But my sorrow turned to anger, and then to resolve." Azara was taken aback by the sudden change in the priestess's demeanor. Beneath her gentle and graceful exterior burned a fire and a frighteningly quiet rage. "That's why I found the scholar, why we freed your man from our prison, and why we sought the Enkeli," Halia whispered, and this time, Azara met her gaze. "To destroy that monster who has robbed us both of our kin."

Halia's revelation caught Azara completely off guard, and she stood a moment in wide-eyed shock. Azara didn't remember drawing her sword, but now she held it extended so that the point was just digging into the flesh on the other woman's neck, drawing a trickle of blood. Halia's surprised expression mirrored her own.

"What are you doing?" Halia breathed.

"What I should have done when I found you in that cell beneath Zin Krafas!" Azara shouted back. "You admit that you are here to slay my god, and you expect what? For me to join you in your vendetta?" Azara sneered. "I should've known better than to trust an Edenian."

"Azara, that creature is no god—it is a demon!" Halia leaned away from the point of the blade, and Azara only allowed her to gain the smallest space before she closed it. "It killed your brother!"

"My brother was killed because he believed in a man who is manipulating my people in his selfish pursuit of power!"

"How can you be so blind—"

Azara stepped forward to backhand the priestess, knocking her to the ground. "Don't presume to lecture me, Halia. You and your companions have been scheming behind my back this whole time," she scowled. How could she not have seen it? "Well, not anymore."

Rustling in the forest behind her drew her attention, and she turned to find Jahzen and a handful of her other soldiers leading Caelum and Flex, along with their newly acquired prisoner. All three of the Edenians were bound.

"Princess Azara," Jahzen said with a salute. "We found these two trying to escape with the prisoner. They had knocked out two of my men to do so, though both should recover with no lasting injury."

"Kill them," she said without hesitation.

"Wait!" a voice thundered.

Simainen and Naranjo walked through the trees, and the crowd of soldiers parted before them. Some of the men gasped as the Enkeli, standing over seven feet tall, made his way to stand before her. He was still stripped down above the waist, showing the bandaged wound on his torso as well as the two strange protrusions on his back.

"Princess Azara, please." Simainen knelt before her, putting them at almost the same height. "Do not do this."

She gritted her teeth. "I am sorry Simainen, but Halia has revealed the Edenians' true purpose among us." She looked beyond the Enkeli and addressed her soldiers. "They seek to destroy our god," she said, raising her voice so they all could hear. Naranjo hissed and stared daggers at the Edenians. "For that, they will die." She raised her sword to strike at Halia, and she heard the ring of swords being unsheathed as her soldiers did the same.

Simainen rose to his feet. "Then as your god, I command you to let them go."

Azara froze. She lowered her blade and turned to look first at the Enkeli, then at Naranjo, who looked as though he'd eaten something rotten. She didn't know what to do.

"I... I can't do that," she said, but her voice wavered.

"Then you would deny a direct command from me?" Simainen refused to back down. In all her interactions with the Enkeli, he had seemed gentle and kind. She hadn't realized just how intimidating he could be. The Razzan soldiers around her were awestruck. Only Jahzen, Hariz, and Naranjo had seen the Enkeli before, and even they were speechless.

Simainen walked around Azara and extended his hand to Halia, who took it and stood, wiping the blood running down her cheek from a cut where Azara had struck her. "It's all right, they won't hurt you," he said gently. The Enkeli silently walked over to the other Edenian prisoners, untying their bonds. The Razzans just watched. She found her voice as they began to leave.

"Halia, if I ever see you or your friends again, I will kill you," she promised. Halia looked at her with a grief that reflected Azara's own sorrow, then Simainen and the four Edenians walked into the fog, fading from her sight.

Chapter 27

The mysteries surrounding the genesis of Edenia and its traditions have given rise to numerous myths and legends. There are stories of wars between gods, foul rituals, and dark magic, but no tale is told so much as the legends of the Unbound, mythical beasts fabled to have once terrorized the continent. Such tales are fascinating to study. While similar stories have been told throughout Edenia for as long as anyone can remember, there is remarkably little written and recorded about these legends. Researchers, collectors, and noblemen are known to offer a hefty sum for any book or document dated before the Great Church Schism that relates to these myths.

-A History of Edenia and Its People
Headmaster Barius
E.A. 627

Azara rode warily into the Harbinger's war camp, escorted by Naranjo, Jahzen, and a dozen of her trusted Guardians. The rest of her soldiers followed close behind them. She was afraid. She had never interacted with the Harbinger personally, but she could never forget the horror beneath Zin Krafas. That was enough of a reason to want him dead, but now, with the death of Azamel, she *needed* him to suffer for what he had done. And she would be the one to make him suffer.

The first battle in the Harbinger's conquest of Edenia was nearly under way, and the camp itself was largely deserted. The few sages they passed were silent ones, but they were able to point the way to the officers' command tent, where Azara's company was instructed to wait. Riders left to fetch the commanders back from the field to meet with them. After a short wait, the tent flap opened and a black-robed sage entered, accompanied by several soldiers.

"Ah, Princess Azara. I didn't expect you to arrive so soon."

Azara didn't recognize the man's face, but she remembered that voice. She had heard him lead much of the dark ritual beneath Zin Krafas, serving as the right hand of the Harbinger. He was in his middle years, with a nose too big for his face and his mostly gray hair already receding. He wore an arrogant grin that Azara found especially irritating, and her frustration was clear in her tone as she spoke.

"Where is the Harbinger?" she demanded. "I wish to speak with him about the murder of my brother."

The sage raised one eyebrow. "Murder?" He shook his head. "I am afraid you are mistaken. The Harbinger is not here at the moment, so I am in command. My name is Koenji."

"Liar!" she snapped. "I have heard the truth of how my brother was manipulated. Your own soldiers attacked me to prevent me from learning what happened!"

Koenji was calm before her accusations. "You may know some of the facts, but you do not know the truth." He pulled out a chair from where it was tucked in under a desk and motioned for Azara and the others to take a seat. She stood defiantly. Koenji didn't seem bothered. "I cannot speak to the actions of that fool, Beljik, for I was not there. The events in the cave, on the other hand, I witnessed firsthand." He waved his hand, dismissing his soldiers, then looked expectantly at Azara. She nodded to Jahzen and Naranjo, who both reluctantly went to wait outside with the rest of her escort, leaving Azara alone with the sage.

Koenji watched them go before he spoke. "Now," he said, folding his hands on his lap, "it is true that your brother was killed back in the cave. A tragedy, it was. But it is not me who you should hold responsible for his death."

"You really think I am going to believe that?" she said. "I know how you goaded him into approaching the raging god, defenseless. I heard how those men who rode with him and survived were then mercilessly slaughtered by you and your men—"

"Once again, Azara," he interrupted, "you know only half-truths." Koenji rose from his seat and poured a drink for himself at the table, then paced as he talked. "Indeed, I did encourage Azamel to approach our god, to stand before him for judgement, as all men must, eventually." He stopped in front of her. "Difficult as it may be to hear, your brother and his men were judged, and dealt with accordingly by the god."

Azara scowled. "My brother was a good man. He honored the gods and lived his life better than anyone I know."

"Perhaps he did," Koenji conceded, "but the gods do not judge by the standards of men, and they do not easily forget the transgressions of their subjects. Their judgement at times may require a son to suffer for the sins of his father. Or," he met her eyes, "a brother to suffer for the sins of his sister."

Azara ground her teeth and had to clench her fists tightly to keep from screaming at the man. "What are you implying, sage?"

Koenji shrugged. "I don't know. I am just saying that the actions of the gods are not always easy to understand. It is possible that Azamel was judged according to his own transgressions, but equally plausible he was punished for his connection to another."

Azara thought back to that damned encounter beneath Zin Krafas when she had killed one of the sages, sprung prisoners free, planned an assassination of the Harbinger….

"No," she said. "That doesn't explain you and your men murdering Azamel's men in cold blood."

Koenji spread his arms wide. "It was mercy!" he breathed. "We granted a swift end to those who were suffering. Those who were too afraid to face the god's judgement in this life were granted an easier death than those who faced judgement and were found unworthy." He continued pacing, edging out of her field of vision for just a moment, long enough to make her nervous. "Azara, you must understand, not a single man who marched with us from Razza entered this land without facing the god's judgement, and many were deemed worthy. Even now, we prepare for battle beside our god, where we will gain victory and Edenia will spiral toward utter destruction."

Azara hated how reasonable the sage sounded. He had an answer for everything, and yet… something still seemed off. She wished she could pinpoint what it was. Koenji smiled at her, almost sympathetically.

"Come, Azara," he said, extending a hand toward her. "Come with me to witness the beginning of a new era, where the chosen of the gods will rule and all else will cower before us."

Daric stood beside Lord Mantell upon a ledge in the lower foothills of the Elys Mountains. Below them stretched the forests of the Almanis Valley, once a lush emerald landscape as far as the eye could see, now scarred black from the fires of the beast terrorizing his homeland. He could make out a pillar of smoke rising from the trees, less than a league away and coming closer.

This was the moment they had waited for. The journey here had taken longer than Daric expected, since Lord Mantell had instructed them to keep to the foothills of the mountains, where travel was more difficult but there was less vegetation. Daric supposed that was wise, for they had heard of the Unbound's fiery breath, and they didn't want to engage the beast while the forest burned around them, especially given how dry the season had been.

The men around Daric shifted nervously. Lord Mantell trotted his mount forward and turned to face them. "Today, men, you will become legends. The heroes who defeat the Unbound!" He drew his sword and pointed at the approaching cloud of smoke. "No matter what happens when that beast comes through those trees, you stand your ground as warriors of Edenia." The men cheered, Daric among them. "This threat to our kingdom ends today. First spear, to the front!"

At his command, three hundred men wielding heavy spears marched down the slope in formation, a couple hundred yards from the edge of the forest. Two more detachments of spearmen flanked the first on either side.

It was a good plan in Daric's estimation. The first spear detachment would take the initial charge from the Unbound, while the second and third would surround the beast and cut off any escape. Unlike the first planned assault led by Captain Bradford, they would focus first on restraining the creature. Lord Mantell's engineers had altered the several ballistae they had brought with them on their march from the capital. Rather than launching standard bolts, these custom ballistae were fitted to launch bolas, a weapon favored by the inhabitants of the wildlands west of Edenia, which consisted of two-to-three weighted balls connected by a cord. When thrown, the bola would entangle the limbs of its target. Lord Mantell took that basic concept and made it bigger and stronger. Their bola launchers hurled massive metal bolas connected to a length of steel chain that could then be reeled in by a powerful crank, allowing for the capture and restraint of the creature. Of course, they had yet to be tested on anything like what they would be facing today.

After the spearmen surrounded the creature and goaded it into position, the bola launchers would restrain the Unbound while the third group, which Daric was a part of, would then engage the creature, seeking to find any way to inflict damage while avoiding the fiery breath it was known to unleash.

The smoke was close now, and Daric could see the rustling of trees marking the passage of the oncoming Unbound. Lord Mantell issued a quick order, signaling the first spear detachment to adjust to its path, and suddenly their quarry was upon them. It was a creature out of a nightmare, a giant, serpentine demon glowing red, charging mindlessly at the spearmen.

"Steady!" shouted Lord Mantell from their ridge above.

Daric had never been a pikeman, never had to stand his ground as cavalry charged toward him, blade pointed at his heart, confident that his spear would prevail against his enemy. Would he have been able to stand before such terror?

The first rows of spearmen stood no chance against the creature as it crashed into them with a mighty roar. Others rushed to fill the gap left by their fallen comrades, thrusting their spears to keep the creature at bay. The flanking spearmen moved into position to encircle the Unbound as it continued slashing and whipping its long tail at anyone that came too close. Daric was so intent on the battle below him that he didn't notice Lord Mantell had moved to stand beside him.

"I had my doubts about this creature, but it seems the legend has proven true after all," said Lord Mantell. Daric nodded, still absorbed in the struggle below. The Unbound was nearly surrounded. "It is enough to make a man question what else he may be ignorant of." Daric glanced thoughtfully at his commander.

An earsplitting roar jerked his attention back down below, as the Unbound breathed its deadly fire, spinning around and annihilating most of the spearmen surrounding it in a ring of fire. Daric cried out in anger and drew his sword, desperate to rush down and avenge his brothers, but Lord Mantell yanked him by his collar and stopped him short.

"Wait, Daric!" he shouted. "It's not over yet." He turned to an officer, who nodded and raised the standard signaling the ballistae to fire.

Several loud cracks filled the air as the eight bola launchers fired at the great beast. The first bola slammed into the creature, staggering it for a moment, but it bounced off its scaled body without grabbing hold. The next two bolas found their marks and secured themselves around the creature's forelegs, the engineers on the ballistae quickly reeling in the slack on the heavy chains. The Unbound struggled against the restraints, pulling at the chains and dragging the ballistae forward.

Another bola missed, but the next two latched onto the creature's left hind leg, followed by another grabbing its right. The Unbound continued to struggle, but with five of the eight bola launchers latched on, it was unable to free itself. The engineers of other three bola launchers reeled in their chains, firing again so that eight taught chains now held the Unbound tight.

Lord Mantell smiled wickedly. "It's ours now. Infantry, march!"

Daric hefted the heavy war hammer he was carrying. Few men in their army possessed the strength necessary to wield such a weapon effectively. But if the creature's scales were nearly impenetrable, they needed to find some other ways to damage it, and if the scales couldn't be pierced, perhaps they could be cracked. Of course, he still carried the sword Lord Mantell had gifted him, should that prove to be a more suitable weapon.

Before he had gone more than a few steps, he and the men around him came to an abrupt halt, muttering nervously. There, emerging from the forest line below them, were hundreds of men wearing black robes, more appearing with each passing second.

"My lord?" Daric asked, turning back toward Lord Mantell. The commander stared down at the newcomers, brow furrowed and eyes afire.

"It would seem we have company," he said coolly.

The black-robed men began sprinting up the hill to the Unbound and the surrounding spearmen, eerily silent as they came, each wielding a long, curved sword. Razzan weapons.

Daric growled impatiently. "We have to get down there!"

"No, Daric!" Lord Mantell shouted after him, but it was too late. Daric was already running down to engage the new enemy below. The spearmen had been caught unaware and out of formation, and they were suffering heavy losses. Daric passed near the Unbound, ducking under the chains that held it and feeling the intense heat the monster radiated as he did so, before he entered the thick melee.

The nearest Razzan was removing his sword from the gut of an Edenian spearmen when Daric swung his war hammer with all his might, sending the black-robed man flying. Two more Razzans attacked, and Daric countered a blow from the first, kicking him in the chest and knocking him back enough so that he stumbled over a corpse behind him. He jabbed the second man in the face with the shaft of his hammer before spinning to deliver a crushing blow to the first Razzan, who had been scrambling to recover to his feet. The remaining black-robed attacker thrust his blade at Daric's chest, but Daric dodged to the left, feeling the blade graze his right shoulder and leave a shallow gash, then slammed the heavy head of his hammer into his enemy's spine. The Razzan collapsed.

Daric scanned the field, breathing heavily as he braced himself for another attack, but none came. The spearmen around him had managed to regroup into a defensive formation. Daric's wild charge had inspired some of the other men on the hillside to join the fray, and their involvement in the skirmish had been enough to fill the gap in their comrades' lines.

He felt a swell of pride in their small victory, but it vanished when he surveyed the larger battle around them. Black-robed bodies lay scattered around the Unbound in a failed attempt to set the creature free, but there were too few of them to have ever stood any chance of success. The Razzan's frontal assault had been a feint.

"Spears, reinforce the bolas!" he shouted, and he sprinted toward the nearest of the bolas. Razzan soldiers had somehow snuck around to flank the bolas while the Edenian forces were distracted. He cursed himself for not catching it sooner. The Razzans were outnumbered; their only advantage was the element of surprise. They had no chance of victory in any prolonged battle. If they managed to release the Unbound, however….

The small detachment of engineers and guards manning the bola were already slain when Daric arrived, and the Razzan assassins were soaking the massive wooden war machine in oil, one of them preparing a torch to set it aflame. Daric hurled his massive war hammer at the torchbearer, striking him in the chest and sending him flying backward, knocking the torch out of his hands and away from the bola launcher. Daric drew his sword and screamed defiantly as eight Razzan soldiers drew their blades and rushed him.

Azara stared in wonder at her god, the second out of the nine that she had witnessed. The Enkeli had demonstrated impressive strength and resilience, but the being before her now was truly spectacular, other-worldly, and much more representative of what she would expect from the nine gods. And yet, this celestial being was now being threatened by the armies of Edenia, the enemy of her people. Her thoughts drifted to Halia and the other Edenians who had once been her companions. How could they have plotted behind her back? After what they had been through together, she had started to trust them, had even been growing fond of some of them. Perhaps her father had been right. Maybe the Edenians were simply an evil people. And the Harbinger….

Her god let out another anguished roar, and Azara's heart ached for it. Next to her, Naranjo growled. "We should go help it," he said, echoing Azara's own thoughts.

"Patience," Koenji said calmly. "Look there." He extended one hand and pointed at one of the strange machines the Edenians had used to entrap their god. From this distance, it was hard for Azara to see much of what was happening there, but soon the machine erupted in bright yellow flame. Six others followed, burning brightly and sending small tendrils of smoke to join the hazy gray cloud above the battlefield. Only the eighth Edenian war machine remained conspicuously unaffected.

"Hmph." Koenji scowled. "Well, no matter. The damage is done."

Daric fell to his knees as he gazed out upon the burning bola launchers all around him. His was the only one that still stood. The Unbound continued its violent thrashing, shaking free of the slackened chains of the sabotaged war machines.

"It's dragging our bola launcher!" shouted one of the nearby spearmen who had helped him fend off the Razzan saboteurs. Daric dove for the lever securing the heavy chain and released it. The chain unwound and pulled free of the machine, snapping toward the unholy creature as it tried to free itself.

"What do we do now?" asked the spearmen.

Daric looked back out at the battlefield. The Razzan soldiers were falling back, having successfully freed the Unbound, and were regrouping into a supportive formation behind the creature. The main Edenian force thundered down the hillside to engage the enemy, led by Lord Mantell. Daric turned to face his small group of soldiers. It wasn't long ago that these spearmen served as the first line of defense against the Unbound, where they witnessed the beast's fiery inferno engulf their brethren. Now he was about to lead them to face the demon again, and likely to their deaths.

"Everything that we can," he said. The men around him nodded determinedly. He gripped the hilt of his sword and took a few slow steps forward, then quickened his pace until he was in a full sprint, shouting along with the men around him as they charged the beast once more.

As Daric and the other Edenian forces closed in on the Unbound, the foul creature suddenly crouched low and leapt up off its powerful hind legs, spiraling into the air. Daric and the others slowed to a stop near where the beast had been, their battle fury fizzling as they stared up in wonder at the creature now suspended in the air above them.

It can… fly.

"Daric, look out!"

Daric looked toward where the voice had come from and saw Lord Mantell sprinting toward him. Lord Mantell dove at him, slamming hard into his chest and knocking him backward. It was the last thing he remembered before there was only fire.

"Magnificent," said Naranjo beside her as they witnessed another of their god's miracles. "It is as I suspected," he continued. "It is the second of the nine gods, the Lord of the Sky. The Dragon." Naranjo knelt and pressed his hands and face to the ground, chanting one of the many prayers to the nine gods. Azara had never known anyone as pious in their devotion to the nine gods as Naranjo. She herself had always believed the stories, but had never considered their existence to have any significance in her own life. To bear witness now to the full might of one of the nine was incredible, and somewhat frightening.

The Dragon had broken free of its chains, and now it flew above the battlefield, unleashing its fiery fury on the Edenians below, decimating their forces. Those who had escaped the flames fled in terror into the mountains.

Koenji stepped up to her wearing an arrogant smile. "Well, Princess. Do you now believe? It is just as the Prophecy has foretold. The Harbinger has come. He has forged a link between our people and the gods, and he will lead us through the mountains to war against the evil that is Edenia."

Azara ground her teeth. The more Koenji talked, the more sense he made. The prophecy of the Harbinger was sacred among the Razzan people, spoken over a thousand years ago and passed down for generations. She had never expected that it might be fulfilled in her lifetime. If the Harbinger's intentions were true, and they were really fulfilling the prophecy...

"Not yet," she said. In the distance the Dragon descended slowly back to the ground. She met Koenji's eyes, determined. "I will stand before the Dragon and face its judgement." She stared over the battlefield toward the Dragon and narrowed her eyes. "And he will face mine."

Koenji smiled. "As you wish, princess."

Koenji signaled for his men to advance. Azara, Naranjo, and Jahzen accompanied them on horseback as they approached the Dragon. The celestial beast was scavenging the field around it, devouring Edenians that had survived the blast. She felt her stomach churn as she watched the Dragon tear into one of the survivors, silencing his anguished screams. She thought back to what Koenji had said when she had confronted him about killing their own men in the cave, that it had been a mercy. As she surveyed the carnage around her, noting the terrible burns on those nearby who were still breathing, she had to wonder. Was it mercy then? Was it mercy now?

They reigned in their horses and came to a stop, dismounting no more than fifty paces from the Dragon, whose back was to them. Koenji, smiling smugly atop his black warhorse, extended one hand toward the dragon. "Now is the time, Azara. Stand before your god and face judgement. Those faithful to the nine have nothing to fear."

Azara took a breath to steady herself and stepped forward. She felt Naranjo's hand upon her shoulder, stopping her.

"Princess," he said, stepping in front of her. "Let me be the first to stand before the Dragon."

She raised an eyebrow at him. "Is even your faith wavering now, Naranjo, that you would doubt the gods?" she asked with a hint of sarcasm. Naranjo's entire life had been lived in service to the gods. He shook his head.

"It's not that, princess. It's just… habit, I suppose," he said, subconsciously rubbing at his still healing forearm, where he had taken a dagger meant for her. She smiled and nodded.

Naranjo laughed. "Many have longed to see this day, but it is we who are here." He grabbed her hand and kissed it. "Remember this day, Azara."

Naranjo backed away from her and walked slowly to the Dragon, escorted by a score of Koenji's black-robed sages. The Dragon craned its neck to look at them as they approached, then turned to face them. It crouched low and growled, head swiveling between the approaching men as if searching for something. When its menacing yellow eyes locked on Naranjo, it froze. Naranjo fell to his knees before the great beast, spreading his arms out wide.

"O Lord of the Skies," he said, "look upon your servant with favor, and let me be found worthy to serve faithfully at your side."

The Dragon roared and reared back on its hind legs. Naranjo recoiled in the shadow of the towering beast, raising his arm to shield his face, but that was all the time he had before the Dragon lashed out with one razor-sharp talon. Naranjo fell to the ground, lifeless.

"No!" Azara screamed, rushing forward to the man who had been her loyal Guardian in her youth, who had saved her life more times than she wanted to admit. But Jahzen, already mounted, stooped down and wrapped one strong arm around her, hoisting her onto his horse and setting off at a gallop in the opposite direction, away from the Dragon.

"Stop them!" Koenji shouted behind them as Azara struggled against Jahzen's hold.

"Let me go!" she screamed. "We can't leave him!"

"He is gone, Azara!" said Jahzen, shouting over the thundering of the horse's hooves.

"I have to go to him!" she begged.

"We have to get out of here, or we will be dead next!"

She clung to Jahzen and looked back at the Dragon through her tear-filled eyes. The god had resumed scavenging the field of corpses, dispatching the poor souls still clinging to life, leaving her friend and protector to be picked clean by the crows. She closed her eyes to erase the picture from her mind.

The horse slowed with a sudden jolt, sluggishly plodding a few feet before collapsing and sending Jahzen and Azara sprawling to the ground. She pushed herself up to her knees and brushed her braids out of her face. Their horse lay panting nearby, the hilt of a dagger sticking out from its flank. Black-robed sages approached from all sides, surrounding them. Koenji was among them, and his blade was drawn. It was one of the opalescent blades of the Nafretiri family.

"At least your brother had the courage to stand before his god," Koenji sneered. "I hadn't expected you to be such a coward." He raised his blade, pointing it at her throat. "If you will not face the gods' judgement in life, then you will face it in death."

Azara scowled and spat, pushing the sword point away from her neck. "I didn't run from judgement," she said, gesturing her head to Jahzen. "This fool grabbed me and rode off like a mad man." Koenji looked at her quizzically, then at Jahzen.

"You're saying you still desire to stand before the Dragon?" he said.

Azara nodded. "I do." She walked over to stand in front of Jahzen, still on his knees. "As for you, Captain," she said. "Don't you *dare* presume to prevent me from doing that which must be done."

Jahzen looked up at her, a mixture of hurt and confusion on his face. "Princess Azara, it is my duty to—"

"It is your *duty* to do as I command!" she said, striking him with the back of her hand as Koenji and his sages watched.

"And right now, I command you to leave." Her tone left no room for argument, but she pressed him further. "You have brought disgrace upon me, and upon yourself. I can only imagine the contempt your men would feel if they were here now." Jahzen stared at her, unblinking, as she continued her tirade. "Pray my father never hears of your shame this day, and your betrayal."

"Azara…" She cut him off before he could say any more.

"Leave, now."

Jahzen got to his feet slowly, then turned and walked away. The circle of black-robed sages around them opened for him to pass, and he looked back once more before continuing into the forest and out of her sight. Koenji approached her, sheathing his sword.

"Well Azara, it seems I have misjudged you," he said.

"You aren't the first," she said. "But enough talk. Take me to the Dragon."

Chapter 28

The Knights of Radiance, like the Edenian nobility, hold a considerable amount of prestige and influence in Edenian politics. It is tradition for six Knights of Radiance to serve at one time, and once appointed, a knight holds that rank for the entirety of their life. The origins of the Knights of Radiance are somewhat mysterious and debated amongst scholars, but generally it is believed the position was created to provide the people of Edenia with a voice of their own in governmental affairs. Unlike the nobility, the title Knight of Radiance is not granted based on familial ties, but rather for exceptional merit and adherence to the four fundamental virtues of Edenian society: courage, temperance, wisdom, and justice.

-A History of Edenia and Its People
Headmaster Barius
E.A. 627

Caelum emerged alongside Simainen from the tree line into a scene from a nightmare. In the distance were thousands of bodies scattered along the smoldering hillside, most of them Edenian, though some wore the black robes of the Razzan sages. In the middle of it all stood a creature he had dedicated years of his life to study: the Unbound. The beast unleashed a stream of deadly fire, engulfing a group of Edenian soldiers attempting to flee. The wind picked up, bringing with it the smell of cooked meat.

Simainen gagged and covered his nose. "This is the horror you spoke of. So many dead... it shouldn't be like this." The Enkeli fell upon his knees. "It shouldn't be like this." The others caught up to them, and Caelum heard Halia gasp behind him.

"Are we too late?" she asked.

Flex stood beside Halia, blood drained from his face as he stared out at the destruction. "I should have been with them," he said softly.

Caelum gripped the hilt of his sword so hard that he began to shake. "Daric was out there..."

Captain Bradford grunted and limped forward to the front of their small group. The carnage was all too familiar a sight for him. "Maybe we are too late to save these men," he said, "or perhaps some have survived. Either way, we have a job to do."

Caelum bowed his head. He had tried to tell Daric not to come, that they stood no chance of victory over the Unbound, but Daric hadn't listened to him. Caelum cursed himself. He should have done more to stop his friend.

Halia placed a comforting hand on his shoulder. "Daric knew what this mission might cost him," she said. "Don't blame yourself for his sacrifice."

Caelum could only nod. He looked back over to the Unbound and noticed a band of Razzan soldiers approaching the creature. He cleared his throat. "I doubt we will be able to fight our way through all of those soldiers."

Bradford nodded his agreement. "Perhaps we won't have to." He pointed to their right. "There's an unmanned ballista over there." He grinned maliciously. "A good shot should be enough to get the beast's attention."

"Then that's where we'll go," said Caelum, drawing the sword given to him by Simainen, its opalescent sheen glimmering in the sunlight. "Bring the Unbound to me. I am ready."

Daric woke with a terrible headache. He was lying on his back with Lord Mantell atop him, unconscious. The normally pristine silver cloak had charred in places from the blast of the Unbound, but other than that, the commander showed no outward signs of injury besides a few scrapes, and he was breathing.

Daric rolled the man off him as his memory returned. The Unbound had flown into the air and unleashed a fiery blast, but Lord Mantell had dived to protect Daric. He couldn't believe that they had managed to escape that inferno relatively unharmed.

He could hear the growls of the Unbound a short distance away, so he kept his movements small to avoid detection. He rolled onto his stomach, grabbing Lord Mantell's collar with one hand, using his other to crawl forward slowly while dragging the commander. Daric glanced back over his shoulder as he crawled. The beast was scavenging the dead, and a small Razzan force approached it from behind.

So many dead…

Neither the Razzans nor the Unbound noticed his presence. *That's good,* he thought, straining as he dragged Lord Mantell behind him. *But what am I supposed to do now?*

He kept a slow but steady pace, doing his best to look inconspicuous. A commotion broke out behind them, and he saw two of the Razzan soldiers galloping away from the Unbound, pursued by the rest of their countrymen. As Daric continued onward up the shallow slope, he began to recognize the terrain around him. *That rock formation there... I remember seeing it just below the bola launcher. That means...*

He crawled a little further, angling slightly to his left, and there it was. Situated another twenty meters up the hillside, partially hidden amongst the brush and the rocks, was the bola launcher he had fought to protect. The blast from the Unbound must have knocked them farther back than he realized. He dragged Lord Mantell the rest of the way and laid him gently behind a large boulder.

Now that they had distance and cover, Daric tried to think of what to do next. They were alone. The rest of the Edenian force was either dead or scattered, and he had no way to contact them. What could he do, alone? He should just pick up Lord Mantell and make for the cover of the forest, not stopping until that demon and the Razzans were far behind him. Yet, if he were to do that, the Unbound would just continue its terrible rampage, first into Almanis Village, his home, and then into the heart of Edenia. He and the other soldiers under Lord Mantell were the last line of defense, and he couldn't give up now, no matter how hopeless the situation.

Daric stayed crouched low and went to inspect the bola-launcher. Nothing seemed broken, but there was no ammunition. Daric had loosed the long chain attached to the bola before the Unbound ripped it free itself. Fortunately a spare bola and chain hung along the side of the war machine on two large hooks. Daric hefted the heavy chains onto his shoulder, grunting under the weight.

This is impossible, he thought. The bola-launchers were constructed to be manned by a team of engineers, not a single soldier. The bola and chain were too heavy for him. Even if Lord Mantell were to wake, he didn't think the two of them would be able to manage the machine on their own.

"That looks heavy," a voice said behind him, startling him enough to drop the chain on the ground.

"Caelum!" Somehow, his friend was standing there, still wearing that ridiculous red coat and smiling widely. Standing with him were the last three people he would have expected to see here, besides Caelum himself. There was Flex, short, dark, and severe, and then Halia, the priestess, who smiled brightly at him. At first, Daric didn't recognize the last of their group, but with shock, he realized it was Captain Bradford, though he looked terrible. However, he looked a great deal better than dead. Behind the people he knew stood a giant, gravely wounded man, his appearance so pitiful he made Captain Bradford look like he was dressed for a ball. "What are you all doing here?"

Captain Bradford clapped his shoulder. "The same thing as you kid. Probably dying, but hopefully taking that devil-spawn down with us." Daric was overwhelmed with emotion and didn't know what to say. Caelum spoke first.

"Daric, I have so much to tell you, but there is no time now. Just know that I found what I was looking for, and I believe I have a way to defeat the Unbound."

Daric didn't think his eyes could get any bigger. He had always trusted his friend, yet still he had found some of the things Caelum said about the Unbound hard to believe. When

Caelum said their mission would fail, Daric had refused to listen. How could any creature withstand the full might of the Edenian military? Now, at great cost, he knew, and he finally believed.

"What do we need to do?" he asked.

Caelum gestured to the bola-launcher. "Get that thing loaded and use it to draw the creature to me. Caelum drew his blade and a metallic ring echoed through the air. But the blade didn't look metal; it seemed perfectly carved, point to hilt, from some sort of opalescent stone—just like the blade Lord Mantell had given Daric.

"Where did you—" Daric started.

"Forget about loading the ballista," Halia interrupted ominously. "It's coming."

Caelum looked down at the creature that had been haunting his dreams since he first witnessed that brilliant flash of light in the crater with Daric, what seemed a lifetime ago. It was terrifying. It charged with a feline grace, but its eyes were filled with nothing but mindless, insatiable rage. The ethereal crimson glow emanating from the creature was a near-perfect match to his scholar's coat. He wondered if it were coincidence.

Caelum gripped the hilt of his sword with both hands, raising it over his shoulder and taking a few slow steps forward before breaking into a full sprint down toward the oncoming Unbound, screaming as loud as he could, hoping to drown out his fear. The Unbound reared its head back and Caelum immediately altered course, diving behind a large boulder and narrowly escaping the blaze of fire erupting from the creature's mouth. The Unbound ceased its charge, maintaining its fiery blast on Caelum's cover.

On their way here, Bradford had coached Caelum on everything he knew about the creature's battle tendencies, and so he had been able to recognize the signs in time to avoid its deadly fire. Despite that, he was pinned down. The heat from the blast was beginning to burn, shielded as he was, and he couldn't breathe. Through the shimmering air he saw Flex charge down the hillside. The beast halted its bombardment on Caelum and instead unleashed a new stream of fire at the other man, but Flex swiftly ducked behind another boulder. Bradford had told them that the creature wasn't too bright. It was relentless in its pursuit of its prey, but it was easily distracted, and could be goaded into pursuing a decoy.

He had to move fast. Flex was now in the same position Caelum had been in moments before, and now it was Caelum's turn to draw the creature's attention. Caelum leapt out from behind his cover and dashed at the Unbound. He needed to close the distance quickly, before those deadly flames were redirected at him. The beast was just out of sword range when it suddenly spun to face Caelum, growling and raising one of its deadly talons in the air. Caelum rolled under the slashing claw, coming to his feet and swinging his sword back over his head, slashing down into the side of the Unbound's exposed neck.

His blade bounced off the creature harmlessly.

No! he thought, panicking. His blade, given to him by the Enkeli, was supposed to be the last piece of the puzzle. It should have worked. Caelum brought his sword up just in time to block the Unbound's retaliatory backhanded strike, but the blow was so powerful he was knocked through the air. He landed hard on his back, knocking the wind out of him, and his head whipped back and slammed into the ground behind him, blurring his vision. His sword tumbled out of his hands and beyond his reach.

As he lay there, dazed, he could hear the slow steps of the Unbound as it approached. The beast stood over him, and he could feel the heat radiating from its body. He tried to shuffle back, but it was no use. He was going to die.

The creature reared on its hind legs, letting out a fierce roar as it prepared to feast on its prey. Caelum was vaguely aware of Flex racing down the hill to rescue him, but it didn't matter. Flex couldn't do anything to the creature. None of them could. Caelum had tried so hard to find a way to stop the Unbound, but he had failed, and the world would burn.

He heard a loud crack in the distance, followed by a whirring sound and a rush of wind as the Unbound was struck by the heavy chain bola, which wrapped itself around the beast's neck and sent it crashing to the ground. He looked up at the bola launcher and saw Daric manning the weapon. Simainen was beside him, his muscles straining as he reeled in the slack of the chain connecting the Unbound to the war machine. A moment later and Flex was there, helping Caelum to his feet and away from the beast.

"Come on, move!" Flex yelled at Caelum, who was still sluggish from the impact of the Unbound's powerful blow and his subsequent hard landing. Caelum stooped to pick up his sword as they passed it, and the two of them worked their way back up the hill to the others, where the boulders and rocky landscape provided at least a little more cover. The Unbound roared furiously as it scrambled to its feet, straining against its chain restraint. It swiveled its head left to right until its eyes locked onto the bola launcher. The Unbound roared wildly and charged uphill past Flex and Caelum. Daric and Simainen dove out of the way before the beast pounced on the machine, crushing it and tearing it to pieces. With another mighty roar, the beast leapt again, staying airborne and gliding out over the deep ravine.

Caelum's mind raced. Without the bola launcher, they would be completely helpless against the Unbound while it was in the air. The chain around the creature's neck glinted in the sunlight, giving him an idea. The length of the chain stretched down behind the beast, still dragging on the ground below. Daric pushed himself to his feet near the wreckage of the bola launcher, and as he stood, he locked eyes with Caelum. He could sense that his friend was thinking the same thing, but only Daric was close enough to the chain to act on the impulse. "Daric, don't!" Caelum shouted to no effect.

Daric lunged for the chain, grabbing it with an outstretched hand. It dragged him until he dropped off the cliff edge. Caelum and Flex ran to the edge, Caelum's stomach fluttering as he looked down into the ravine. Daric was hanging onto the chain, swinging below the Unbound as it flew, and the beast was now aware of its unwanted passenger. The Unbound gnawed on the chain, trying to free itself, and Caelum's heart sank as he watched his friend dangling perilously, knowing that if he were to lose his grip, he would fall to his death. Caelum tried frantically to think of some way to help his friend when Halia shouted from behind him.

"Caelum!"

A group of black-robed sages, weapons drawn, climbed up the slope toward them, led by two figures that Caelum recognized. One was the hook-nosed sage who had led the dark ritual Caelum witnessed in Razza. He wore one of Simainen's stolen blades sheathed at his side. The other was Azara, wearing her gold and black scale armor, otherwise unarmed.

"Hello, Caelum," she said coldly.

The Razzans spread out, surrounding them. Halia was a short distance away from him, crouching over Lord Mantell, who was beginning to stir. Simainen and Captain Bradford stood protectively on either side of Halia. The man beside Azara turned and spoke to her.

"You know this man?" he said.

Azara nodded. "They were my prisoners. They managed to escape just before we arrived at your camp. You should kill them all now."

The sage smiled wickedly and addressed his men. "You heard the princess. Kill the—"

Quick as a viper, Azara reached for the sage's sword, pulling it from its scabbard and plunging it into the unsuspecting man's stomach.

She growled through her teeth. "For my brother, you murderer!" The sage groaned, clutching at the blade in his gut, then collapsed to the ground.

The scene erupted into chaos. The sages surrounding them charged at Azara, eerily quiet. Flex drew his sword and rushed toward Azara as well, who withdrew the sage's blade from the body at her feet and screamed a challenge at the foes around her. Caelum hefted his own blade as he prepared to face the attackers.

Behind them, the Unbound roared. Daric had steadily climbed up the chain, making his way closer to striking distance of the beast's body, managing so far to dodge or deflect its attempts to swipe at him. With a sudden howl, the beast spun rapidly, whipping Daric around and off the chain, launching him through the air until he crashed into the cliff wall below Caelum.

"Daric!" Caelum cried, scrambling to his knees to peer over the cliffside, fearing the worst. Yet Daric had somehow managed thrust his sword into the mountain side upon impact and was hanging precariously from the sword's hilt. He swung to grab hold of a small ledge and pull himself up. Caelum couldn't believe it.

The Unbound hovered out over the ravine, circling until it was looking right at Daric. It roared furiously and flew in a frenzy, intent on its trapped prey. Daric rose to his feet and held his sword high, but it was futile. He would not survive. Caelum didn't know what to do. Nothing he could do would matter.

But he couldn't do nothing.

He gripped his sword tightly and gritted his teeth, then took a few steps backward before launching himself off the cliff.

"No, don't!" Caelum heard Lord Mantell shout, but it was too late. The voice faded along with the clamor of battle, and Caelum could only hear the wind rushing past him as he fell, gripping his sword in both hands above his head, blade pointed down, directly in the path of the charging Unbound.

The man watched as the Dragon decimated armies. He watched as it terrorized the innocent. And he watched now as the last spark of hope for mankind was about to flicker and die. He had even watched what was to come should things continue as they were, and he had watched the entire world burn.

Prelt. That was his name.

Across the cell there was a faint green glow, almost blinding after so long in the darkness. Then it faded, and Roland breathed his last. He had done it.

that was responsible for Caelum's pain and the pain of countless others. All Caelum needed to do was kill him. The man writhed in agony, tormented by something unseen. *He deserves this,* Caelum thought to himself. *For my suffering, he deserves his pain.* Caelum approached the man and prepared to strike him down. "I can endure this pain no longer," he said to the man.

But you can. He wasn't sure where the thought came from. *You have endured this pain almost your entire life. The pain of loss.* Caelum remembered himself as a little boy, tears streaming down his face as he lay awake at night, mourning his parents' deaths. This, he was sure, was his own memory.

His vision cleared. He looked down at the pitiful man convulsing in pain, but something was different. He still sensed an evil within the man, but now he could see amidst the darkness there shined a faint light, beautiful in its radiance and undeniably pure. Caelum drew back, horrified by the savage impulse he had nearly succumbed to. The light inside of the man was precious, and he had almost destroyed it. The man threw back his head and screamed, and Caelum stared in horror at the face he saw looking back at him. It was his own.

Suddenly, the world became quiet. He opened his eyes and the beast was gone. Furthermore, Caelum found himself levitating in midair, still a few meters above the treetops. He still felt the agonizing heat, but something had changed. With a little bit of concentration, he could expel the heat from his body, and a flame manifested in the palm of his hand.

What is happening?

Caelum willed himself forward in the air, and he began to move, first slowly, then faster. It felt… natural, almost as easy as it had been when he lived the dragon's memory. He heard a scream. Caelum concentrated on flying higher, back up to his companions, and he shot upward, faster and faster, until he was well above the battlefield. From his vantage point he could see the torrent of black-robed sages as they pressed his friends. And there was something else. He rubbed his eyes and looked again to be sure that he wasn't imagining things. That same radiant light he had seen in himself during the vision, he now saw in his companions below him. In the attacking sages, however, the light was absent, and Caelum suddenly had a chilling thought. During the ritual he witnessed beneath Zin Krafas, he remembered seeing a light leave those men's bodies, as if it had been drawn out by the Harbinger's blade into the bodies of the ones who were sacrificed.

He had no more time to dwell on the significance of that revelation; his companions needed him. The sages were being driven forward as a second, smaller force of Razzans, which he assumed to be Azara's men, assaulted them from behind. Caelum hoped they were on his side, but they would not be able to force their way through in time to save anyone. His friends were gathered into two small groups amidst the sea of black. The first group was holding their own well enough. Simainen's incredible strength kept the sages at bay, with support from Bradford, Lord Mantell, and Halia. Nearer to the edge of the cliff, however, Flex and Azara were being overwhelmed.

Caelum dove down through the air, impaling one of the sages attacking Flex as he landed before he turned to face the oncoming horde. He stretched his hand out and expelled the heat built up within himself. A stream of fire erupted from his palm, setting his enemies ablaze. He turned slowly, directing the deadly flames in an arc around him until he had annihilated them entirely. Then Caelum leapt into the air and flew to his other companions, quickly dispatching the sages there with another wave of fire. To their credit, none of the Razzan sages retreated. To the last man, they charged at him, and each one fell writhing in flame. After the last black-robed sage fell, Caelum stood, breathing heavily, looking out at the devastation he had wrought. He turned his palms up slowly and stared down at them in horror.

Now I have become the monster.

He felt a hand upon his shoulder and turned to find Simainen looking down on him with a solemn yet understanding expression. Behind him were Halia and Bradford, both staring at him as if they thought he might turn his fire upon them next. Lord Mantell was beside them, and Caelum felt as if the man were debating whether to cut him down where he stood. Daric, who must have managed to find a way back up the cliff side, headed toward them, supporting Flex and Azara, who were both covered in blood. Caelum wasn't sure whether it was their own or not, but they were both able to stand when Daric released them. The big man ran toward Caelum, embracing him and nearly cracking his ribs.

"I thought you were dead, Caelum!" Daric held him back at arm's length, looking him up and down in wonder. "That stunt you pulled was crazy! What were you thinking?"

Caelum managed a small laugh. "I guess some of your thick-headedness finally rubbed off on me."

Daric grinned. "It's about time. Are you going to tell me what happened after you struck the Unbound down like some hero? And if that wasn't enough, then you flew up here and saved us all!"

Caelum thought back on what he remembered after he leapt off the edge of the cliff. "I… didn't really have a plan," he said, and he laughed. "But it was the strangest thing. I'm still not sure what is real," he admitted. Everyone was quiet, waiting for him to speak. "After I jumped, the sword in my hand felt warm. I struck the Unbound, and I began to burn everywhere." He paused, still not sure what exactly *had* happened. "Then I closed my eyes, and for a moment I felt as if I *was* the dragon." He left out some of the details, not wanting to relive the horrific temptation he had felt, had almost given in to. He had wanted to kill that man, had been willing to do anything to gain vengeance for the pain he felt, a pain that hadn't belonged to him. He knew that if he had killed that man, he would have died. A cold shiver ran down his spine. "Then the heat changed from something I experienced outside of my body, and it became an internal burning. I opened my eyes and the beast was gone, and then…" He gestured to the battlefield.

His companions stood wide-eyed around him. Daric clapped him on the back. "Well, whatever you did, you saved us all." Daric's lighthearted cheer spread among his companions. Halia was smiling at him now, and Captain Bradford walked over to him and grasped his shoulders. If Caelum didn't know better, he would say the man had tears in his eyes.

"I had lost all hope that that devil would ever be slain. So many men have given so much…" His lips quivered as he shook his head. "You did good, son."

Azara and Flex both sat on the ground, looking terrible. Halia began treating their injuries. Caelum walked over to them, and Azara looked up at him cautiously. He knelt beside them.

"Thank you, Azara. Without you and your men, today wouldn't have been a victory."

She narrowed her eyes curiously. "My men?" She looked around until she noticed Jahzen and her soldiers approaching. She got up and limped toward them. "What are you doing here?" she snapped.

Jahzen was completely taken aback, and he threw his arms up in the air. "You told us to come here!" he replied. "You said—I can only imagine the contempt your men would feel if they were *here now.*" He scratched his head. "I thought you were hinting in front of the enemy that you wanted me to fetch the men and bring them to the battle."

Azara's face flushed. "That's not what I…" She stopped and just growled. "Well, anyway, I am glad you are here now."

The ground had been trembling since the moment Caelum leapt from the cliff, but now it suddenly stopped. Something pulled at his mind and made him look southeast, toward the crater that he and Daric had been exploring when all this began. A beam of light stretched up into the clouds. His heart sank, and Daric came up behind him.

"The trembling began when that light appeared, and I felt the wind pick up at the same time," he said solemnly. "Just like that day in the crater."

"No…." Caelum said. "It can't be. We just defeated the Unbound. There can't be another! Not now…" He walked to the cliff's edge again, along with Daric, Halia, Azara, Bradford, and Flex.

"At least we know they can be defeated," said Halia.

Caelum shook his head. "I still don't know how I was able to defeat it."

Daric looked as if he was about to speak, then stopped and drew his sword. Caelum was shocked to see that it was another opalescent blade, just like the one he had, and like all the others that belonged to Azara's family. Daric handed it to him.

"You said you felt like your blade was growing warm as you fell. Did it feel like this?"

Caelum grabbed the sword and felt that same gentle warmth radiating from the hilt. "Yes," he said. "It felt just like this." He raised an eyebrow at his friend. "Where did you come by this blade?"

"I gave it to him," said the deep voice of Lord Mantell. "That blade has been passed down in my family for generations." Lord Mantell looked as astounded as anyone. "I had no idea there were others like it."

Caelum was trying desperately to put all the pieces together, but there was still so much he didn't know. He looked at Azara, who held another of her family's blades.

"Azara," he asked, "may I hold that blade for a moment?" She hesitated, but handed him the sword. It felt cold. Caelum shook his head and handed it back to her. She put her hand out and refused to take it back.

"I want nothing to do with that sword," she said. "It is nothing but a lie."

"No Azara," rumbled Simainen, who had joined them at the cliff's edge. "The blade may have been stolen in the past, but now I give it to you freely. I want you to have it." Caelum held the blade out to her again, and she stared at it. She still seemed unsure, but she reached out hesitantly and took it this time, avoiding meeting Simainen's eyes.

The Razzan soldiers under Jahzen began clearing out the bodies of the fallen, making giant pyres and setting them ablaze. Lord Mantell retreated from their group, setting out to gather whatever Edenian troops might have survived their encounter with the Unbound and its sages. Simainen was taken by some of the Razzan medics for treatment. The remaining Edenians, along with Azara and Jahzen, stood silently staring out at the pillar of light, preparing for the storm that they knew was yet to come.

Epilogue

Paholainen was furious. He beat his wings viciously, flying down into the dark cavern where his prisoners were kept. He tore the iron door that led to their cell from its hinges and threw it to the side, crashing loudly against the stone walls of the cavern. He entered the chamber and saw two corpses hanging limply from their chain bonds where there should have been only one.

One of the other prisoners was smiling sickly, and with two large strides, Paholainen stood directly in front of him, grabbing him by the chin to look in his eyes. The prisoner couldn't see him in the darkness, of course, but Paholainen wanted to look in the man's eyes when he killed him.

"You," Paholainen spat. "You betrayed me."

"I... betrayed them." The man's voice quivered as his eyes flickered around the room.

Paholainen scowled. The seer had served him well, had shown him what he must do in order to succeed. This recent betrayal was a setback, to be sure, but nothing more. He had preferred a more subtle strategy up to this point, but it appeared that the time for subtlety was over. He took one step backward, then drew his sword and, in one swift strike, slit the throats of the four remaining prisoners.

"Let it be chaos."

The ground shook violently beneath Caelum's feet, and he floated up a few inches into the air to avoid losing his balance. The others around him had no such option, so Caelum reached out a hand to steady Halia. She grabbed his arm and smiled at him, then she stared past Caelum and all expression faded from her face.

"Creator help us," she said. Caelum looked back out at the pillar of light and his heart sank. Four more beams of light had joined the first.

"Seven hells," he heard Bradford mutter.

"It can't be…" he breathed.

"Caelum!" Azara shouted, holding out her blade. "It's warm."

* * *

Steven Sandy
UNBOUND

A Message from the Author

Thanks for reading *Unbound*, the first book in the Radiance Trilogy. If you enjoyed the story, please consider leaving a review on amazon.com. Self-published authors live and die by the reviews we receive from you, our readers, and I would greatly appreciate the support!

Be sure to check out the second book in the Radiance Trilogy, *Unwrought*, which will continue to follow Caelum and his companions as they seek to end the threat of the Unbound.

If you would like to stay up to date on news related to upcoming releases and other relevant information, check out my website at stevensandy.com.

Made in the
USA
Columbia, SC